Harold Myers
July 12, 2023

BLANTON ARMS

HAROLD MYERS

20 Twenty
Literary Group

ISBN
978-1-961250-03-1 (Paperback)
978-1-961250-04-8 (eBook)
978-1-961250-02-4 (Hardcover)

BLANTON ARMS

Chapter 1

The history of Jack Hudson remains safely locked in the vaults of the CIA. He had dedicated his life to serving his country and he had recently considered retiring.

He had been out to dinner in the evening and as he walked towards his rented apartment in Moscow, he felt the heat of a bullet whiz by his head. He did not know who would be shooting at him although the GRU, an offshoot of the KGB, had a large bounty on him and he knew others wanted him dead.

He quickly ducked into a nearby alley and hid behind a trash bin with his loaded Glock ready to fire and waited. Seconds passed and the sound of footsteps on the graveled alley alerted him of the danger lurking not far from where he stood. A body ran past him shouting in Russian before realizing Jack had hid behind the trash bin. The Glock exploded and body fell to the ground with a single bullet to the head and Jack's next shot killed his accomplice as he ran towards him.

Jack quickly departed the area and hurried on side streets to avoid a direct path to his apartment. When he arrived at his building, he carefully searched for other possible assassins. Seeing no suspicious activity around his building he entered through a rear door and ran up the stairs to his third-floor apartment. It took him less than ten minutes to disguise himself as an old man, gather a backpack containing various identities and leave via the fire escape.

He made his way to the US embassy to safety and for an easy exit out of Russia. It became the last of his many dangerous missions and he retired after 25 years of service.

Two years had passed since his last brush with death and he lived in Arlington Virginia and had settled into a comfortable retirement When he received a call from a former CIA executive.

"Jack, I have a job offer for you I think you will find very interesting. I am not sure you know; I am now Director of the Secret Service."

"Congratulations sir but you realize, I am retired and enjoying my new life."

"I know Jack but by now I felt you may be bored and want some challenging action."

"Possibly sir. I will listen to you, but you better be convincing."

"Jack, did you ever think about how someone might kill the president?"

"Excuse me sir. You're not asking me to kill the president, are you?"

"No, no but I along with others in the government have become concerned about domestic or foreign terrorists using sophisticated technology to kill the president or other high-ranking members of the government. I don't believe the current Secret Service protection is adequate."

"How do I fit into this equation sir?"

"The opportunity I am presenting would require you to plan and manage a very high-level secret operation and I know you, from your previous experiences, possess the skills to do this job. The operation would remain invisible to the public, all US government agencies, and especially the Secret Service. There will be no back-ups, no safety nets and you will be a one-man band. The only caveat would be if you were arrested for attempting to harm the president."

"It does sound really interesting and challenging sir. Do I get paid for doing this?"

"You will have access to a secret bank account for your spying necessities and you will be compensated with a large consultant's fee. I will also provide you a weekly schedule of presidential visitors and travel."

"When would you expect me to start sir.

"Today would be fine."

"I accept the challenge Sir, but I will need four weeks to prepare a workable plan including my obtaining multiple identities, technically advanced computers and the clothing and disguises needed to initiate the operation."

"That is acceptable. Any further questions?"

"Can you reconfirm what you consider my primary objective?"

"Your objective is to determine how you could successfully kill an American president."

Chapter 2

Jack accepted the assignment and while generating his plan and obtaining the variety of items needed, he contacted a representative from the tenth district of Texas to furnish an invitation to visit the White house.

He received the invitation as a tourist from Texas and he could visit in three weeks. The Secret Service required a background check prior to the visit and Jack provided all the information requested per the instructions accompanying his invitation.

Jack had gathered notes on all aspects of the White house tour. He figured the Secret Service had to use facial recognition software to keep track of all the visitors and to determine if some had previously toured the site. It also alerted them if a person did not exit with the tour group they had joined upon entrance and an immediate search would begin to locate the absent visitor.

Visitors are encouraged to carry small cameras or cell phones to photograph the areas they visit. Thus, Jack carried a cell phone with a special telephoto lens to photograph or video distant objects particularly for his use on the external grounds of the White House.

A few days prior to his visit to the White house, he had practiced the nuances of a Texas gentleman and the typical dress, so he would blend into the crowd. When the day of his visit arrived, he dressed casually and playing the role of a true Texan, he wore cowboy boots to increase his height by two inches. He had gone to a tanning studio to achieve an outdoors look and let his beard grow for two days. He wore a Stetson Stallion cowboy hat which gave him the appearance of increasing his height another two inches. Everybody would think of him as just an old Texas cowboy.

Like all tourists, he started his visit at the visitor's center on the day and at the designated time specified. The tour started with a fifteen minute video overview of the complete tour. After viewing the video, Secret Service personnel joined the group including Jack and they led the entire group on a typical public tour of the White House. It included the beautifully decorated public rooms in the East Wing, and all of them had been exceptionally maintained.

Many of the tourists in his group began to ask questions and the Secret Service agents accompanying the group would provide them the answers. Jack asked the agent "Is this the only part of the White House we get to see?"

"I'm afraid it is sir. We have too many groups visiting daily and not enough time to accommodate a detailed tour. Now if the group will follow me, we will move on to the Rose Garden."

As the group entered the Rose garden, Jack noticed a variety of flower gardens and noted the total area to be much larger than he ever imagined. He heard the Secret Service guide explain, "the area is typically used for presidential press meetings, visiting heads of state and private party entertaining. It is also where the presidential helicopter, Marine One, takes off or lands whenever the president leaves or returns from his travels."

Jack began to wonder how this large area could be successfully secured but he would not ask such a question, but he did manage to casually shoot a short video of the entire area.

The tour, although interesting, ended less than one hour after he had arrived. The Secret Service guides did not allow the group to stay in one place very long and after the short visit to the Rose Garden, the group walked back to the visitor's center and the people slowly exited through the visitor's gate.

Jack returned to his home and began to summarize what he had observed on his first White House visit. Although it had been brief, he had been very impressed with the Secret Service coverage within the White House. He quickly reached an early conclusion from his observations; there are too many eyes watching and with instant communication, it would be impossible to harm the president, while within the confines of the White House.

This shifted his focus to the external areas adjacent to the White House where the president frequently is exposed to the public. He studied the video he had shot while in the Rose Garden and his thoughts kept returning to the large number of trees he had seen plus the expansive size of the area. The video also exposed two large buildings fairly close by on either side of the White House and partially overlooking the Rose Garden.

He then began to formulate a plan using only technology to enter the Rose Garden space covertly. But he knew he had to acquire more information regarding the safeguards maintained by the Secret Service to accomplish a realistic scenario which offered any opportunity to succeed.

He accessed the Internet to gain information regarding security of the White House and adjacent grounds to determine if a safe approach existed to enter the area clandestinely.

He learned Washington D.C has a strict no-fly zone. Any plane not scheduled or following a strict path into Ronald Reagan National Airport is first given a warning by aircraft controllers. If the intruders do not respond or show any sort of compliance immediately, they'll be quickly destroyed by one of the countless surface-to-air missiles located around the capital.

The perimeter of the White House inside the fences, is surrounded by skillfully placed infrared lasers to detect even the smallest threat against the White House. They cover all areas from the surface to the sky and even beneath the surface.

The level of security is sensitive enough to recognize birds landing on the lawn or squirrels running from tree to tree which not only break the laser beams but also activate motion detection cameras. The Secret Service agents on duty are instructed and required to investigate each intrusion incident and treat it as a possible threat.

As he learned of all the security devices in operation, he reminded himself, this is not meant to be an easy assignment. They can't protect it all; he thought; 'I have worked and spied in many places and no place is ever without weaknesses.'

Again, Jack talking aloud to himself; 'I am going to have to study hard to overcome the number of obstacles and the reason for this investigation is to find which obstacles do not provide complete protection. I will find the one that gets me close enough to kill the president.'

Chapter 3

The next morning as he drank his coffee and read the newspaper, a small but relevant article in the business section caught his eye. Amazon, the online retail giant, had begun investigating the possibilities of package delivery to their hordes of customers by drones. What a brilliant idea. If a drone can carry a package; why not a gun, an explosive or a deadly germ?

The Secret Service had a capability of using drones, Jack knew about them but, the use appeared to be limited to a space within the White House grounds. Could they detect a drone 100 yards or a mile away from the property? Did the drones they employed stay active day and night and what about bad weather use?

He began to research drones and made the decision to purchase one to see if he could successfully operate it. Learning to operate it would then allow him to evaluate how he or anyone else would use the device to access to the White House grounds and attempt to assassinate the president.

Three days later, on a hot D.C. summer day, he chose to drive the roughly one hundred and fifty miles to Philadelphia, where on the Internet he had found a hobby shop specializing in drones for multiple applications. Using one of his many aliases, he planned to purchase a model capable of remote control from a distance, with relatively high speed, quiet operation and capable of carrying at least a two to four-pound item.

It took him about two hours to reach Philly and due to traffic, another half-hour to find the shop where he could purchase a drone for experimentation.

After parking his car, he entered the shop and immediately, a young man approached him, who introduced himself as Mel and offered to assist him with his purchase. Right away, Jack recognized Mel, as a geek who would be very helpful in providing important knowledge which would assist Jack in purchasing a suitable drone.

"Mel, I'm Jack and I love indoor and outdoor photography and although I have shot some scenes from many high places, I began to wonder what I could possibly do photographing with a drone.

"Hi Jack, nice to meet you. It's interesting, you actually have a pretty common request and honestly, for something decent with a carrier mechanism for your camera, you'll spend about six hundred but using a low-cost model may limit your potential objectives. For this model, your range will be limited, and the controls are just so-so.

"Here is another suggestion. Let me show you a model we have in stock which should serve your purpose. We offer this model running about $1200 and it really is easy learn for beginners and relatively simple to fly. The controls are easy to use but, you have to get used to using them and practice a lot. I would equate them to controls used by some of the more common video games.

You can also add your own camera to the drone and there is one more interesting feature I think you will like. The manufacturer has an app so you can learn to control the flight from your computer and review the shots from your camera in live time. Maybe, you may also want to add the GPS function to provide guidance if you want to fly from point A to point B and to tell you the exact location where you took your picture?"

"Great, two features I never would have anticipated. You sold me. Do you sell the GPS feature here?"

"Yes, we do, and I can add it to your order. Anything else you feel you may need; you can always order from our web site. Thanks for visiting us today and you can always call me for advice." He then handed Jack a business card.

"Thanks for your help Mel and if I get stuck on a problem, I will call you."

Jack paid in cash and used one of his fake identity cards to register the drone purchase. He then left the shop for his casual ride home. He had gotten exactly what he needed to test the Secret Service for his first mission.

Chapter 4

Jack woke up at his normal seven am time. Gulped his first cup of coffee and began to plan his day. His only thought today would be how to learn to fly the drone he recently purchased.

He had checked the local area for a large enough place to test the drone and selected a large park a few miles away which also had a good-sized lake. The selection of the big park at Lake Barcroft south of Arlington should be a reasonable training ground. Lots of open spaces and trees because it might be necessary to learn how to land the drone in a tree.

However, before he would leave, he decided to sit down with the instructions and try to understand how difficult or simple it would be to make the drone fly and control it. He opened the box containing the drone and removed it from the box along with the instructions. 'It's always good to read the instructions first' he said aloud.

Jack finished reading the manual and then packed the unit and instructions into its container. He grabbed a beach chair and cushion, then into his backpack he added a package of batteries, a bottle of water and a protein bar and headed for his car to drive the 15 miles to Lake Barcroft.

Upon reaching the Lake, Jack using binoculars, looked for a deserted area close to the lake where he could begin his practice sessions. He sighted one about a half mile away and drove to the location.

He grabbed his chair, the backpack and the carton containing the drone. He planned on practicing his flying over a small beach area and he could see very few people within a couple of hundred yards.

He sat in his chair and loaded the batteries into the compartment beneath the drone and then placed the drone on the ground and started the rotors and let them run a few minutes while he got comfortable with the controller.

He increased the speed as recommended in the manual and depressed the up control. The drone slowly rose up into the air and when it reached ten or more feet, he increased the speed and steered the unit towards the water edge and then slowly reversed direction. He listened but he could hardly hear any noise from the rotors turning as he practiced left to right movements over a relatively small space.

When he felt more comfortable with the controller, he began to fly the unit higher and then brought it down to about twenty feet and reduced the speed to see how it reacted. The first attempt almost caused a crash landing but he skillfully increased speed and hovered the unit overhead for a short period.

He continued practicing for over an hour before he repeated his experimenting but this time using his iPad to control the practice flight through the same routines, he had completed using the supplied controller. He quickly learned controlling the drone with the iPad required more concentration than the regular controller. 'It is just a matter of time and practice' he thought.

After practicing for more than another hour he decided he didn't do too bad for day one. Only one near crash. He knew though, he would need at least twenty to thirty hours of experimenting if he were to become skilled enough to accomplish his objective.

He spent numerous hours during daytime and nighttime over the next few days practicing flying the drone and he replaced a lot of batteries. He greatly improved his ability to control the drone and fly to a specific area in less than one minute. He felt, this would be the amount of time needed to reach the Rose Garden and land in a tree or hover above a tree. He had awareness of the many obstacles just to get inside the fence surrounding the White House, let alone reaching a tree undetected.

He had mounted a video camera and GPS unit underneath the drone and using the app, on his laptop, he could now control and observe the many things the drone would capture on video as it cruised along, including zooming the lens onto targets of high interest.

His next experiment with the drone would be to practice flying in a city environment with numerous obstacles he had to avoid. otherwise the drone would crash. He located another park in Arlington not far from his house surrounded by residential homes and decided it might be a good spot to see if he could fly the device around houses and shoot a video of various objects, he would select along the flight path.

The next day about an hour before sunset, he went to the park with his drone device and situated himself about twenty or thirty yards from the housing development. He then launched the drone and guided it near the closest row of houses and began videoing the backyards of about twelve homes with the drone about thirty feet in the air. He surprised himself how easy he could control the drone and simultaneously video the back yards.

He sensed this had been good preparation for what he would have to face approaching the White House. One question remained to be answered. Can I get inside the grounds without being detected?

Chapter 5

The next Jack had intended to again review possible obstacles in his way but, before he could think any more about obstacles, he received a phone call from the Director.

"Jack, I want you to attend a quick one-day presidential rally in Columbus, Ohio in three days. Your objective is to monitor all Secret Service actions before and during the rally and see if you can spot any possible weak points in the Secret Service coverage. I'm sending you an attendance ticket today."

He learned the site was about 450 plus miles from D.C. to Columbus Ohio and he figured he could make the drive in about seven hours. Assuming he left early tomorrow, he would have a day and a half to survey the site and to plan what he might do while in attendance.

He immediately began to pack the clothing and disguise he might need while attending the rally. He definitely had to get a MAGA hat and perhaps a Trump tee shirt. He filled his overnight bag along with his clothing collection and his personal cleaning products so he could arise early and get on the road about six am.

He awoke at five-thirty and washed up and then dressed and headed for his car. He left his house at just about six am and drove the route to where he would get onto I-68 and eventually take I-70 into Columbus.

The rally would be held in the afternoon, the day after tomorrow, at the Shottenstein Arena close to Ohio State University and he decided to stay at the Renaissance Columbus Downtown Hotel, not very far from where he would attend the rally.

He checked into the hotel just eight hours after he left his home and would use the balance of daylight hours to survey the arena area. The drive to the arena took about ten minutes and then he drove around the area a couple of times.

He knew what the Director expected of him and it is all part of the learning process. He knew the arena only held about 19,000 people and dependent on the seating arrangements, it would probably be less then maximum capacity.

He had a full day and one-half to figure it out, so he returned to the hotel to rest. Upon entering the lobby, he noted a number of Trump supporters gathered at the bar and decide to join them to see what he might learn.

He picked a seat between two obvious supporters, sat down and told the bartender to bring him a Glen Fiddich on the rocks. The drink arrived rapidly and the guy next to him asked if he planned upon to attend the Trump rally.

"I am sir. I live in Virginia and I am waiting to see and hear Donald speak tomorrow. By the way, my name is Peter."

"I'm Tom. Do you have tickets?"

"Thanks, but I already have one."

As he sat at the bar, he looked around and had a good idea that most of the people in the bar area supported Trump.

"Peter, here is a bit of advice: Be there at least two hours early or you will be sitting in the nosebleed section. They are expecting a full house crowd."

"Thanks Tom and maybe I'll see you inside or maybe tomorrow after the rally."

"Thanks Peter, but I am heading back to Kentucky after the rally as I have farm chores to do."

"Again, thanks and be safe."

Tom left and after Jack finished sipping his drink, he left to go to his room and make it an early night.

He woke about eight and after he showered, he went downstairs to eat his free breakfast. The hotel had a good spread and Jack took advantage of their good selections. He finished eating and went upstairs to his room where he would do nothing but rest and pack his stuff and checkout by one.

He would then drive to the arena, get in line with the other 10,000 or more people and await the opening of the doors. He carried very little on his person except his phone and wallet. He did wear steel toe shoes to test if they set off the magnetometer, if not, they would probably pass through at security. If he passed the shoe test, then he knew he could sneak a deadly weapon onto the premises. If he failed the test, then security did okay.

He expected the doors to open in about twenty minutes after he arrived, and he had a good spot in the line. He felt he would probably be close to the front of the arena and have a good look at the president.

The doors opened before the twenty minutes passed and he got in quickly and passed the shoe test. A number of vendors had booths selling everything Trump. Besides the tee shirts and posters, bottles of Trump wine and Information about various Trump properties could be found.

Jack bought a Trump tee shirt with the slogan; Trump in 20/20 and along with his MAGA hat and he fit perfectly in with the crowd. He found a seat about ten rows from the front and settled in for the long wait until Trump would speak.

The music blared as more and more people filled the arena and then the music stopped, and the head of the Ohio Republican party welcomed everybody and stressed the importance of Trump being reelected. "Another words, get out and vote and drag your neighbor with you. We need a strong showing and we all depend on you."

Jack eyes did not focus on the speaker but rather he carefully reviewed the stage and surrounding area. First counting Secret Service agents and what he saw as possibly local security staff. The setting appeared very well protected.

A large plexiglass screen hung raised above the podium where Trump would speak. Jack guessed it would be bulletproof and Trump would remain behind it at all times.

After about twenty minutes of redundant speeches by party dignitaries, finally one of the speakers introduced President Trump.

At first, he welcomed everyone in attendance and told them: "it is the biggest rally I ever had in Ohio" and the crowd cheered. He continued by knocking the Democrats and then discussed problems caused by Obama and he went on and on with his rally rant.

Suddenly, Jack heard a loud voice, "Trump you're an idiot." Then there appeared to be a skirmish in the middle of the arena between the protester and one of the faithful. Jack never turned around but kept his eye on Secret Service personnel and the president. Trump moved from behind the plexiglass shield and yelled at the faithful, "take the jerk down."

Arena security quickly ejected the protester and the room quieted down enough to allow Trump to speak once again.

Jack knew if he had a gun, he could have killed Trump instantly. He more than likely would also have been killed but the President would be dead.

The rally ended shortly thereafter, and Jack slowly made his way back to where he parked his car. He began driving back towards home knowing he had his first success but still had seven hours to go before he would reach home and get to his bed.

Back to my mission tomorrow.

Chapter 6

Jack slept for a good part of the day after returning from Columbus and the Trump rally. He sent a report for the Director about the knowledge he had gained and his ability to possibly smuggle a gun into the arena and his high probability of killing the president. He ended the report providing recommendations for plugging the security gaps.

He then returned his thoughts back to studying the various areas leading to the White House, and he decided to start his surveillance in the Ellipse because of its location being closer to the rear of the White House and an area where it would be easier for him to observe the Rose Garden with its numerous trees. He might also be witness to some of the president's press briefings periodically held in the Rose Garden.

Two days later, he packed what he needed into a knapsack and carried a small blanket so he could relax on the Ellipse lawn and try to blend in with the rest of the tourists. He drove his car and parked near the West Falls Church area to ride the Metro Orange Line. He exited the Metro at the Federal Triangle stop at the intersection of E Street.

Then he leisurely walked towards the Ellipse taking zoomed in photos of the Rose Garden area just like the many tourist walking in the same direction. He picked a spot on the Ellipse lawn and spread his blanket where he intended to relax for an hour or so while observing and recording activity at the White House entrances.

He used phone for not only taking pictures but also as a recording device. He spoke into the phone whenever a vehicle entered or left the property and recorded the gate description, the time and the type of vehicle entering or leaving. He did note around lunchtime, a larger number of vehicles entered or left the property. He could only assume they were people coming to have lunch in the White House or on their way out to have lunch elsewhere.

He had been there about forty-five minutes when a couple walking nearby spotted him and called his name. "Jack, it us Randy and Bette."

Jack jumped up and immediately recognized his old friends and former CIA agents. "My god, I haven't seen you two in ages. How have you been?"

"We're great and retired like you and what a nice surprise to see you."

"Well, the same here. I decided to leave my house today and get some sunshine and enjoy the wonderful view of the White House."

"Jack, what have you been doing with yourself as we haven't seen you since your retirement." said Bette.

"Just hanging out doing nothing of any consequence. It's a lot more sedate than my previous life, yet it is also a lot more boring."

"We feel the same. It's almost too quiet at times."

Bette then interrupted them. "Jack we are on our way to lunch at Scotts. Do you want to join us? We can share some old war stories."

Jack laughed and said, "sure. I didn't realize lunch time had almost arrived."

He then picked up his stuff, packed it into his knapsack and off they went to Scotts. It wasn't more than a ten-minute walk from where Bette had sighted him, and the surveillance of the Ellipse area would have to wait for another time.

Scotts is a well-known DC bar and grill and an after-work hangout for many current and retired CIA types. Jack, Bette and Randy had been there many times before because the food was good, and they had a decent range of liquors and they might always meet someone they knew. Jack particularly liked their broad range of single malt scotches.

Bette and Randy ordered their favorite martinis while Jack ordered one of his favorite scotches on the rocks.

Slowly sipping their drinks, they studied the menu. "The place hasn't changed much in the years we've been coming here, has it, Jack?" said Randy. It's where I convinced Bette to marry me. Of course, I had to promise her, we would come here often so she wouldn't have to cook."

Bette laughed and then the waiter appeared to take their order.

Jack, Bette and Randy had served together in Europe on a few occasions on various assignments. They shared stories as well as remembering friends during their wait for lunch. They continued to talk during lunch and rather than dessert, they had ordered another round of drinks.

As they finished their drinks, Bette invited Jack to a small party at their home with common friends in about one week. "I am sure you will know a number of the people and you should have a good time."

"I appreciate the invitation Bette and I enjoyed seeing you folks once again and I need to socialize more frequently. Again, nice to see you both and I look forward to your party."

I definitely will attend their party and he had to admit to himself, being alone is not fun.

Chapter 7

He left Scotts after two o'clock and it wasn't too late to go back to the Ellipse, but he decided he would skip working outdoors this afternoon and return home and begin studying the large number of photos and videos he had accumulated.

Although he appreciated the time spent with his friends, he had gathered a lot of information prior to their meeting, while he had lazed on the Ellipse lawn. He had taken numerous photos, recorded the vehicles entering or leaving the various gates he could observe and shot a short video of the trees encircling the Rose Garden, at the rear of the White House.

It is a good time to closely assess if the photos and videos could enlighten me on how to successfully accomplish my first priority. I will not succeed unless I can safely get into the Rose Garden. I must find my way around this puzzle and hopefully the pictures might guide me to a workable solution.

As he studied the photos and video, he realized the trees he observed belonged to a presidential tradition of planting trees. Many of the trees were full-grown and would not be the ideal place to land a drone into as the foliage would interfere with the line-of-sight to see the president or anyone else standing in the Rose Garden. Once more he had to rethink his plan although he knew his options were dwindling.

Maybe, I should think about not landing the drone but rather hover for a very short period external to the White House grounds. Then, take the picture and get out of the air space as soon as possible. Hopefully, the sensors only activate within the confines of the grounds. This might be tricky, but if I can find the right site, perhaps it might be doable.

The other option might be to land the drone on a high place with visibility of the Rose garden and shoot pictures or videos from the selected spot.

Two options do not give me much room for success when I have to consider all the sensors and alarms in my way. Maybe I need to relook at the information I already have gathered and find safer options.

As he once again reviewed the various photos, he saw buildings on both the eastside and westside of the White House. He then remembered on westside of the White House sits the Eisenhower Executive Office Building, and on the eastside sits the Treasury Department Building.

Both of these buildings are tall and face the White House and the Treasury Building faces a large portion of the Rose Garden. He wondered, would it be possible to land the drone on one of the rooftops and observe from there and it is in bullet range to the middle of the Rose Garden. He thought his odds suddenly improved and this could be an attractive alternative option and one of his few chances for success.

He stayed busy the balance of the week including a couple more trips to the Ellipse and one to Lafayette Park. Again, he just observed how vehicles arrived and left the White House area and how frequent the agents stopped cars or did searches of the vehicles.

He also became more serious of studying with binoculars, the Treasury Building and the Eisenhower Building and whether they offered a safer option then landing the drone in the Rose Garden.

He had never been approached for questioning during his visits to the area, but after his last trip, he decided not to press his luck any longer and he would stay away from the area for a couple of weeks to avoid any suspicions.

On Friday, he remembered he had accepted an invitation to Randy's and Bette's party. He shaved, showered and dressed in his better casual attire. He had not partied for quite a while, but he figured it would be good to mingle with people he previously knew from the CIA. Maybe I'll meet someone new he thought.

Bette and Randy had a house just south of Arlington VA close to the Potomac River. Jack arrived at the party about seven and picked the house with a few cars parked in front of it and guessed it would be the correct address. He walked to the door, rang the bell and suddenly Bette opened the door to greet him.

"Jack, nice of you to come. Let's go in and meet some of your old friends."

He entered with her and heard people laughing in the other room as he entered the house. She escorted him into the area where a few people had gathered. Surprisingly, he knew at least half of the people there and immediately he felt at ease. It had been too long since he had renewed contact with any prior friends or had even attended a party.

Randy introduced him to those he didn't know. "Jack this Debra. Bette and I worked with her for a time in the Netherlands and meet Pete Carlson who spent a few years in Poland with us. Jack, the bar is in the other room. Go grab yourself a drink and come back."

Jack headed in the direction of the bar and fist pumped a few companions he knew from the old days at the CIA. He poured himself a scotch on the rocks and then he wondered back into the group to join in conversation with old friends.

Tony, another one named spy, grabbed his arm and pulled him into the group. They discussed recent events in Russia, Syria and Turkey and how the United States had possibly made a mistake by not being involved in the equation.

One story lead to another one and the group departed from serious tones to ones of laughter. Each person in the group had a different story and they all recounted instances of fright and terror and also the funny side of things occurring in the hush-hush world of the CIA.

Debra had joined the group and apparently had spent most of her service life in the Baltics and Middle East. However, she listened more than talked and stood there sipping a glass of red wine.

She is a pretty woman and Jack wondered if she was married or more of a loner like himself.

Bette rang a bell to get everyone's attention. "We have finger food and dessert in the dining room" she announced, and the group casually headed into the room to enjoy some treats.

By chance or by mutual attraction, Debra sat next to Jack at the dining room table. While the rest of the group began recounting stories of long-ago wars they fought. Jack decided to learn more about Debra and her relation to the CIA.

"What did you do while member of the company?" he asked

"On my last assignment, I became the team leader for a medium sized group based in the Netherlands, but our real assignment included the Baltics and the Middle East. I spoke Hebrew and Arabic, so I spent a lot of time in Israel, Jordan, Saudi, etc. It never really got boring. What about you?"

"You probably lead a cozier life than I did. I primarily worked in and around Russia and some of its proxy states posing as a businessman in the arms business. It wasn't a comfortable stint. But like you and the rest of the group here, I survived and finally decided to retire two years ago."

"Do you miss it? You know the concern of always being someone else and the thought of being exposed. The periodic briefings, debriefings and then, the new assignments."

"No, I don't miss any it. I get to sleep late sometimes, not worrying what disguise I need today or if there is a sniper tailing me. And you?"

"I enjoy the quiet of home, my dog and being able to go into a store without taking out my mirror to see who might be following me. Sound familiar?"

'Well enough about our past and he suddenly blurted out, by any chance, would you be available for dinner later next week?"

"Wow, where did that come from, but I like it because I am also tired of cooking for myself? You name it, when and where?"

"What kind of food do you favor?"

"Actually, a good steak or Prime Rib would suit me just fine."

"Got it. Have you ever been to the Sizzling Steer in D.C.?

"I've heard good things about it, and it would be okay for me."

"Let's exchange telephone numbers and I will text you our reservation time for Thursday. Is that ok?"

"Sounds good and I look forward to a good dinner."

Other people in the group had left the table and had started to call it an evening. Jack and Debra agreed to meeting on Thursday and then parted to say their goodbyes to other guests.

Jack slowly drove home and could not stop thinking of the lady he had just met. It brought back memories long hidden away about Anne his first love in high school. She also had that infectious smile like Debra.

'Don't go gaga Jack,' he told himself. 'There is something special about this lady but what should I do next?'

Chapter 8

He awoke the next morning and continued to think of the lady he had met last night. But then, he remembering he still had a job to do and he switched his mental gears back to his Secret Service game plan.

He felt there had to be at least three or four important aspects he had overlooked but he could not identify them yet. Hence, he decided to begin a list of the unknowns. He had already determined the drone would be his primary weapon and he would have to concentrate on how he could get it into the White House area without being detected.

He returned to the idea of landing the drone on one of the rooftops of the adjacent buildings. The more he thought about it, he began to favor the Treasury Building because it had a larger view of the Rose Garden then the Eisenhower Building. He didn't realize it yet, but the Treasury Building option would become his only chance of real success.

First, he would also try to solve a few of the questions about sensors and alarms by landing the drone on the roof of the Treasury Building facing the White House and Rose Garden. It hopefully would answer a number of his questions.

He would attempt to park the drone on the roof or the small wall encompassing the roof of the Treasury Building and within sight of the

Rose Garden. If no alarms or lighting systems activated, he could turn on the camera and remotely operate it to zoom in or out dependent on the resolution needed.

In order to accomplish such a bold attempt, he would have to try to find a safe area about a mile or two away from his target to launch the drone and a different area to retrieve it. He would control it with his laptop using GPS locations and with the drone providing visual sightings.

He checked the weather and the Wednesday night forecast called for clear skies and no rain. Before Wednesday, he had to do a drive though surveillance of areas about one mile from his target to find safe areas where he could park his vehicle and control the drone without being observed.

He also remembered to make the reservation at Sizzling Steak for his date with Debra and to text her the reservation time.

On Wednesday evening, after he had again studied Google maps, Jack finally decided the best spot to park the drone would be on the Eastside of the White House where the distance from the Treasury Department to the Rose Garden is five to six hundred feet and the visibility, weather permitting would be good between the drone landing site and the Rose Garden.

He had also done surveillance on a number of spots approximately one to two miles from the White House. Once launched and the drone safely parked on the roof, he could drive his car to a Wal-Mart Supercenter, approximately one mile from where the drone landed and where he could park his vehicle to control the drone from his laptop.

He expected these actions to take no more than ten minutes and then he could safely sit in his car and use the drone to photograph or video the Rose Garden at night. He had not heard from the Director about any Presidential functions taking place or the Presidential helicopter having a scheduled landing, thus the area would probably be in total darkness.

He parked his car in a relatively dark quiet place near the 14th Street Bridge and had practiced in advance the ability to quickly launch the drone. He loaded fresh batteries into the compartment, turned the drone on and steadily increased the RPM's until lift had occurred. The drone took off perfectly and he guided it into the dark skies and then directed it via the GPS onto a straight path to the Treasury Building. It took three and one-half minutes to arrive there and he slowly controlled it up to the roof level. Lowering it to the roof a few inches at a time he would try to land it and observe if alarms of any kind activated.

About one foot above the roof flooring, lights suddenly came on and not only startled Jack but also a flock of pigeons roosting on the ledge of the building. Jack diverted the drone from the roof flooring to the ledge and carefully landed the drone on the small wall surrounding the roof where the roosting birds had just vacated the space. To Jack's surprise, the lights went off.

The roof is certainly covered with sensors but not the perimeter ledge surrounding the roof. I knew there had to be some weaknesses, he thought. But, let's see what I can do now but only after I drive to Wal-Mart's parking lot.

He had turned the drone and camera off and ten minutes later he pulled into the parking lot and picked a space between an SUV and a large pick-up truck. They would serve as a good cover for him while he manipulated the drone on a series of actions to test whether the Secret Service could determine the presence of the drone.

He activated the drone and moved it about on foot above the ledge of the wall and rotated the drone so the camera would be pointing in the direction of the Rose Garden. He then set the drone back onto the ledge and turned the camera on.

Jack sat up instantly as the view from the camera showed the lights in the Rose Garden and a congregation of people either standing or sitting at a number of tables. Jack had no idea about the event, but he laughed at his luck.

He slowly panned the audience and by zooming the camera began to realize judging from the dress and VIPS in attendance, it had to be an event for a visiting dignitary. Panning the camera to another spot, he saw the American flag and besides it stood the French flag.

He then began to pan the camera towards what appeared to be the head table to find the President. There sat Donald Trump, chatting with the President of France and I am only 500 to 600 feet away. Two shots and both would die.

He quickly adjusted the camera and began videoing the scene. The camera recorded frame after frame of the VIPS, the Presidents and other dignitaries in attendance and all in range of a potential sniper.

Jacked continued to video the event for another ten minutes before he decided to end his mission. He shut off the drone and drove to another nearby mall, parked in a dark deserted location. He then quickly turned on the drone, lifted it into the air and safely retrieved it three minutes later. After packing the drone, he headed for home where he would provide the director some 20 minutes of video and additional camera shots to show how close to death Presidents can be at times.

When he arrived at home, he quickly uploaded the video and other shots to the Director's web address with a short note. "Not too bad for about one hour's work!"

In less than ten minutes, he received a call from the Director. "Jack, I knew you eventually you would have another success, but this is excellence at its best. Where and how did you do this and how far were you from the scene you shot?"

"I sat a mile away in my car but the drone I used sat on a roof ledge of the Treasury Building about 500 to 600 feet away from the Rose Garden. It would have been an easy shot for any sniper, who set out to kill the president."

"Could you have substituted the camera with a gun?"

"No, I needed the camera to see but I could have added a gun. Using a gun though the accuracy might suffer a little. My choice would have been a small missile outfitted to explode about three to four feet from the target and thus causing massive damage and death to many people."

"What's next on your agenda?"

"Finding another hole in the fabric."

"Goodnight Jack."

"I thought so sir."

Chapter 9

The next morning Jack awoke with a smile on his face for two reasons. First his mission last night ended very successfully, and he took pride in his accomplishment. Tonight, he had a dinner date with Debra and who knows, maybe I'll be lucky two days in a row.

After arising and having his much-needed cup of coffee, he began to think about what comes next regarding his presidential project. I have proven very strongly the ability to use a drone to get close enough to the President Trump to perhaps harm or kill him.

He tried to keep generating thoughts, which could possibly lead him into another successful mission. Some definitely farfetched but as he continued to generate ideas, he just might hit upon a winning strategy. As the day wore on, and his thoughts became more ridiculous, he finally conceded, he might have to face defeat.

He then turned his thoughts to other matters which of course included Debra and his evening's dinner date.

Debra and Jack had agreed via text messaging to a 7:30 dinner date at the Sizzling Steer. I know she likes steak or prime rib and also drinks red wine, which means, I had better catch up on my wine lingo so I can possibly make a good impression.

He went on the Internet and pulled up the site for the restaurant. Then, for the next ten or so minutes, he studied the wine list from the restaurant and noted they favored Cabernets and Merlots with a sprinkling of Zinfandels.

Quickly, he consulted Goggle for this months' hot wine and Old Vine Zins won out.

Around six-thirty he finished showering, shaved and put on some classier clothes then what he had worn to the party. He didn't fancy a tie, but he did wear a nice-looking sport jacket and when he stood before the mirror, he thought he looked pretty spiffy.

He slowly walked to the garage and drove his car to the restaurant for the first date he could remember in about five years. He arrived about ten minutes early and as he entered the restaurant, he saw Debra waiting for him. He walked over to her, took her hand and said hi."

"Thanks for being on time she said. I am hungry."

Together, they walked over to the reception desk to get seated and appeared happy to be rewarded with a table in a quiet area of the restaurant. "Would you prefer a drink or some wine he asked?"

"I prefer wine and mostly I prefer reds." Debra replied.

At that moment the waiter appeared and asked them if they would like to order drinks. Jack asked for the wine list and within seconds, the waiter handed him a large leather-bound wine list. He casually opened the thick list in such a way as to sort of imply to Debra: I'm good at this and I know what I'm doing.

Proceeding to scan through the numerous sections, he stopped in the Zinfandel section and asked Debra if she liked Old Vine Zinfandels.

"Well, yes and if fact they rate high among my favorites. Did you learn about them in the company?"

"No, I just happen to like them myself."

The waiter returned and Jack ordered a bottle of his selection. The waiter told him it would be a few minutes but, in the meantime, he brought them glasses of water and a small basket of fresh rolls.

Trying to make conversation, Jack asked Debra if she would like a roll.

"Sure." He passed the rolls to her and she took one. Then she asked him, "tell me what you did today?"

"Well not only today, but lately, I have been studying the various sights of D.C. and I am amazed that I worked here for so long and never visited 90 percent of what is available and fascinating."

"That is pretty neat because I also feel, here I am among some of the best museums in the world and I sit a home complaining of nothing to do."

"Debra, you have probably hit the nail on the head because as I started to read about many of the attractions, I became overwhelmed with of my lack of knowledge of what sat right in front of me for so long.

"It is called retirement Jack. We have become preprogramed or brainwashed to sit back and do nothing after we retire. In fact, if we have our health and the will, then we should try to get a life beyond the sofa. Do you need a partner to motivate you? If so, I'm interested in seeing a lot of what you have been researching. Let's team up once in a while and go see and enjoy the sights."

"Debra I would love to do it."

Sorry to interrupt said the waiter, "but I have your wine and I have brought menus for you to select your meal. Let me pour you a small sample of the wine." Jack pointed to Debra and told the waiter, "She is the official taster."

Debra smiled and accepted the glass of wine. Took a sip and swished it around in her mouth and gave it back to the waiter. "Excellent she said. Good choice Jack."

They both laughed and Jack raised his glass to toast Debra. "Here's to us and some new adventures."

"Thanks Jack. Now let's satisfy our hunger."

The waiter returned shortly and told them about the specials of the day and then asked them what they wanted. Debra and Jack placed their orders and they continued their conversation until the meal arrived and then they paid more attention to the food then to each other.

"How was the prime rib Debra?"

"Great and how was your steak?"

"Tender and tasty."

Both agreed, it exceeded their expectations.

The waiter returned again to ask about a dessert selection and both passed on dessert, but they gradually finished the bottle of wine.

Jack asked Debra if she would like an after-dinner drink, but she declined and then she said, "I've had a good time and we should meet again. Jack, I was serious about seeing the sights of D.C. and I think it would be more interesting to share it with someone like you. So please keep me in mind for a future adventure."

"Thanks Debra. I also had a good time and yes, I would be happy to explore this town with you. I'll call you soon to set something up."

Once more the waiter appeared and set the bill on the table. Before Debra could reach out, Jack took the bill and said it would be his pleasure to treat her. I'll let you pay the entrance to the Smithsonian Aerospace Museum, he said with a laugh."

"I accept and thank you for the fine dinner, the wine and the good conversation."

They casually left the restaurant and headed for their separate cars to take their long drive home alone.

Chapter 10

Jack arrived safely home and had a soft glow about him. 'I haven't felt so relaxed in a long time and I owe it all to Debra, she is a special person.' he said aloud to the four walls of the empty living room.

He sat and read a mystery spy novel for a short time and then headed upstairs to go to bed.

He awoke a little later than normal then went downstairs for a cup of coffee and after finishing his first cup of coffee, he brewed another one and the walked into his den to consider his next mission against the Secret Service.

His choice for a third mission had become clearer as he had decided he would again use the drone but this time he would enter the White House grounds.

It would be a lot trickier than landing on a ledge, he thought. I need to practice flying the drone underneath a vehicle entering the manned gates used by the Secret Service vans to ferry agents to and from headquarters during shift changes. If in the evening, it should go unnoticed as I have never seen any of the gate agents look under a vehicle.

He had noted the vans used be the Secret Service to transport the agents before or after a shift change, had been slightly raised about two to three feet off the ground. The drone stood about fourteen inches high including the camera beneath its body.

If I can fly it a few inches off the road for about a few hundred feet, the drone will be safely in the area. Then I must get it behind all those trees and find a good hiding place without disturbing sensors and alarms.

He had saved some area maps of the White House lawn leading to the Rose Garden to get some distance measurements from the entrance gate and translate this into time to release the drone from under the van. The release point would happen at the shortest distance from the entry road to the trees. These factors mattered because every second counts and the minimum used becomes my advantage, Jack thought.

He then estimated, a van entering the authorized vehicle gate in the SW corner close to E street and moving about five miles per hour would travel 1000 feet to the front of the White House in about three minutes. Jack would release the drone from under the van two minutes after leaving the entrance gate and then fly it sixty feet behind the trees. What he would do from there, he still had to figure out.

Jack estimated distance from the roadway of fifty or sixty feet to the trees and the lasers may not pick up the drone movement before they could identify the object. It would quickly land in the trees and the Secret Service might treat it as a stray squirrel or a bird roosting for the night.

Tomorrow, Jack planned on going back to Lake Barcroft where he could practice landing the drone in a tree. He also needed to see if he could control the drone ten inches off the ground and hold it steady for about 200 yards.

What he planned on doing at the White House put a lot of stress on Jack and resulted in many fitful nights of sleep. Yet he continued to try and achieve something most people would think would be unachievable.

He practiced his routine for a few days and had gained some confidence he would succeed in his effort. Little did he know, his test would come in three days.

He received a phone call from the Director concerning the president's schedule.

"Jack, President Trump would be attending fund raisers most of the week and his schedule showed he would return on Thursday evening approximately at 8:30 to 9:00 pm. Maybe you can arrange to observe from the Ellipse and see how the agents act.

"Okay sir. I am familiar with the area and should be able to get a good look."

"Let me know what you see."

"Yes sir."

The call ended and Jack confidences dropped a notch but maybe, it's time to do it and test my skills against theirs. I have two more days to practice and get ready.

Early to bed tonight and then back to the lake tomorrow. By six am he had already had his coffee and packed his knapsack, grabbed his chair and headed for the car and his trip back to Lake Barcroft and begin test flying the drone.

He arrived at the lake put out his stuff and sat in his chair and then turned the drone on. He placed the drone on the ground increasing the rpms, the drone slowly rose, and Jack worked to maintain control while the drone followed a straight line ten inches above the ground for about 200 yards. He then turned it around and followed the same path back and maintaining ten inches above the ground. He repeated this sequence two more times.

Now, I have to try to land it on a tree limb about thirty feet high. The park at Lake Barcroft had many trees thirty feet and higher and it did not take Jack long to find one for his practice tests.

He selected a tree almost forty feet in height and it had numerous long broad limbs and it appeared to be similar to one standing on the right side of the Rose Garden. Once more he revved up the drone and as he increased speed the drone rose to the height of the limb and gently eased the drone onto the limb He continued to practice for another hour before he became confident of his ability to land the drone on the limb.

He then flew the drone off the limb and returned it to land just in front of his car. He repacked all his stuff and placed the drone back into its container. With everything in the car, he headed for home.

Wednesday, he returned to the Ellipse and using binoculars, he carefully studied the trees closest to the White House and close to the helicopter landing site, He finally spotted one tree which had a large branch extending out with little foliage on it. He had found his target. He then spent the rest of the day rehearsing his routine.

He would leave home about seven-thirty and drive to the fourteenth street bridge again where he would launch the drone to a location on E street Where the drone would sit on a building with the camera on and wait for the van to pass with the eight pm shift crew heading for the White House.

The drone would be relaunched and follow the van. As the van moved to about a hundred yards from the entrance gate the drone silently slipped beneath the chassis and moved as the van moved. When the van stopped at the gate. The drone continued to run but remained in a hovering position until the van started to move up the road to the front of the White house. As it slowed on the final curve, Jack slowed the drone speed and suddenly the drone hovered above the roadway, no longer beneath the car.

Jack immediately increased the RPM and headed the drone towards the trees while simultaneously raising it to the height of a limb he had spotted from the camera view. Within 20 seconds after clearing the van the drone settled on a high limb to await the President's arrival on the Marine One helicopter. He couldn't believe no alarms went off, no lights quickly turned on and yet the drone set upon a limb with a clear view of the area the President's chopper would set down.

He didn't have to wait long because suddenly the area lit up like daylight and he saw the helicopter slowly being lowered to the ground. It safely landed and the ground crew put into place the portable stairs. The helicopter doors opened and there stood Donald Trump waving to his staff.

All of this being captured on video onto his computer and it continued to record as the President greeted staff at the bottom of the portable staircase. An easy hundred and fifty-foot shot for any sniper.

Jack shut the drone off and then drove his car back to the mall where he had landed the drone on his last successful venture. He parked the car in a dimly lit corner and restarted the drone through his laptop and increased the rpm to lift the drone up very fast like a bird in flight and it flew over the fences in less than five seconds. He weaved around the Treasury Building and headed for the mall where he quickly landed and retrieved it. Then he rapidly departed the area and headed home but along the way, he stopped for a minute to forward the video to the Director.

"Jack, your batting three for three. It appears you were very close when you took this video. Where were you?"

"My toy sat in a tree one hundred feet away. You should get Trump to wear a bulletproof vest."

"We will reinforce our tree coverage. What's next on your plan?"

"It wouldn't be a surprise if I told you."

"True, enjoy the rest of the evening Jack. We will talk again soon."

"Good night sir."

Chapter 11

Jack had now successfully gained access to the president on three occasions. He wondered if a fourth attempt could be tried and could it be successful?

What he didn't know, about the same time he had successfully gained access to the Rose Garden, an event took place relevant within the FBI, ATF and CIA which did not involve Jack and his Secret Service assignment.

In late 2017, the FBI learned of a shipment of sophisticated weapons produced by Blanton Arms was being held for inspection in an export control area scheduled to ship to a Baltic country. The weapons had been identified on export documents as low-grade weapons acceptable for export to the named Baltic country. The grossly inflated dollar value for the type of weapon listed on an invoice tipped off the export agents into thinking the shipment had been priced in error.

When they opened the crates and began to inspect the goods, they discovered totally different weapons and immediately notified the FBI to inspect the shipment. After inspection, the FBI determined the product did not match the weapons shown on the Bill of Lading and other export documentation.

In fact, the type of weaponry discovered in the shipment had been banned for shipment by the US government and could only be exported with clearance from a security board. The actual weapons listed in the export documentation cited lower grade weapons and It became obvious, the export documentation signed by an executive of Blanton Arms had been falsified.

Further review of a number of previous shipments to the named country and other countries by Blanton Arms, reveled numerous shipments of the same item with high dollar amounts had been shipped to other areas and the documents had been signed by the same executive.

The FBI didn't stop the shipment but did start an investigation of Blanton Arms and notified their agents in the Baltic area of the suspected problem. Within days, a message sent from the Baltic country revealed the shipments had been destined to be collected by a known regional arms trader who in turn had close ties to Russian intelligence.

The FBI knew the named country to where the goods had been scheduled to ship but most likely it would not be the ultimate destination for the shipment. Unfortunately, there had been no obvious evidence as to where the arms would eventually end up.

This revelation set off alarms within the intel agencies responsible for keeping restricted arms from reaching foreign enemies and set into action a secret FBI investigation of Blanton Arms and its executive staff.

In the initial investigation, the FBI found George and Priscilla Blanton, principle owners of the Blanton corporation donated large sums to congressional members mostly engaged in military spending. They further learned of numerous international trips by the pair not only to the Baltic country in question but also to other known European countries identified as possible illegal arms deal hot spots.

Hence, an expanded investigation of the company and the foreign intermediaries received an Intel priority to determine the extent of the fraud and illegal arms exports. Other experts from different agencies would be selected to assist in bringing the case to a speedy conclusion to avoid further damage to the United States government, its military and its allies.

A meeting led by the Director of the FBI including high level executives of the FBI, ATF and CIA took place to determine how extensive the damage could be if Russia and other rogue nations had the ability to purchase key American weapons through a network of illegal arms dealers.

"Gentlemen, we are here today because of the recent findings of our Export agents in conjunction with the FBI and our ongoing investigation of Blanton Arms. I believe it is incumbent upon all of our relevant agencies to not only look at Blanton Arms but our entire American arms business. I believe the need exists for a broad investigation of our American manufacturers, but It is also important, we investigate foreign arms dealers involved in corrupting and harming American interests.

I know we have the skilled people to do the job domestically, but I am not sure we have the talented personnel to provide important investigations internationally. Therefore, I would appreciate all of you to review your employee databases for a talented individual with international experience in the arms trade. We need one or two of these personnel as quick as we can make them available."

"Anybody here have knowledge of some of our agents who may have the experience we now need?"

"Sir, I spent almost twenty years in the CIA before joining the ATF and I can give you one name who I consider to be the most qualified agent the CIA ever had for monitoring arms shipments internationally. He speaks four languages including French, German, Chinese and Russian, is a computer genius and a master spy. The only name he has ever used is Jack."

"Sir, as a former FBI agent, I also knew Jack well enough that he wouldn't come back to the same old job. But he is extremely patriotic and if we offered him a job as a special assignment in investigating an American company internationally, to help America he would probably jump at the challenge."

The Director of the FBI replied "It sounds like he would be especially beneficial to all of us because of his proven skills and if we can identify an accomplice with similar skills so they could work together as a team, we will have a win-win situation. Thank you both for your input. I will find Jack."

The next day the FBI director, had searched their database and up popped Jack. The director read about his long history and the successes he had on many dangerous assignments. He definitely is an ace thought the director. Now I will try to contact him. But before he did that, he searched the database for another person he also knew to be very capable and would serve as a good partner to Jack and would fit into the scheme the Director had been visualizing.

He then went back to Jack's file and a further search revealed Jack had been consulting to the Secret Service for about four months and reported to the Director of the Secret Service and he immediately called the director who he knew personally.

"Jeff, Paul here at the FBI. How are you?"

"I am fine and yourself?"

"I am good but the reason for my call is to determine the status of Jack currently in your employ. What is he doing and is he available, for another more dangerous assignment?"

"Jack is a wonder and he has been working to find out gaps in the Secret Service which may bring harm to the president or other high-ranking officials. He just, for the third time outsmarted the Secret Service and obtained photos of the president on the White House grounds close enough for a sniper to easily kill him.

"Interesting. Can you give him up for a few months for a high priority assignment in Europe?"

"Can you tell me a little bit about it?"

"It involves shipping of illegal arms to rogue dealers in Europe, who more than likely, then to ship these weapons to our enemies."

"That is right up Jack's alley but, I suggest you call him and discuss it with him in detail and he might like the challenge."

"Thanks Jeff, I will call him today and I owe you one."

"Your welcome, I only drink Jack Daniel's."

In a few minutes the Director of the FBI placed a call to Jack.

"Jack, this is Paul Baron of the FBI and if you have a few minutes, I would like to talk to you."

"Hi Paul, I believe we met once before about four or five years ago in England."

"Yes, we did. Good memory Jack. The reason for my call today is we have a major problem here in the USA and in Europe involving the sale of unauthorized arms being shipped to our enemies by an American company. Quite frankly we need help and you have been recommended by a few agents as the guy for the job."

"Can I ask the name of the American company?"

"Jack, this is top secret, but I know you can be trusted. The company is Blanton Arms."

"Interesting. What would be my role?"

"We need you in Europe to determine who is receiving the arms and their final destinations. But first, we want you and a teammate to meet the Blantons and see if they would hire you as a European sales agent."

"How would I be able to meet them and who would be my teammate?"

"If you're interested, here is how we can arrange the meeting. In two weeks, there is a big shindig at the White House for Medal of Freedom Honorees and our suspect, and his wife will attend. We can get you and an escort an invitation and arrange for you to be at the same table with the suspects.

The escort I have in mind is also is a woman about your age and also retired CIA. She is very knowledgeable of international arms dealers and the European area we need to investigate. I have been informed you know of her and I believe the two of you could help us solve our problem."

"Is her name Debbie?"

"Yes, and if you are still interested, arrange a meeting with her and try to assess her level of interest."

"I assume the need is ASAP?"

"You are correct Jack. We have only two weeks to get our act together."

"I will call her today sir."

"You have my private number. Call me and let me when you have reached a conclusion."

Chapter 12

Within an hour he called Debra and asked her if she could possibly meet him soon to discuss a consulting project he had been offered by an Arabian Prince and knowing she had Middle Eastern skills, perhaps she could advise him. He suggested they meet somewhere convenient and discuss the project in either your car or mine because of some classified details. She hadn't expected to hear from him but happily accepted his invite and they planned on meeting at the Potomac Mall fountain around one o'clock today.

Now he would have to convince Debra to attend the function with him which also meant being open and honest about his current role of spying against the Secret Service.

He arrived about ten minutes before the meeting time and waited next to the fountain for Debra's arrival. She suddenly showed up about two minutes after he arrived and looked pretty radiant and appeared happy to be seeing him again.

They walked to her car and after they were seated, she asked, "Well, what is this big deal with the Arabs you are contemplating?"

"It's a little longer story than what I told you on the phone and I want to assure you; what you are about to hear from me, may seem a little spooky. I don't want to scare you away as I do enjoy your company."

"Sounds intriguing. Keep going."

"The reason I preferred we talk in your car is because what I have to tell you is highly classified."

"Your right, that does sound spooky and is even more intriguing."

"Thanks for your understanding."

"Here goes; for the past three months, I have been engaged in an active spying operation against the Secret Service. I accepted this job after the Director of the Secret Service personally asked me to help the organization. I report only to the Director of the Secret Service and up till now, my role has been unknown to probably less than three or four people. I am the sole agent assigned to a project to determine holes in the Secret Service armor and how it could affect the life of the President or Vice President. In other words, I have to use my prior experience and imagination to determine how, via nefarious ways to bypass the myriad of detection devices and controls used by the Secret Service, and then harm or kill President Trump."

"You what? Did I hear you correctly or did my imagination play a trick on me?"

"You heard me correctly and now you know about my project, whether you accept it or not, you must promise to keep it secret."

"I am in shock, but I can keep a secret, but I must ask, why your telling me such a big secret?"

"Well it seems, I suddenly need an accomplice for a couple of reasons. I really need someone I can bounce Ideas around with and someone who has experience in the spy game. And by the way, I didn't suggest the need for an accomplice, it was tossed to me suddenly on my restricted line today when the Director of the FBI called me. It seems they need you and I for an assignment and it begins with us attending a White House function."

"You are inviting me to a White House function. Of all the dates I ever had, nobody ever asked me to attend a White House function. I feel I'm now travelling among the elite of our nation. How can I say no. By the way, what kind of function will we celebrate?"

"It's for recent recipients of the Medal of Freedom. We can expect the usual VIPS plus a number of important people in attendance. Strictly a black tie and stunning gowns event with lots of VIPs and the President."

"You mean Donald?"

"Yes, also him.

"Now, let me digest once more what you have told me. You say you're a professional assassin being funded by the government to take out the President. Isn't it called a coup? And you now want to recruit me to assist you?" She had tears in her eyes and laughed while she spoke.

"I hope your car is not bugged. I haven' t dated in so long, I thought I could win your heart by wining and dining you at the White House. That my dear, would be called a coup."

They both laughed at that comment.

"Jack, you have a record as a good CIA agent, and I know you to be a serious and dedicated worker. What you are doing is tough and I realize it must be very lonely having to question yourself day after day on every decision you make. I've been there a couple of times and it can be very stressful.

Hence, rather than sit around deciding whether to rearrange the one couch and two chairs at my house, I would be happy to do something good for our country, ourselves, collect a paycheck and forget about retirement for a while. I accept your offer, but I am not sure of what I can contribute but I will try. There is something else you should know about me Jack. Your boss, the Secret Service Director is a close friend of my dad who by the way is also a retired CIA executive."

"Your dad is retired from the CIA?"

"Yes, and so was my mom before she died of cancer."

"You must have had a great education long before you joined the company? I certainly know how to pick partners."

"When do we start Jack?"

"Welcome aboard partner. We already have started. I will call the Director of the FBI and start the process."

I'll be waiting for your call. Ciao."

Chapter 13

After their conversation, he casually drove home with warm or maybe hot thoughts about his new partner. She had a very impressive upbringing with parents both working for the CIA. In addition, she understands the stress and strains of being a spy and she also acquired success herself by serving as an important member of the company.

A nice-looking lady, good conversionist, intellectual and a former CIA agent and willing to be my partner. It's almost as good as winning a jackpot at Vegas. I hope she can start soon because we have a lot of work to do and maybe I won't be so lonely now.

He had just concluded his thoughts when the restricted phone rang.

"Jack, Paul again. I wondered if you connected with Debra?"

"I did Paul. We are ready to go."

"Fine, you will begin to receive additional information in the next couple of days. In the meantime, you and Debra begin planning immediately and as a reminder, the White House function is two weeks from tomorrow."

"Thank you, sir. I will call her after we end our call and we will start tomorrow."

"I'll stay in touch."

Jack immediately called Debra and explained the urgency of their getting started.

"Where do you want to meet Debra."

"Text me your address and I'll be there about nine tomorrow morning."

"Sounds great and I will have fresh coffee ready. I will also bring you up to date on my escapades thus far."

"Any success?"

"Yes, and I will fill in the blanks tomorrow.

"See you tomorrow and sleep well."

The phone went dead and he replaced it back in its cradle on the desk.

I can hardly wait for tomorrow he thought.

Jack arose early and began preparing a list of items they may need prior to the White House function. Certainly, both of them would need the proper clothing attire but D.C. had numerous rental shops for all occasions. They would also have to study the recipient's resumes to at least have some minimal knowledge about their work. They will also need some knowledge of the guest list and what room would be used for the function.

Just around nine, the doorbell rang, and Jack rushed to the door to greet Debra. "Good morning and glad to see you once again. Can I get you a cup of coffee?"

"Thanks, just black please, it would be great."

"Nice place you have and in a pretty nice location. Lived here long?"

"I bought it about twelve years and since then prices in this area have become simply outrageous."

"Housing in this area is a good investment. Tell me about your Secret Service job."

"My first attempt to get at the President worked out better than fine. I shot a twenty-minute video showing clear views of the Presidents of France and the United States and other VIPs in attendance all within shooting distance.

"The second time I had a clear shot at the president at a rally in Ohio and for my third attempt, I gained access to the Rose Garden and sat my drone on a tree limb and watched the President exit Marine One. It would have been a very easy shot from about one hundred feet.

"You've been very busy and successful but now since we will be working for the FBI, we have to do something more dangerous, Correct?"

"Yes Debra, I fully expect this assignment will harder than the last one.

"I assume you have already prepared a to-do list, what are your priorities on the list?"

"We are creatures of habit, aren't we? Well, we start by reading some resumes of the recipients and then we go to some rental shops to dress ourselves for our introduction as Mr. and Mrs. Aldridge. We got invited because we donate reasonable sums to the Republican party. We should know which room will be used for the function and the list of invitees, so we'll know their names when we see their faces. The Director will send us the proper identity documents early next week. Something is beginning to trouble me, I'm not sure what but I will now share those thoughts with you."

"Thanks a lot Jack. But before you do share with me, let me say, you have been honest about everything and maybe the two of us sharing the burden will lower the stress. So, let's start and get at it because time moves ahead regardless of what we do."

"Thanks Debra, here is what I know about this assignment. The FBI will sit us at a table with the Blanton's, the founders of Blanton Arms. The government has evidence of them exporting restricted items to known illegal arms traders in Europe. The Director wants us to befriend them and to see if I can get them to employ me in Europe to gather evidence of their illegal acts."

"Jack, I know a couple of good sources with knowledge of these activities in Europe but to me, the difficult part will be getting the Blantons to accept us and hire you."

"You are correct, and we should begin planning and figure out what approach might work best for us."

"Good time to break for lunch Jack. Did you prepare a gourmet meal, or do I just get a half of an old Subway sandwich you have laying around?"

"Neither, I have prepared Tuna Fish salad on a bed of Lettuce served with Hawaiian sweet rolls and homemade Arnold Palmers."

"You certainly know how to treat a lady."

"Sit here and I'll get the food."

During lunch, they chatted about the economy, the state of the stock market and other things without talking about work or each other. They finished lunch and Jack set the dishes in the sink to be washed later.

They moved into the den and sat in separate chairs and began discussing information gathered about the Medal recipients. The deeds performed by the recipients had been well documented and quite easy to remember since all had been newsmakers for some time.

"Jack, I think we have done enough for today and I am ready to head home, but I promise to try to put together a possible scenario as to how we might operate with the limited information available to us. We can only hope the Director offers more information as to what we have to investigate."

"Yes, I agree, having little information allows us to overthink this and muddle up our thoughts until we crash and burn. Let's step aside for a few hours and sleep on it. Travel safely and I'll see you tomorrow. Maybe, we should go shopping for some fancy duds, so we won't be taken for street people at the function."

"Sounds good. Ciao." and she quietly closed the door.

Chapter 14

The next day, Debra arrived back at Jack's house; they greeted each other, and each had a cup of coffee. They limited their talk to a summary of the previous day and decided it would be better to go shopping for their outfits rather than dwell on what ifs.

They decided to take the Metro and Jack drove to the station and parked the car. His instinct told him they had been followed as he watched a car park a few spaces from his car. He didn't want to alarm Debra, but he kept an eye on the person exiting the vehicle.

He had also exited the car and walked around to greet Debra and quietly said, "take my hand and snuggle a little. I believe someone followed us."

She immediately took his hand and leaned into him as lovers often do. They started to walk to the station and behind them followed a tall nondescript man. Suddenly, Jack stopped and said aloud "I forgot my phone. I'll be right back."

The man behind them continued towards the station and passed Debra but she got a good look at him and knew from his clothing and manner, he did not come from America.

Jack returned to where Debra stood in less than a minute and had carefully watched the man walk past her and continue to the station.

They also continued but they both became a little more cautious of their surroundings.

"Am I dreaming, or did this really happen?" He said. "The car had been following us since we left my street. I watched it in the mirror and although the driver had numerous opportunities to turn off or pass us, he didn't. His eyes and his car followed us all the way to this place."

"Jack is the Director having us tailed or could there another reason?"

"Maybe another reason. Maybe someone in the Secret Service has caught on to my surveillance and they have begun to follow us?"

"Let's not take the Metro but pay close attention to our friend. Once he enters the Metro, we will turn around and head back to the car pronto. He probably won't notice for at least a minute or two that we did not enter the station. It will give us time to get his license number and get out of here."

"Jack, I've already got my phone out to grab a photo of his license plate, so keep walking to our car."

They quickly entered the car and drove out of the station parking lot but stopped in a spot with a clear view of the station entrance. Jack watched the doors of the Metro station waiting to see if the man came out. No one exited the Metro station and so Jack drove back to the parking lot and saw the stranger's car remained where it had been originally parked.

"I'm getting paranoid Debra."

"It's okay Jack, I have the license number and it is easy to check and you are not paranoid."

"I guess I am not, but I did enjoy holding your hand and you snuggling next to me."

Debra laughed and gave Jack a big smile.

"Well let's start over again and they exited the car and walked back to the Metro station.

Once they boarded the Metro, they relaxed some and about three stops later, they exited the train and headed towards the mall. They entered the shop of "Mario's Tux and Gowns for all Occasions" because it had a reputation of being one of the better events and wedding rental places in D.C.

A voice greeted them upon their entry. "What a stunning couple. Let me guess, you came here to arrange for your wedding or maybe just for another party?"

"Thanks for the stunning couple bit but we are not getting married but came here to rent a fancy tux for him and an elegant gown for me. We will be attending a function at the White House soon and we don't want to disappoint our fellow attendees."

Mario and Jack laughed, and Debra just smiled. "I'm sure I can satisfy your wallet and your look. Said Mario."

"Who wants to start?"

"I'll start because tuxedos almost always come in basic black and I will stick to black."

"Step over here please and let me get some measurements and my assistant Eva, will tend to your lovely bride."

"Sorry, we are not married."

"My apologies. I should stick to measuring."

"It's ok Mario. No harm done. Let's start looking at what you have to offer me."

Meanwhile, Eva had taken Debra to a large rack of gowns and she began picking her selections. She then would hold them up to her chin to see how the color suited her.

Jack selected a tux, a cummerbund, a bowtie and matching handkerchief for the tux pocket. He had black dress shoes at home and so he had quickly found what he needed and ended his search.

He then walked over to where Debra looked over the numerous gowns on a large rack. He found a comfortable chair and settled in to watch the fashion show.

"Jack, you have it too easy. Me, I have to select a gown based on fit, color, style and wondering if there will be someone attending the function with the same dress. You talk about pressure; I have a lot of it right now."

Jack just sat and smiled.

Finally, after about fifteen minutes, Debra had selected three gowns and disappeared with Eva into a fitting room. She soon reappeared with her first choice and waltzed over to where Jack sat.

"Well partner, do you think this one will turn heads?"

"You look very elegant but let me reserve my opinion until I see the rest. It has been a long time since I judged a beauty contest."

"Ok, sounds good, I'll be right back."

In a few minutes, she returned in a more gorgeous gown and did a slow walk around where he sat.

"That is very special and makes you look great, but I still want to see number three."

"I'll be back."

Jack smiled and had to admit, Debra looked stunning in both gowns and he would have a difficult time selecting what looked best.

It wasn't long before she appeared in her third choice and Eva the shop assistant closely followed her. This selection, a lilac satin gown with sequins outlining her hourglass figure topped the other two and all Jack could do was stare. Debra looked positively beautiful. The color, the fit and the smile on her face said; this one belongs to me.

Eva just nodded her head and pointed at Debra. "Honestly, the gown had been definitely made for her. We didn't know her when we purchased it but by just looking at her, we and she couldn't' be more pleased."

"What's your feeling Jack?"

"I feel you are going to be the most beautiful stunning lady to attend the function and I am happy and proud to be your date."

She smiled broadly and said, "thanks Jack and thank you Eva for helping me."

Debra and Eva walked back to the fitting room and returned in about ten minutes and joined Jack at the checkout desk. He had already made the required payment and told Mario they would pick up the gown and tux in about ten days.

Chapter 15

Debra and Jack left the shop hand in hand and headed for a casual lunch somewhere within the mall. He found a small Chinese restaurant in the mall and picked a table away from other diners. As they sat down, Debra pulled out her cell phone to read a couple of new messages.

"Jack, here is a message which should interest you. It's from my dad and he traced the license number of the car who had followed us to the Metro Station. The guy lives on 39 Virginia Lane. Sound familiar?"

"Oh, my god. The guy lives three houses down from me and I thought he tailed us."

"That's okay, I thought he was a foreign agent. Why do I think we have been in this business too long?"

"Maybe, it's time for us to hang up and retire."

They had not noticed the waitress standing at the table sheepishly looking at them. "Now what do you two fancy for lunch?"

"I have a bowl of Udon soup with chicken and with chopsticks and hot tea," said Jack.

"You can bring me Mongolian beef, said Debra.

"Brown or white rice?"

"White."

"Shea shea sojai." replied jack.

"What did you say to her Jack?"

"I said thank you miss."

"You speak Chinese?"

"Yes"

'What other languages?"

"Russian, French, Spanish, some Hungarian and a smattering of English."

"Sorry, I only speak Arabic, Hebrew, Slovakian, Polish and also English."

"We are going to have a tough time communicating, said Jack while laughing."

"Oh, I can also sign."

At that moment the waitress delivered their food.

"Let's eat," said Debra.

"Now this is good food said Jack and how is yours Deborah."

"Just fine, just the way I like it. You seem to know how to use those chopsticks Jack. Do you always eat Chinese food with chopsticks'?"

"I try too. It's what I learned on some of my trips to China. It becomes a habit after a while."

They had finished their lunch and sat sipping tea from small cups and not speaking but rather trying to interpret the thoughts of each other based upon body language.

"Well I am full, and we have had a busy morning avoiding neighborhood spies, trying on tuxedos and gowns and then having a fine lunch. We now have two choices. Go to work or quit for the day. What is your choice Debra?"

"I have enjoyed the day thus far but, I do believe we still have to grasp what role we are going to play at the White House function. Nothing has changed since yesterday but we have to keep asking ourselves questions which may lead to plausible answers."

"Your right. We'll have lots of time when we retire. Let's get on our way and we only have a short ride to my house. The right answer will arrive sooner or later."

They left the mall and got back on the Metro to the station where Jack had parked the car. They then drove the short distance to Jack's house to immediately began planning their line of attack to support what the government expected of them at the White House function.

Chapter 16

They settled in at Jack's place and started discussing their plan.

"Here is a part of our plan which we had better start considering. Since we are meeting someone new, then who are we, where do we come from and where do we call home? Have we got kids in college, grandkids, jobs, etc?"

"Good point. Living in D.C. may be okay, and I could be a partially retired arms dealer. I know enough to pass a test. Maybe you can be a consultant to the Middle East advising on political and intelligence matters or a housewife. You decide what you think is best and believable."

"Since our goal is known, this sounds like the ideal path to take. You are the arms dealer and I consult as you mentioned but only periodically. We have no kids because this would raise additional questions difficult to answer. Right now, I am in favor of quitting for today and maybe tomorrow will bring more clarity because today, it is very hazy."

"Good suggestion. Why don't we have a drink. Would you like a glass of wine? Zin or cab?"

"Cab would be fine."

They sat opposite at Jack's small kitchen table thinking of their previous discussion. They toasted each other when Debra suddenly set her glass down and looked straight at Jack.

"You know, this is as stressful as I have been in a couple of years since I retired." Here I am in another stressful situation and not knowing why. Actually, maybe I do know why. I met this handsome guy who twisted my arm and promised me he would wine and dine me in luxury at the White House.

What he didn't tell me, he is a confirmed top-level spy chaser and who continues to work even as we sit here. But today, the myth got shattered when he convinced me of a strange car following us driven by a foreign looking man of evil who turned out to be one of his neighbors."

"Most of what you say is true, especially the handsome part. But even a good spy chaser makes a mistake some time, particularly when distracted by a beautiful woman."

"I like you very much Jack and hope we continue to have a good relationship. We sit here as two adults caught between doing right and carefully trying to avoid letting their true feelings for each other get in the way of their commitments to their job responsibilities."

"I like you too Debra and again, you are correct in your assessment. Me, I want to take you in my arms, feel the warmth of your body and savor the taste of the first kiss. But I can wait, and I can say to you it was worth the wait because if I didn't accept this FBI challenge, I would have never met the love of my life."

Debra stood up and walked slowly over the where Jack sat. She offered him her hand and he rose from his chair.

"This is what the warmth of my body feels like and now I want your lips to savor the first kiss."

They embraced for a long moment as their lips joined in a passionate kiss and they continued to hold each other close long after the kiss ended. Debra gently let go of Jacks hand and returned to her seat. Jack stood silently with a wonderful smile on his face.

"Jack, think of the kiss as a down payment to be paid in full at a later date to be determined."

"I will always remember this moment and I want you to know, you can make partial payments at any time."

They both laughed and then rose to hug each other once again.

Chapter 17

He was just finishing his first cup of coffee when the restricted cellphone rang at eight o'clock. The Director was calling him.

"Good morning Jack. I hope I did wake you."

No, I have been up and about for an hour or so.

"Good. I want to remind you and Debra, will try to become friendly with a couple who both maybe spying on the United States and selling arms illegally to various groups in Europe and elsewhere.

This is a serious situation and needs your and Debra's full attention. You will receive a dossier within the hour. You and Debbie should study it, then have a conference call with me later this afternoon.

"I can tell you it will be time consuming and you will travel to Europe more than you may want too but you and Debbie will get to have some relaxing time too on government expense in high rent districts. Talk to you later today Jack."

"Bye sir," but the phone had been disconnected.

He quickly called Debbie to tell her some of the news.

"Good morning. I hope you slept well. I just got off a call from the Director and by the time you can get here, I will have a rather large dossier on who we will be meeting. I will provide full details when you arrive. Fresh coffee ok or to do want it after I kiss you good morning?"

"We'll see but it sounds like we are going to have a very interesting day. See you in about thirty or so minutes."

No sooner had he hung up his cell phone call to Debbie than the doorbell rang, and a government courier handed him a thick envelope. He signed on the iPad to indicate he had received the package. and the courier quickly left.

Jack could hardly wait to open the envelope and determine what awaited him and Debbie. He opened the thick covered envelop and pulled out a large sized manuscript with a big TOP SECRET stamp on the front.

This is serious stuff and he set the document on the end table, sat down in his comfortable chair, picked up the manuscript and began to slowly turn the pages of a bound manuscript about three inches thick. After getting past the Top-Secret jargon and the index pages, he came to page one.

In bold print he read; The information you are about to read is highly classified and is not to be shared with anyone without TOP SECRET clearance.

His eyes continued down the page and he got his first look of who he and Debra would be encountering at the upcoming White House function. George and Priscilla Blanton.

He had just begun to read the dossier when Debra rang the doorbell. He ran to the door and quickly opened it, grabbed her hand and Said good morning."

"What, no kiss, no coffee?"

"Sorry, I just started to read the dossier when you rang the doorbell."

"Sit down here and let me get you a coffee and then we will talk."

In about three minutes, Jack returned and handed Debra her coffee. He then settled into a chair close by and once again picked up the dossier from the end table.

"Before I begin to talk about the dossier, I just read the first couple of pages, but first, I must tell you about my call from the Director this morning."

"Actually, he called about thirty minutes ahead of me to stress the importance of this assignment. He concluded by telling me, we would be travelling to Europe frequently and staying at ritzy resorts at government expense and he expects us to read the dossier today and call him later this afternoon to have a discussion."

'Wow, lucky me. Not only did I meet a handsome guy with a job who is taking me to a White House function but now he also wants to treat me to a European vacation. Do I have to work?"

"Unfortunately, yes dear. The Director said they chose us because of our previous successful experiences, and they expect us to bring a conclusion to this case. We better start reading and learn all we can about George and Priscilla Blanton."

"Please hand me the dossier and you rest for an hour while I read. Do you have a legal pad for me to write down my concerns?"

"Ok, here is the manuscript and I'll get you a pen and paper. Have at it."

Debbie immediately flipped past all the warnings to get to the real story. George and Priscilla Blanton are suspected of possible treason and spying for a foreign entity(s). The facts are spelled out throughout this dossier and had been gathered over a period of the last 24 months with the help of numerous intelligence agencies.

The facts will speak for themselves and although they have not yet been charged with a crime, the government believes additional executives of Blanton Arms know of the clandestine activity and could be charged themselves with abetting the crime.

In the initial investigation, the FBI found George and Priscilla Blanton donated large sums to congressional members mostly engaged in military spending. They further learned of numerous international trips by the pair not only to the Baltic country in question but also to other known European countries, which have been identified as possible illegal arms deal hot spots.

Hence, the investigation has been expanded and is ongoing. Other experts are being made available to assist in bring the case to a speedy conclusion to avoid further damage to the United States government, its military and its allies.

Jack had been sitting nearby on the coach for about thirty minutes waiting for Debra to give him a summary of her findings. When he saw her look up from her reading, he suspected she had completed her own investigation and now I guess it will be my turn.

"Jack, I'm done and from what I read, we have become the primary investigators for the FBI and other intel agencies. The case is complex and far reaching across most of the known arm's hot spots throughout Europe. We definitely are going to have a convoluted vacation, but we'll be together."

She then gave Jack a summary of her reading of the dossier.

"The case is pretty clear cut, but we still have a lot of work to do before even going to the function to greet our new friends, George and Priscilla."

"I don't think I really have to read the story as you have summarized it enough for me to get the drift of what is going on at Blanton Arms. Some of it seems amateurish but maybe it is done purposely. Companies of their size usually have very competent people at the top to carefully manage the short, and the long-term issues. I am sure selling arms illegally is never discussed at a board meeting.

I guess we now must sit and plan who we are and how can we get in the good graces of the Blantons."

"Jack, I don't think you can introduce yourself as an arms specialist. It seems George has too many senators on his payroll and it is easy for him to see through our made-up stories. We have to be a little more creative about our respective personas."

"Your right. Let's study George and Priscilla a little closer. What are they like and what appears to be their passion? Are they just doing it this thing for money or is there another reason for their actions? Where do most of their travels take them and how frequently? Who are their deal makers? I might even know some of them and this would be tough since they know me only as Jack."

"Then we will stick to the name of Jack and if I am to be your wife, where is that big diamond I should be wearing?"

They both had big smiles on their faces but deep down they knew they had started a journey and would enter the shady world of arms dealers and killers without any compassion. The story they had to concoct had better be bulletproof and well-rehearsed, as each of their lives truly depended upon it.

"We'll get the diamond tomorrow as Wal-Mart has a discount for seniors on Tuesday."

"Good because I found a good wedding band for you in a Cheerios box this morning."

They both laughed but, they both knew whatever they had gotten themselves into had danger written all over it. Neither one of them did not want to see each other being compromised, harmed or even dying. Now is the time to get their act together and it better happen rapidly became obvious to both of them.

"Okay its serious time." Said Jack. "I must stick to the name Jack because of my previous history. What is the most common name you used Debbie because we will be working in your old stomping ground and you may be recognized by one of the characters we might be introduced too?'

"Mostly everyone knew me as Clare, and which should work ok. My maiden name won't mean anything since we have become a married couple; aka, Mr. and Mrs. Aldridge."

"Ok Clare it is. I will begin calling you Clare in the right situation, so it won't be any big surprise to people we don't know. I have an extra laptop here and my desktop computer as well. Let's start some serious in-depth research about George and Priscilla Blanton."

"I'm ready. Let's keep each other informed of what web site we're using because there is no use in duplicating our efforts. Also, if it's important, print out the relevant info and bookmark it. We may have to find it again."

Jack decided to search the business side and Debra the social side of the Blantons and it wasn't long before they both had settled on web sites to explore their unknown foe.

Per their agreement, they began to find interesting information and bookmarked and printed articles as they moved from web site to web site. After about thirty minutes, they settled back and saw the pile of copies sitting on the printer. Both had been engrossed into their readings and what they had found separately would be of interest to both.

"Let's relax for a few minutes. I'll make us a lunch of turkey sandwiches and brew some tea for iced tea."

"Need an assistant?"

"Not for this job."

Chapter 18

Lunch showed up real soon and they sat at the table with a pile of printed info besides each plate. They read the printouts while eating and would discuss their findings after lunch. About twenty minutes elapsed during their lunch and it was close to four when Jack remembered they had to have a conference call with the Director.

"Let's plan on calling him in about ten minutes and let him know what we have learned and together, we can draw some preliminary conclusions. When we call, I'll start on the business side."

"Good afternoon sir. I also have Debbie, on the line. We studied both the business side and their private life side."

"Obviously, you two have read the dossier, so give me some feedback."

"First something unusual. The Arms subsidiary's cash on hand grew rapidly in the fourth quarter of 2018 yet their sales versus previous years remained about the same. It amounted to over 650 million dollars and it raises questions as to where these funds came from because sales did not contribute to it. But interestingly, over the next three quarters, this surplus gradually disappeared and yet the fixed costs remained stable and there did not appear to be any major infrastructure additions. So, where did it go and to whom? It's probably the most suspicious of the findings on the business side, which I have found. I think a money man should look at it in detail and we will probably need some number crunchers to investigate it further. Here's Debbie."

"What Jack found was Interesting and suspicious. I learned they both actively engage in Republican politics and contribute large amounts to Republican causes. He has strong relationships with a few senators, and she is also actively involved at the state level being the Republican state Chairperson in Alabama where they both grew up and attended college. They travel quite a bit and own homes in Alabama, Florida and Long Island. In addition, they travel frequently to Europe stopping in the Baltics, Italy and Germany and they have attended government affairs in Russia. Lastly they control a charitable trust fund endowed for fifteen billion dollars."

"You did say fifteen billion?"

"Yes, I did."

"Thanks Debra."

'One other thing, sir, can you send me a restricted phone? I may need one when Jack and I separate."

"Thanks Debbie I'll get you a phone. Jack how much money suddenly showed up on the balance sheet?"

"Over 600 million."

"That's a lot of guns and ammo."

"I'll get a bean counter involved. OK, for now, I will send you more recent info about the Blantons tomorrow. Until then, keep honing your individual roles because we don't want to alarm the Blantons. Bye for now."

Jack hung up his phone and stared out into space for a moment.

"Something troubling you Jack?"

"Maybe, I am trying to figure out why two elderly people worth zillions of dollars are acting like petty thieves? What do they have to gain or maybe they are hiding something or maybe they are being pressured to protect their name and wealth?"

"Are you suggesting they might be involved in a black mail scheme?"

"I can't be sure of anything at this stage."

They continued to discuss the Blantons and the facts they knew about them. They still couldn't figure out why somebody in the billionaire class would commit the crimes specified against them. Did it involve money or status or just plain stupidity?

All difficult questions to answer and in reality, only the Blantons could provide creditable answers if we could talk to them.

"Maybe we will know more tomorrow Jack. I'm getting sleepy, so ciao."

"Sleep well Debra and we'll continue tomorrow."

After Debbie left, Jack poured himself some Scotch over a glass of ice and sat in his den for a long time rehashing the Blanton facts. He felt he had run into a brick wall and at this point, he had nowhere to go.

At ten o'clock, he finally decided to go to bed and maybe a good night's sleep would refresh his thinking.

He awoke early the next morning and still had remnants of the Blantons running through his head. He found it hard to shake these thoughts thinking maybe he had missed a clue or two which could perhaps shed a little more light on the case. He then decided to return to the dossier and slow read the information which had been provided to see if anything suddenly came to light and changed his thought process.

He started at the very beginning where it assumed the Blantons to be guilty of treason and spying. What constitutes treason and if spying, who does it benefit, a country or themselves? Puzzling assumptions without any statement as to why. Jack doubted if these assumptions would stand up in a court of law.

Treason is defined as giving away top secrets to an enemy and nothing referencing or proving such activity had been stated. The dossier fails to mention who they might be spying against. Is it the US military or the government and what kind of information could they steal and who is receiving the information?

As Jack read page after page it still did not reveal to him any incriminating information which could point to treason. He also had doubts about the spying part. Maybe the information the Director is sending today will be more direct and revealing.

He put down the dossier and once again began to wonder what this whole situation is about. They are rich, they travel, they have friends in high places but treason and spying. 'It just doesn't add up for me.'

Before he could think any more, the doorbell rang and again a government courier handed him a large envelop, for which he had to sign on the iPad to show receipt of the package.

He headed back to the comfort of his chair and opened the package. Once more there was a rather thick manuscript inside for him to read. Like the previous dossier he had read, it contained the warning about being Top Secret.

He flipped the pages until he had reached the page titled CHARGES. Well, I should get some answers now. He began reading the new manuscript under the charges heading. And his senses heightened as he began to read.

George and Priscilla Blanton said Husband and Wife jointly and individually are hereby charged with Treason against the United States of America. The Blantons both jointly and individually have been in possession of highly sensitive information which in turn has possibly been carried or transmitted to known foreign agents. These crimes occurred domestically and internationally over a period three years.

George and Priscilla Blanton said Husband and Wife jointly and individually are hereby charged with spying against the United States of America. The Blantons jointly or individually spied upon US military bases, sights and organizations and had frequent access to military locales unavailable to others. They then possibly transmitted or otherwise passed this sensitive information to known foreign adversaries.

Before Jack could continue, the doorbell rang again and as he headed to answer the ring, he sensed it would be Debra. Upon opening the door, she stood there with a happy smile upon her face.

"Come on in. I had just finished reading the charges being prepared against the Blantons and they are very startling. Treason and spying and If all these are true, we will meet a couple who will challenge our intellect and skills."

"I assume, without being told, the Director wants us to become a part of the Blantons clandestine network and probably more internationally than here. We better prepare how we can convince them we can be useful to them for a price and inform them, we have done this before."

"Yikes! All that huh? Well it certainly enlightens us puts things more into perspective. I know how we are going to be spending the next few days."

"Oh, before we begin our rehearsal, did you notice what I have on my hand, as she waved it slowly in the air?"

"Wow, what a gorgeous ring. Much better than I would have given you," he said smiling.

"It belonged to my mother given to her by my dad for their wedding and has sat in my jewelry chest for too long and since I needed a wedding ring for our so-called adventure, I am donating it to our cause."

"Debra it really is beautiful and so are you. I am going to be proud to be your husband, even if only for a few months."

"Thanks Jack, you do make me happy. Unfortunately, we have other things to do and I believe it is Important we start preparing now since we have a clearer picture of the challenge."

Chapter 19

After Debra had come into the house, they moved to the kitchen table with note pads to begin casting their roles as people with experience internationally who could contribute to the Blanton's business. They had international arms experience, they knew a number of buyers and sellers and they could speak most of the key languages.

"Jack, I suggest, we go slow on giving the Blantons information. Let's not be too anxious or pushy but let's be friendly.

"Understand. We should not volunteer anything unless a specific question is asked and then let's not overdo it."

They decided to stick with Clare and Jack who met in Europe a few summers ago and actually got married in Paris besides the River Seine. Both had prior marriages and neither had any children.

He worked as an independent arms dealer in and around Russia and the Baltics. She had a degree in international business and felt more comfortable working for herself as a free-lance translator mostly to Arabic and Israeli commercial entities.

They had left Europe a few months after their wedding because Jack may have been involved in a couple of shady arms deals to the wrong people or at least, he had been accused of it by the US government.

They now lived in a large house in a nice neighborhood in Arlington and chose to work only periodically or when a special opportunity came along. Mostly, it involved Jack, when somebody needed a few weapons and most of these shipped to South America. He bought his products only through gun shows throughout the United States.

Returning to Europe for extended periods had always been their goal because they enjoyed the European lifestyle and believed more business opportunities existed for the both them in Europe.

They received an invitation to this affair through a congressional friend of Jack's who could not attend but sent us on his behalf.

"The rest we can fill in with BS but let's not over do it."

They both agreed this information should be passed to the Director for approval and if he has any recommendations for us. We should also ask him to us the name of the congressman or any other person who provided the invitation.

They had only four more days to firm up their story, pick up the dress clothes they had rented and to gather additional information about the Blantons.

They practiced the routine frequently, taking turns asking tough questions to each other. They believed their introductory remarks would work well but from then on, the questions would be tougher, and both had to be able to answer quickly with a safe answer. They realized they would be playing in a high stakes game and one mistake could cost them the opportunity to assist the government in the case against the Blantons.

Three days before the function, Jack went back to Mario's to pick up the tuxedo, accessories and the gown Debra would wear. Mario added a boutonniere for Jack and a corsage for Debra.

Later, they talked to the Director, who thought their approach sounded good and he happily dropped the name of Senator Robbins from Iowa who knew the Blantons and would vouch he gave Jack and Debra the invitation to attend the function.

They spent the rest of the day doing more rehearsals and continued to ask each other difficult questions. As the day progressed, they sensed they had mastered the lines for the upcoming performance.

"Debra, do we have recent pictures of the Blantons? I want to be able to recognize them and try to avoid them during the cocktail session at the function. I believe if we searched them out or pushed ourselves upon them, it would be a mistake."

"What's your reasoning for that approach?"

"Well, put yourself in their shoes for a moment. This couple wants to monopolize us during cocktail time and suddenly shows up at our table sitting next to us. This could set off alarms and they would be polite, but we would never see them again.

But if we get introduced to them during the cocktail party, keep it short and move on to talk to whoever is alone. Then, when we show up at their table, it's "Oh hi again." and we go on from there."

"Debra left about 8:30 and Jack continued to think if they had overlooked any aspic of their sting operation. Suddenly, he had another thought which could ease the meeting of the Blantons considerably. Why not have someone the Blantons know introduce us as someone who could possibly help their business in Europe.

I'll call the Director in the morning, but we only have one full day left to make such arrangements, but it would be a dynamite approach.

Jack called the Director exactly at 8:00 am. Sir, I believe I have a way to smooth the path to success and told him of his wish for someone who the Blantons knew who would be attending the function to introduce Debra and me to them."

The Director wholly agreed and said he will call him back within an hour.

Debra showed up around nine and Jack told her of what he had requested of the Director and he should get a response shortly. He had just finished saying this to Debra when the restricted line rang.

"Jack, you are going to love this. Senator Bosch, who is a key member of the Armed Forces Committee and also is a member of the Appropriations Committee. He personally knows them and also is aware of the investigations into the Blanton's corporation. He will be happy to introduce you and will tell George, he should know you because of your past history in the arms business. Hopefully, it will grease the skids."

"How will I meet Senator Bosch?"

"You will both have name tags and he will be near the right side of the bar at 6:20 sharp. Good luck and we'll chat after the function."

"Well, the Director knows his way around and will have Senator Bosch introduce us to the Blantons. He is a key member of a couple committees the Blantons try to influence, and his introduction should help us quite a bit."

"I guess all I have to do is put on my fancy gown, dab on some make-up and waltz in holding the hand of my hubby and enjoy being in the magic castle."

"Something like that. I am sure we have prepared ourselves well, and we have two key introductions, Senator Robbins and Senator Bosch, who both know the Blantons. All we have to hope for is the Blantons to show interest in us. Then, we'll take it one step at a time, but both knew the stress starts tomorrow.

Chapter 20

The big day finally arrived, and as usual Jack woke early, got a cup of coffee and sat at the kitchen table just thinking of the daunting task facing him and Debra this evening. He could only hope they had covered all the material they needed to know, and all would go well for their opening act.

About two hours after he awoke, Debra arrived bringing her gown and other necessities for this evening's performance. It became evident, her nerves were acting up. Jack took by the arm and sat her down, gave her a little pep talk.

"Debra, tonight, you and I embark not only on a new adventure but, a new chapter for us. We have never worked together before and although we both have faced adversity in our past, tonight will be no different from previous experiences.

We should keep this in mind. There is no immediate danger to our lives. We have aged but remain healthy and I assume have decent bank accounts. We will be going to a place where few of our fellow citizens have rarely even visited let alone, received an invitation to a White House function. We have prepared ourselves extremely well for this occasion and if it fails, it's not the end of our lives.

In fact, it maybe a new beginning. Just remember when we first met, none of your other boyfriends ever invited you to the White House. Yet here we're ready to go. So, let me see the beautiful smile which stirs my emotions."

She quickly smiled and almost instantly her nerves steadied.

"Jack, whether you realize it or not, you just gave me a few more reasons why I should not be nervous but rather I should be full of smiles and my new husband holds my hand as we enter the White House for act one. From that point on, it's just remembering our cues and our lines and at the end of the evening, we hope the audience applauds."

"We have worked hard to come this far, and we will do well Debra. We should start getting ready about three-thirty as the limo will show up at five. In the meantime, let's turn on the TV and relax."

They watched mostly news programs until the time to get ready arrived. Jack went upstairs to shower, shave and put on his tux. Debra used the guest bathroom to prepare herself. They both dressed and met downstairs within an hour, complemented each other on their good looks and then sat waiting for the limo to arrive.

The limo arrived as scheduled and since the White House function started at six and because of the typical D.C. traffic, it would take forty-five to fifty minutes for their limo to reach the White House. It would take another five to ten minutes to clear the guest gate and be dropped off at the front entrance. Debra and Jack sat close together during the ride and remained silent most of the time. They arrived at the front entrance just about six.

They stepped out of the limo on to a carpet leading to the entrance where they presented their invitation and had their identifications confirmed and then they walked through a metal detector to ensure they had no weapons.

They then walked with an escort and entered into the Green room already partially full of other guests. It served as the room for smaller cocktail parties and sometimes small dinner parties but for today's function, it would serve as the bar area.

After cocktails, the group would move to the State Dining Room for the dinner and presentations. Jack looked at his watch as he wanted to meet Senator Bosch at 6:20 sharp as the Director had advised him. He still had about five minutes to go when he glanced over to the right side of the bar, Senator Bosch had arrived right on time. Jack and Debra slowly walked over to the Senator and greeted him like they were old friends.

"Hi Jack, you may not remember me, but I sat on the intel committee when you gave your Russian overview in 2017. Nice to see you again and happy to assist you. Who is this lovely lady holding onto your arm?"

"I am his wife Clare, and it is a pleasure to meet you. I want to thank you for your generous offer to assist us."

"It's all my pleasure but before I introduce you, we should get a drink and enjoy ourselves. Besides, I'm buying." and they all laughed.

The Blantons have already arrived and in fact, they waved hello to me a short time ago. We'll stand around and sip our drinks for a minute or two and then we'll stroll over to meet them. I will introduce you as an old friend who had previously helped the intelligence committee about Russian arms trades. It should work and I will leave the rest to you. Good luck."

"Thanks, sir, for the drink and certainly for your assistance."

"Glad to help Jack. Let's go meet the Blantons."

"George how have you been and Priscilla you look radiant tonight. I would like you to meet an old friend and his wife. Let me introduce Jack and Clare Aldridge. Jack has been a friend for a few years, and he was a sharp arms dealer in many locations including Russia, South Africa and quite a few other areas. I saw you and thought you might want to meet this guy and chat a bit. I'm off to get another drink and to meet some other friends. Nice seeing all of you."

"Nice to meet you Jack and Clare. You folks live in D.C?"

"No, we have a nice place In Arlington and we actually don't come here very often. Another old friend, Senator Robbins received the invitation for tonight but had a conflicting appointment and asked me if Clare and I would like to go to a White House function. We have never been to one and jumped at the opportunity."

"Senator Bosch said you had been an arms dealer?"

"Yes, I still am but now, it's mostly small amounts to South America. I am very familiar with Blanton Arms products and sold quite a few in the good old days."

Just about then the call to dinner was announced.

"Nice meeting you folks, maybe we will meet again sometime, said George."

"Nice meeting you and Priscilla, George."

They went their respective ways and Jack and Debra took their time and dropped off their drink glasses at the bar and then casually followed the crowd to the State Dining Room.

As they entered the room, they were again asked for their invitation and they received a card showing their table and seat assignment.

"So far so good. We hope it stays that way," Said Jack.

"There is our table."

Without really looking at the other invitees, they glanced at the name place cards until they saw Aldridge Party. When they began to sit, they noticed the Blantons next to them.

"Well hello again." said George.

"Hi, we only know a few people here and now we know two more," said Clare.

Priscilla talked first. "Clare, I love that gown. Where did you find it?"

"I bought this in Italy some years ago from a small boutique in Florence. I am actually surprised it still fits."

"It is lovely on you."

"Thank you."

Jack, since we plan on being here for a while, "why did you leave Europe?"

"I sold a couple of large orders to a group in Bulgaria where I thought the arms would remain. Instead, they were quickly resold to a rebel group in South Africa and Interpol only knew my name and they thought, I had sold the weapons to South Africa. I proved it wasn't me, but I also got the message and it didn't take much to convince me to leave France and return to the states."

"Another words, Interpol and possibly the FBI would keep tabs on you?"

"Correct."

"I still maintain contacts there, but I find it difficult to export arms from here versus what I could do in Europe."

"Would you ever consider going back?"

"Clare and I both love the European style of living. We like the art, the landscape, the people, the food, etc. Maybe, but we have a nice home here, we have friends and frankly, we have enough in the bank to do whatever pleases us. Still it's a maybe."

"Just wondering, said George."

The salad had arrived, and Debra and Jack began to eat without paying much attention to the Blantons. They asked for glasses of red wine and casually chatted to themselves while eating and drinking. They knew they could not be too pushy, or the apple cart would tip over.

Debra began talking to the lady on her left while Jack focused on his salad and wine.

George reached over and passed Jack his card. Jack reached into his tux pocket and handed his card to George.

George read his card for a short time. It said, Jack, International Arms and Weapons Sales www.jack.armssales.com. It had no address and no telephone number.

"You do business using limited information? You don't use your complete name, address or phone number?"

"All my friendly contacts know me as Jack and they also have my email address and phone number. They trust me because I have never cheated them nor missed a promised delivery. The group of reliable contacts is small, but they buy a lot of goods and pay handsomely when the deal goes through. It's the way they and I like it."

"Sort of a cartel of arms dealers?"

"I am not sure how any government classifies us as we tend to stay well hidden."

"You're an interesting guy Jack."

"My wife keeps me honest, but she also has been a great help to me."

"You both are interesting. Where did you meet?"

"Actually, I met Clare on a trip to the Baltics. She had a translating service for Arab and Israeli businesspeople, dealing in the area. We got married in Paris and lived there until we returned to the USA."

The main course appeared; Jack and Debra again ignored the Blantons while they ate. Jack commented once about the food saying, "They eat good on taxpayer dollars."

The dinner ended and the waiting staff removed the dinner plates and replaced them with dessert plates and coffee cups. The presentations began and Debra moved a bit closer to Jack and they held hands beneath the table.

The Vice President served as the emcee and introduced each of the recipients along with a short video of their work. The recipients remained on the small stage and the guests rose and applauded for the President's introduction.

"He then spoke. "First, I want to congratulate each of the recipients for the fine work they have done for a long time. I also offer my sincere thanks on behalf of all Americans for the contributions each of them has given to our great country. We all consider it an honor to be in your company.

Lastly, I want to thank all of you attending this evening and sharing these precious moments with us. Again, thank you."

Debra and Jack sipped their coffee and ate a small amount of dessert. After the president had concluded his remarks, people began to say their goodbyes. Jack told the Blantons it had been a pleasure to meet them and shook George's hand.

Jack and Debra stood up and said goodbye to other guests at their table and began the slow walk to exit the building. Jack had texted the limo driver and they like everyone else would wait until their car arrived.

It didn't take long for the limo to get them home. The exited the limo and Jack took Debra's hand and held it tightly.

"I believe we did well tonight, but I don't want to dwell on it now. We'll have time tomorrow to dissect what occurred and just guess at future possibilities. Now, I just want these moments for us. I enjoyed every moment of the evening but to me, the most beautiful part had to be you and I sitting together."

"Jack, at first my nerves acted up, but your confidence lifted my spirits and I studied everything about our sitting in the White House, so I could always remember this night. It may have been a job, but it will remain the nicest job I have ever had. You made it special for me and now is the time for us to enjoy our own special event."

That said, she took Jack's hand and lead him into the house and up the stairs. They rushed up the stairs, like two lovers in lust.

Chapter 21

Jack and Debra did not leave the bedroom to after nine in the morning but both of them smiled broadly and they either hugged each other or held hands. They went downstairs to have the first cup of coffee and to review their meeting with the Blantons at the White House function.

"Jack, what questions did George ask you? He seemed very interested in you and his body language demonstrated he had a strong interest in what you had to say."

"He asked a couple of key questions. He wanted to know why we left Europe, and would we consider moving back there again. He did react to my business card not having a complete name, address and telephone number, but I believe my explanations on all questions, satisfied his curiosity."

"So, what conclusions can we draw from this first meeting?

'Debra, it's a toss-up but I believe I whet his appetite and he will call again with a pretext of us going to one of their parties. Here's why. George may know he is being watched and he thinks we can possibly bail him out.

We accept a sweet offer from him to relocate back to Europe and mange some of his unsavory arms dealers and ensuring Blanton Arms get it's, fair share of the booty."

"Jack, I didn't mention this to you, but I think George recognized me. How, I am uncertain, but I just have a feeling."

"Did your family know him?"

"I am not sure but let me call my dad and ask."

"Dad, it's me your favorite daughter. Yeh, I know, I am the only one. Dad, I have a question for you. Did you know George Blanton?"

"Know him, he and I fished together whenever we could break loose from business or our families. He is a hell of a nice guy. We haven't spoken in a while, but I know about him and Priscilla donating more than 500 million dollars a year to more than 2000 charities across the USA. If you rate people on a scale, they would be a ten. Why do you ask?"

"Oh, Jack and I met him and his wife the other evening at a White House function. I thought I recognized him, but I wasn't quite sure."

"You used to call him Uncle George. If you see him again, send him my best wishes. Bye now, I am watching Jeopardy."

"Bye dad."

Debbie, you looked shocked. What is wrong?"

"What I said before is correct. I knew him as a little girl, and I called him Uncle George. My dad told me Priscilla and George donate more than 500 million dollars a year through their charitable trusts. He also rates them on a scale and says they deserve a ten. Jack, something doesn't smell right because these could not the same people we have read about recently."

"George showed no signs he knew you but maybe he is to polite. What your dad just told you is quite different from what the dossier claims. These people do not match the ones we read about. People stealing money do not donate anything, let alone 500 million dollars a year."

"Let's hope they will contact us to meet again."

"I had planned for us to maybe go to the Smithsonian today but maybe we have some other chores to do involving the Blantons."

"Jack, the charges maybe real or someone has plans to cover their tracks while blaming the Blantons. We can only guess as to why and if we can uncover the culprit, we could probably answer the question."

They went back to reading the dossier and other manuscripts they had received from the director. It dawned on them at the same time about an executive of Blanton being investigated and maybe, the link to all of the troubles.

They spent the rest of the day discussing the probable reasons, but they did not have access to all of the facts and therefore but could not decide guilty or not guilty.

Soon bedtime arrived and they continued to toss thoughts back and forth until they fell asleep in each other's arms.

They awoke early and wondered down to the kitchen to have coffee and watch the morning news cast. About nine o'clock, Debra's phone rang.

"Hello, Debra, this is Priscilla Blanton. We got your number from your dad and George and I would like to meet with you and Jack, today if possible."

"Jack and I have no plans, so sure, today would be okay. Let me give you our address and what time is convenient for you?"

"How about ten o'clock. Does that sound okay?"

"Okay, we live at 33 Virginia Lane in Arlington. See you at ten."

"Who called Debra?"

"Priscilla Blanton and she knew my name and got my number from my dad. They will be here at ten."

"Well they now know about us and what we do but, there is always the possibility we will get some answers and solve some problems or have new questions and more problems."

"First, let's get dressed quickly as it is almost nine-thirty."

About fifteen minutes later they returned downstairs and heard a car drive up. They opened the door and saw the Blantons walking up the sidewalk leading to their house.

"George, Priscilla, welcome to our home. How can we help you and George?"

George shook Jacks hand and said "Jack I am happy we met you and Debra the other night because we wondered after I told Priscilla I had confidence; I knew Debbie. I knew her as a young child and her dad, and I often fished together when we got the opportunity. Debbie still has the happy smile she had as a child.

Both Priscilla and I suspected something did not appear right. You see, I knew Debbie had been in the CIA and after a couple of phone calls I soon discovered, you also had a long history with the CIA. So why would you two attend a party posing as husband and wife and sit at our table, unless the government had us under surveillance. Quite frankly, it made no sense to us."

"George, we must be truthful, yes, we attended the function to meet the both of you and we had precepts about you and your company, Blanton Arms. We hoped to get to know you better and for me to work for your company in Europe.

"I appreciate your candor Jack, but you have only a small picture of my role in the company. You see, ten years ago, I ceded complete control of the entire Blanton conglomerate to a trusted team. Priscilla and I wanted to pursue another path. The business had been very good financially to us and we wanted to give a major portion of it away.

We formed two nonprofit Charity trusts. One named after her mother and my mother who always taught us to help others. The second trust is in our names and is more directed towards politics targeted to improve the lives of many. You may already know, together, our trusts distribute more than $500 million per year to charitable organizations across the USA. In addition, we also support numerous orphanages in many European countries.

"Thanks, George for sharing the information with us. We know what you said is true information and we believe you. Based upon what you just told me, my instant conclusion is you and Priscilla have been set up for a fall but by who and why, I cannot answer. What I can say, it is alleged, a top executive in your arms division is diverting Blanton products to known enemies and diverting large sums, probably in hidden bank accounts in Europe.

"The lead agencies have asked Debra and I to try and get additional evidence, primarily in Europe. I believe if we act in time and find the true culprits, we can keep your name clean.

I am going to suggest the following: Debbie and I will act on your behalf, but we need a good story, which I can sell to hold off the intel agencies of doing further damage. You will have to give me a job to assist sales in Europe.

"Thanks Jack. What do you need?"

"A bank account because I will need to grease a few palms. I will also need some confidential data about higher level employees of Blanton Arms group, and you must gather it without their knowledge. Debbie and I will stay in the high rent districts throughout Europe only to assist in painting a successful picture. I want my sources to think I am doing pretty well in the arms business.

I didn't tell you, between us, Debbie and I speak eight languages in addition to English; we each have 25 years in the CIA mainly in Europe and I have a master's degree in computer science. I will use this last skill to tap into some of Blanton Arms secrets. But again, all together, it may be very pricey."

"Jack is $300 thousand to start okay?"

"It is more than enough but it depends how many times Debbie has her nails done and her hair set." They all laughed at the remark and it lightened the load of stress on the Blantons.

"Remember, we still get paid by our government and we know you and Priscilla do a lot for others and hopefully we can do a lot for you."

"George, I just had another thought which will add to our credibility in the agency. Fly us to Paris in your private jet because you want to get us on the job as soon as possible."

"When do you want to go?"

"Two days will work for us. We have to inform the agency we will begin to work for you outside of the normal channels. They will assume we will get involved in doing some dirty work for Blanton, so they will have a strong case to delay any charges until they hear from us.

I am guessing we possibly can clear this up in about a month or two."

"Do you mind if Priscilla and I fly with you? We haven't been to Paris in a long time."

"It works for us and we will have some time to do some serious planning."

"Thanks once more for meeting with us and for your honesty. We know what you are doing could be dangerous and we want you to stay safe. Can we take you to lunch now, as all this talking made me hungry?"

"Let's go."

Chapter 22

They dined at a small restaurant in Arlington overlooking the Potomac River. They continued their conversation about the trip to Europe and Jack had confidence he and Debra knew the right people he could trust to gather information for him.

"George, I hope you can get me the names of the Blanton Arms top executives before we leave as I want to start having them investigated in the USA.

"I promise you Jack you will have the needed information by tomorrow and the bank account would also be open and funded tomorrow.

Their flight to Paris would leave around eight at night and because of the time differences, they would arrive in Paris about ten in the morning. Hotel reservations will be made later today and transportation from the Airport will also be booked. If you need additional information, call me at any time.

The Blantons drove them home and Jack knew he had plenty to do prior to leaving for Paris. He needed a good story to tell the director and to hold off any agency actions prior to Debra and him finishing their investigations in Europe. He also had to contact one of his close friends, an arms dealer located in Germany, to meet him in Paris in two days.

Debra and Jack again sat around the kitchen table and worked out a plausible explanation to give the Director. Debra also had some close contacts in Belgium she could rely on to perhaps gather information.

"Debra how strong is your feelings the Blanton's are innocent?"

"One hundred percent Jack and I'll tell you why. There is nothing in either of the two dossiers to prove any of the charges. The real evidence provided by the FBI says the weapons shipping documents were signed by a Blanton executive. Find him and it will prove the Blanton's innocence."

"I agree with you Debra and now we have to mislead the Director for a short period."

"Sometimes that happens Jack but now I have to leave to get ready for our flight. I will check the weather to see how we should dress, and I'll text you the info. Is there a possibility we may need a couple of guns?"

"I didn't think of that, but yes, they may be necessary. Revolvers of any size will be fine."

"Got it, I have to run now but here is a kiss to hold you until I return. Oh, I almost forgot, we are going to have a honeymoon in Paris, right?"

"Maybe in a couple of months, but this will be a hardworking vacation."

"Ciao."

Jack sent a short email to his friend asking him if he could be in Paris the day after tomorrow. He followed up with an email to another friend in Russia asking for a safe number to call him in the next three days.

He then called the Director on the restricted line. "Sir, I have some good news for you. George Blanton made me an offer I can't refuse. He wants me to move to Europe ASAP and I will fly to Paris with Debbie tomorrow on the Blanton's private jet. I suggest holding off on any further actions against the Blantons until we have finished our investigations. I have already lined up at least two reputable sources and Debbie also has one as we start to gather info. We should be able to provide some dirt in about a week to ten days.

I also suggest an investigation of the entire upper tier of Blanton's top executives in the Arms division to include emails, texts and bank accounts. I will give you names of key players tomorrow. George is not doing this alone."

"I have one other request sir; can you keep this information strictly between you and maybe some top executives. I would prefer no one investigating Blanton should know about Debbie or myself.

"I agree Jack and I will put the proper wheels in motion, and we will hold off on all charges until you finalize your pursuit. Travel safe and you and Debra be careful. When big bucks become at risk, bullets usually fly to stop a lot of investigations."

The line went dead and Jack sat and thought about what the Director just said. He did not want anything to happen to either Debbie or himself and they would be very careful who they met and worked with on doing their job.

George Blanton called Jack early in the morning and gave him three names and their job titles. They had all been at the company a long time and he assumed the probability of more people involved as George knew it took a lot to get shipments out the door and through export agents. Jack wrote down the names and titles given to him.

Robert P. Wimsley, GM, Paul f. Silverman, CFO and Lawrence R. Rivera, VP of Production.

George confirmed the bank account had been opened and he would give the info to Jack tomorrow. They would be staying at the Shangri-La Hotel and transportation has been arranged and by the way, we will pick you and Debra up around seven tomorrow evening to go to the airport, Obviously, the plane doesn't leave until we get there.

Jack explained he had spoken to the Director and all actions will be on hold until we conclude our investigation. They said their good-byes and Jack would not hear from them until tomorrow night.

Jack sat down at his computer to send the names of the executives to the director when he noticed he had an urgent email. Opening up his mail app he noted the email from his friend in Germany confirming their meeting and Jack should send him hotel information.

He quickly answered and gave him the hotel information and said he looked forward to meeting him again.

He then sent the names he had received from George to the Director with the caveat; there probably could be more people involved.

He continued working on his computer and using a memory stick, downloaded information which could be of use to him in Europe.

He thought about bringing his Apple Pro notebook but the computer equipment he would need to enter other computers had to be a lot more powerful. His friend from Russia would help him in obtaining the right software and hardware in Europe to meet his hacking needs.

He had not heard from Debra and wondered what she might be doing to prepare for the trip and, so he called her. "Good morning dear. How are you?"

"I'm fine just sorting out what to bring. Do I need anything dressy?"

"Yes. Since we are staying at least for a few nights at the Shangri-La, you may need something fashionable."

"Boy, from the time I met you, you have gone out of your way to take me to all the places I always dreamed about. Now to top it off, we are going to Shangri-La?"

"Only the best for you love."

"Let's hope it stays that way. I'll be over in a couple of hours after I pack and lock up the condo. We'll be alone tonight for some peace and quiet. But I know we'll end up reviewing plans for the week.

I do think we may have to go our separate ways for a couple of days if I decide to visit Belgium but it may be worth it as my contact said she knows a thing or two about arm sales sold to NATO countries being diverted to Russia."

"How interesting. Franz from Germany will meet us in Paris and should also have some useful information. I may disappear probably to Finland to meet my friend Boris from Russia to set up a hacking spot. He is as good as it gets in hacking computers.

I want to try to get into Blanton arms computer system to see if I can get relevant emails from the names I had been given by George. There also might be a European Bank used to funnel funds from one entity to another, we may try to hack."

"Ciao sweets, I have to get moving to finish up. See you for a late lunch."

Jack smiled knowing she is okay, and he will see her soon.

Chapter 23

Debra finally reached Jack's house about two o'clock and she had promised him a late lunch. She had stopped at KFC and got them both chicken sandwiches and fries and they sat in the kitchen eating and discussing various approaches to learn more about the mysteries surrounding Blanton Arms.

"Jack, perhaps the real keys lay in the computers of the three named executives."

"I agreed but I also think if I can learn about the European bank being used to funnel funds between Europe and the USA, then it would be the major breakthrough."

It became more likely the bulk of their proof of establishing the innocence of the Blantons is stashed away in a few hidden computers. Yet, Jack's and Debra's European contacts may offer the greatest possibilities of obtaining answers and reaching a solution.

Jack had enough computer power at home along with the right software which he thought would give him a possibility to trying his hacking skills now. We won't be leaving for another twenty plus hours, so what have I to lose.

"Debra, I'm going up to the computer room to test my skills. We have time to kill and I can't think of better use than to attempt a hack of one of the suspects computers."

"Give it a try dear but don't spend all night doing it."

"Got it."

He then headed up the stairs to the computer room which had stood unused for a few months. He hoped everything still worked and he flipped the main switch. The lights on the computer flashed and soon it entered into the start-up process. He waited about three minutes while it was booting up and suddenly the home screen filled with a couple of dozen icons and he started typing away.

He first went into Facebook to see if any of the names had a membership and lo and behold, to his surprise, all three were listed and shown as Executives of Blanton Arms. Two of them had what appeared to be personal email addresses in their profile and Jack went to work.

Using some very sophisticated software jointly developed by Boris and himself, it took him about twenty minutes to enter into Paul Silverman's home computer while he actively used it and while Jack watched. Jack could see Paul writing an email to the other two suspects asking about a $3,500,000 payment due from the Ukrainian sale. The payment is overdue and the source in Russia says the Ukrainian received his money. I'm not sure what the hell is going on?

"Debbie, get up here fast. You have to see this, now. I can't believe my luck."

Debbie came rushing into the room and Jack pulled her over to a chair next to him.

"You have to read this."

"You can't be serious. You have only been here twenty minutes and you struck gold?"

"Let's hope he doesn't shut his computer down for the night. I'm finished if he shuts down, but otherwise I can grab all his mail, his banking info and whatever else seem relevant. These guys may not be too bright. For now, I will sit and wait, and you can go back downstairs."

The wait didn't last long. In less than ten minutes Silverman had left the computer on and there wasn't any more activity. Jack aggressively and rapidly went to work. He quickly scanned Silverman's files until he found his top priority. The complete email file of received and sent emails to Bob Wimsley and Larry Rivera. He downloaded about three years' worth, without stopping to read any of them and placed them into a folder and hit save on his computer. He would read them later.

He next scanned through email files looking for foreign extensions and found quite a few. He then downloaded those into a separate folder. Now he began looking for banking information. He noted there were four banks listed and one of them based in Poland. These files became a lot more difficult to latch onto.

He began using some tricks he had learned from his friend Boris and soon, he had the ability to read every statement and messages passed between Silverman and all the banks. He created another folder and another download went into a folder on his computer. He felt he had enough of the key info for now and made sure to scrub all evidence of the computer being compromised before he safely exited. He then decided to move to Larry Rivera's computer.

He had a little more difficulty in getting into Larry' hard drive but the software guided him with suggestions and after touching the right buttons he succeeded. Larry had not logged into his computer all day and so it made it easier for Jack to do his thing.

Again, as in Silverman's computer, he scanned for emails from the names he had and easily pulled all the information he wanted into his computer. Next, he checked Larry's bank files and again easily saved them. Larry had practically no communication with any international contacts. Jack again went through his exit exercise to safely end his session on Larry's computer. He then decided to begin reading the files he saved from both Silverman's and Larry's computers.

Debra came back to the room and asked Jack if he had gotten anything interesting.

"I'm not sure but I have four or five large files of data which I will put onto a thumb drive in a minute. I wasn't planning on bringing my laptop but now I have this data, I will take it and read it while we fly to Paris."

"Jack are you telling me, you acquired four or five folders of info from other people's computers and yet you have been up here for only one hour?"

"Good huh? Do I get a special hug maybe?"

"Well stand up. Okay, are you ready?"

She softly pressed her body against his and slowly began rubbing his back while kissing his neck. Jack surrendered, took her hand and they walked into the bedroom.

They woke early in the morning and Jack jumped out of bed. Debra said she wanted to sleep a bit longer. Jack went to the bathroom and splashed some water on his face; dried himself and headed back to the computer room.

I have a few more hours, maybe, I can capture some info from Wimsley. He immediately went to the Linked-In site and found his name and then reviewed his profile. Not much there but there is an email address and it looks more personnel then a business address.

He hit a few more keys and quickly learned he could not easily tap into Robert Wimsley's private computer as it had more than one firewall to stop intrusion. This did not deter Jack, but he had to be a bit more aggressive and cleaver in his approach if he wanted to be successful.

He had a few tricks to try and spent twenty minutes without success before he tried another tactic.

He went back to Silverman's computer and he sent out an email to Wimsley as if it was sent from Silverman but containing malware which would allow him to gain access to Wimsley's computer. Within a few minutes he received a response and he knew the gate to Wimsley computer had been opened.

He then quickly gained access and soon learned Wimsley had a fairly standard set-up and Jack should have no issues retrieving what he wanted as he had done on the previous computers. He scanned folders and files to get an overview as to how the filing system had been established and in about ten minutes later he had all he needed from Wimsley and between the three sets of data he had, it should not be a problem to get a pretty good insight into the work between the three amigos.

He loaded the newly acquired data onto the thumb drive for later use. He then packed it with his iPad and placed it into a brief case to carry onto the plane for the flight to Paris.

He had been finished for about an hour when Debra came down the stairs and as usual had a pleasant smile on her face.

"Good morning sweetheart."

"Good morning dear. I assume you worked again this morning?"

"Yes, I got into Wimsley computer and obtained a few more relevant files. A nice morning of good work."

"You sure no how to tweak my physic. I met you as a presidential assassin, we got married and now you have become a major hacker. I hope they don't give a lot of jail time for these pursuits of yours."

"Nah, they got to catch me first. Would you like some breakfast or is it brunch time?"

"Toast and coffee and love is all I need."

"I know how to make love and coffee, but I usually burn toast."

"Since you excel at the first two, I wouldn't notice the toast."

"You are sweet." They ate their breakfast and discussed more about what further information they would need.

They listed the summary of priorities as follows:

Learn the names of all known arms dealers selling or trading Blanton goods in Europe or elsewhere.

Determine the ultimate destination of Blanton arms once they reach European shores.

Follow the money. What are the names of the banks moving the cash around and the country location?

Contact Interpol for possible assistance.

Contact various hotels or resorts where the George and Priscilla have stayed on their numerous visits to Europe.

What role do the Russians have in some of the transactions?

"This should keep us busy for a while Debra, but possibly, some of this information I have on the thumb drive could assist us in solving our priority needs."

"Do you have a laptop?"

"Yes, an Apple just like yours."

"Good. Let's divide up the workload. I will begin with Silverman's emails and other stuff and you will study Wimsley's stuff. We should be able to do this in a couple of hours before George and Priscilla pick us up."

"I am going to call George now. I need some travel data from him."

"George, Jack here. Do have a moment to spare?"

Sure Jack. what do you need?"

"I would like your and Priscilla's travel itinerary to Europe and Russia the last two years. Please include dates and particularly hotels or resorts you stayed in during your visits. If there is something special to be noted, please add It in a comments section. We want to account for all your trips and activity in the areas you both visited."

'Fortunately, I have a super assistant and she can put this together pretty fast. If we don't have it by the time, we pick you up, she will fax it to us on the plane."

"Thanks George. I want you to know, we have already made some serious inroads into this project and will continue until we get what we all want."

"We have faith in you and Debra. See you both in a few hours."

Chapter 24

While Jack and Debra were preparing to fly to Paris, Paul Silverman, CFO of Blanton Arms had lunch with Adam Sanderson of the FBI. In appearance, they were two suited executives out to lunch. They had previous meetings regarding some international shipments and Adam was doing the investigation, but Silverman had a feeling he could change the relationship in favor of Blanton Arms.

"Paul, I'm sure you are aware your company has pretty good sales and you now have your latest weapon into production and yet I understand the government is restricting shipments to a number of countries. From my viewpoint, I don't understand how you can maintain good sales in Europe without selling your newest weapons."

"Adam, to be truthful, because it is a high price item with a lot of demand, it will reduce our sales dramatically. We are trying to lobby a few senators to ease the restriction but thus far nothing has happened and from what we have been told, there is a good chance the restriction on sales will not be lifted."

"You know Paul, there may be some other ways to get around your shipments. The Export Customs agents are mostly paper pushers and if things are done a certain way, it's possible some good sales can be had in Europe."

"Adam, you are well aware we have tried this before and got caught and in fact it is how the FBI and you came to investigate Blanton. Can you give me an example of how it can be handled without raising concerns by customs?"

"How you guys screwed up was putting a high dollar value on a lower cost product and you got caught. It was a stupid mistake. Some of your competitors packing lists show one product with an accurate price but the goods being shipped in some cases are different products. No inspections are performed, so they go through customs quickly. Some competitors do it to avoid restrictions and others to limit customs duties in Europe or elsewhere. These are not a made-up examples Paul; it is really happening."

"Interesting Adam and I admit the mistake we made was stupid of us. Are many of our competitors doing what you described?"

"Some but not all. It boils down to how devious you want to be and how much money you want to make."

"I know two or three of us who want to make money. Big money."

"Make that four people who want big money. I like fancy restaurants and women who enjoy sex. It's an expensive hobby."

"Your telling me. I got a mistress for seven years now and she wants a new car every two years."

"Paul let me educate you a little. I have knowledge of buyers all over Europe looking for these weapons but can't buy them but would pay triple the price to get them. Right now, the only decent arms sellers are the Chinese, Russians, Iranians and North Koreans and they have nothing resembling Blanton's weapons."

"Triple the price you said. In all cash?"

"All cash and it can be moved to a bank of your choice."

"Adam, would you be willing to meet with me and a couple of other executives to further discuss this subject."

"Sure, I am open to that and I understand it has to remain confidential, but again, I am also interested in making money."

"Understand. Let me see If I can arrange a meeting in the next couple of weeks."

"I'll wait to hear from you."

The next day, Silverman sent an email to Wimsley and Rivera describing the essence of his meeting with Adam. He asks them to start thinking whether Adam's approach would benefit us, and we should meet to further discuss this matter. They all agreed and decided to meet in four days at Silverman's house.

Silverman had suggested the meeting be casual and he offered to prepare barbeque dinner for everyone. They joined together on his patio and after dinner and they began to discuss the issues.

Silverman started first. "Look guys, I see this as a prime opportunity to make ourselves a lot of money. I believe it will dwarf everything we have made up to now and perhaps reach hundreds of million dollars. I realize we have made mistakes in the past with our trying to get around the law, but we learned something and between us have the smarts to grow our wealth. I believe Adam has a workable plan and I'm in favor of having him joining our group as a minority participant. Bob what do feel about this matter."

"Quite frankly, I am for it, but I think we have to pay attention to the details much more than we have in the past. We can't just ship goods without considering the initial destination because the government is well aware of the illegal arm's hot spots. ignoring this aspect will eventually lead us to trouble. Each sale and shipment must be well thought out to ensure it will not come back to haunt us. I agree we are smart enough to do this, but we have to be careful of every action we take. I like the money part, but jail part is unattractive. Your turn Larry."

"What you both said is true and I also agree it is the right step for us to take if we want to increase our holdings. We all realize it's illegal, but we aren't the only ones doing it and besides, it won't be long before there is a Chinese copy be peddled. There are numerous steps for every order, and we must be able to get them right every time. I will prepare a checklist procedure for us to use in the acceptance of any order and future shipment. I should be able to present you both a draft in the next week. Once we approve it, it will be our responsibility to verify each sale and shipment meets our criteria. Lastly, I think we should meet with Adam soon."

After receiving positive responses from his partners, a few days later Silverman arranged a meeting with Adam, Wimsley and Rivera to discuss shipping goods to Europe and avoiding the restrictions imposed by the government. The meeting would be held at Wimsley's home on a Friday evening. They all assembled at the scheduled time and Paul Silverman opened the meeting.

"Adam, let me introduce Bob Wimsley our General Manager and Larry Rivera our VP of Production. They are aware of our previous conversations and we would like to hear from you how we might proceed to increase our European sales. Before we start, Bob wants to take our drink orders.

"Nice to meet you both and Bob if you have Vodka, I will have it on the rocks."

"Thanks Adam, I know what Paul and Larry want and I will return soon with our drinks."

Bob quickly returned and passed the drinks around and they toasted to what they hoped would be a productive meeting. "Let's just have a casual meeting and listen to everyone's ideas. We are all here to make money so we can enjoy our women and our toys." Suggested Bob.

"I agree with your comments Bob 100 percent and I'm here to make a deal that's good for all of us. Paul has previously discussed with me the difficulties Blanton faces because of the restrictions on your newest model. I believe if the restrictions suddenly disappeared your sales would skyrocket, and I mean by tens of millions of dollars yet realistically, we all know this will not happen."

"Your right Adam, I know many of our European resellers want this weapon and we have received numerous inquiries from the shady side of arms distribution in Europe and elsewhere. As GM, I want big sales and maybe if we are smart enough, we can all become rich, including you Adam."

"Bob, unknown to you, I am aware of your deliveries into Europe over the past year and some of them went to as you say, shady dealers. I have some very interested contacts who are not small potatoes and will pay significant amounts to get these weapons. I can help you there and also here because I am the lead agent investigating Blanton Arms. But and this is important, you must work hard to get all your paperwork letter perfect to avoid any questions by customs agents."

"We all agree on that Adam. Would you be willing to act on our behalf for perhaps a fee?" asked Paul.

"It depends on the fee and other arrangements such as banking."

"It is easy to arrange the banking part and let's say the opening fee is one million."

"I can get you one to two hundred million in sales rapidly with a fifty to one hundred percent margin, but I want to start with a fee of two million and then if sales develop as I have said, we can talk about money again later."

"Larry, Bob lets have a little conference now. Adam, excuse us for about ten minutes."

All three left the room and went outside to discuss what they just heard from Adam.

'Did you guys listen to what he said? Two important aspects jump out to me. First, he is the lead FBI guy investigating Blantons shipments and next he says he can get us a few hundred million in sales with a big fat margin. I would classify that as a win-win for us."

"I agree."

"Thanks Larry."

"Paul, Larry I also agree and besides, we already have almost $40 million in our bank in Moldova. Therefore, two million is a bargain and if he does what he says, then he wants a few million more, it will also be a bargain."

"Let's go visit Adam again but before we do, let's have another round of drinks." Said Bob.

"Adam, we all agree to your terms and will deposit two million into our personal bank in Moldova in your name where it will be hidden and safe. Let's raise a toast to our future success."

"Thanks to all of you and thanks for the vodka. As the Russians would say, Nostrovia. Seriously though, in the next few days I will acquire a list of contacts for you to use to start a business relationship. Please be careful that this information is limited to this group as to many people involved raises concerns. Remember, don't give the store away. Let them offer you a price and if you want more say so. They are hot for your product and sales will speed up over time because I know Russia is still stockpiling weapons. I will promise you this, the investigation of Blanton will drag out for a long time and you will know when to cash in your chips."

"Larry, any delivery issues you can foresee?"

"As long as I have some decent lead times and advance notice when we can expect orders, I should not have any problems."

"One other problem which you people may not be aware of is shipment destinations. The FBI has knowledge about certain areas being labeled as illegal arms hot spots. I will arrange shipments to avoid those areas and we will use as many as twenty safe locations to avoid any questions."

"As GM and speaking for the three of us, we promise you Adam, we have the no how to get over many of the anticipated problems, we will limit exposure of this information to the three of us and we will earn the business and will keep you periodically informed. Thanks for meeting with us and I will send you an email about having a meeting at "two" on Friday to indicate the payment is in the bank."

"Adam, Paul, Larry if you want to stick around, we can have another round and maybe shoot some pool. Let's relax as we will have plenty to do once the orders start rolling in."

Chapter 25

Jack and Debra ate lunch while continuing to discuss work. They still had about six hours before they would be picked up to go to the airport. Jack felt he could use the time to study Silverman's emails as he felt it could lead to more meaningful questions, he could ask George. Afterall, they would be on the aircraft for at least six hours before arriving in Paris.

He opened up his notebook and plugged in the thumb drive containing the files he had previously retrieved from Silverman's computer. He entered the folder containing the emails and began reading ones from the previous three years.

At first, the files only contained discussions of normal business information. However, when he started reading an email dated June of 2016 to Wimsley and Rivera, he almost fell off his seat. The email discussed a 40 million dollar deal between a dealer in Serbia and wealthy oligarchs in Moscow friendly with Putin. It further stated, this is a test and we will make a clean twenty million as long as it hits no snags. Remember, all "T's" have to be crossed and all "I's" doted. The next order will be worth one hundred million to us. Be careful and let's make sure we do it right.

I can hardly wait to read more he thought as he opened another email. Once again, the next few only discussed normal business issues and practices. Nothing serious about these but who knows what will pop up on any of these.

He had now reached emails dating in November of 2016 and another one addressed to his two amigos appeared. This time it covered a shipment going to Poland and possible would be trans-shipped to Soviet separatists in the Ukraine. The value only eighty million but with a 28 million dollar profit. He told his friends the money would go to their account in Poland.

Well. I know the location of one bank, and I bet I find more. In fact, four emails later, he began reading another email talking about banks they had been using in Bulgaria, Slovakia and Belarus in addition to the Polish bank. Silverman now proposed to them about buying a smaller bank to make it easier to hide their wealth and move their money around. Silverman would let them know soon as he had been reviewing three banks in three separate countries and he would soon offer them a choice.

The year 2016 offered no further information but he expected 2017 to show much more activity and probably the purchase of a bank.

In fact, in February of 2017, Silverman provided his cohorts three banking options. The countries of Slovakia, Romania and Moldova could all be under consideration. All three relatively close to one another but Moldova appealed more to Silverman because of it being a poor country with rather loose banking laws. The plan called for them to find a suitable partner from the region and one capable of managing the bank.

He further wrote, we want a banker who wants to make a lot of money and yet stretch the rules in our favor. We have to remind ourselves, soon we will have close to 100 million dollars and we want to steer it in the right directions without interference from governments. I for one want to retire wealthy and within the next three years, so let me know how to proceed.

In March, another deal occurred for a small amount of 12 million but the still netted five million to add to their savings. It wasn't until May when a decision to partner with a Romanian banker by the name of Gustav Petrolin, from Eastern Romania on the border of Moldova. The action would have to happen rapidly because additional deals appeared on the horizon and the trio from Blanton Arms had to park their money somewhere safe and untouchable.

Sure enough, over the next six months, emails showed deals worth millions of dollars moving throughout Europe and heading elsewhere as dealers became aggressive knowing Blanton openly skirted laws and could be trusted to deliver.

The dealers used their knowledge of corrupt individuals to keep the goods flowing safely to their destination and the bank also grew large quickly because of the influx of dirty money from both the dealers and Blanton Arms.

Silverman, Wimsley and Rivera relished their success and had no reason to slow down the money train they had created. They just keep wheeling and dealing because they thought nobody would look over their shoulders.

Jack thought about it for a minute as to what had occurred over the last two years and he conceded they had been right up until now. However, good times do not last forever.

He shut down his computer because the time for the limo to arrive would be soon to catch their ride to Paris. He went upstairs to finish packing, and then to bring his and Debra's suitcases downstairs.

He told Debra some of the information he found, and he knew George Blanton would be thrilled. But there still lots to be learned and the emails only contributed a small piece of the puzzle. More facts and documents had to be uncovered for them to claim success.

Twenty minutes later they entered the limo, said hello to Priscilla and George and headed for Ronald Reagan Washington National Airport and then soon, they would be onward to Paris.

When they arrived at the airport, George and Priscilla led them into the private terminal. They all had their passports checked by security and cleared TSA to board their flight. Priscilla led the way towards the aircraft which Jack thought looked like either a G550 or G650 Gulfstream. After boarding, he learned from the information sheet in the seat pocket, showed it as a G650 worth about 60 to 80 million dollars.

The plush décor included sofas, tables for eating, large screened TVs and individual large seats which would convert into full sized beds. The interior could easily accommodate up to 18 people with room left over. The luxury of the Blanton's plane equaled or exceeded the equivalent of any five-star hotel presidential suite.

On board, two well dressed and manicured attendants to serve the passengers from the moment they entered the cabin. Debra and Jack sat on the long leather sofa on the right side of the jet. The coffee table in front of them held a copy of today's Washington Post and Wall Street Journal in addition to a small tray of delicious looking chocolates.

While the pilots continued their checkout procedures, Priscilla gave Debra and Jack a tour of the plane. A separate cabin in the rear of the plane contained a full-size bedroom, sitting area with TV and a well-appointed bathroom including a standalone shower. The front portion of the plane had a mini-kitchen, large refrigerator and a well-stocked bar and a good-sized wine cooler. All the comforts of home.

After the tour, the pilot announced the plane had been cleared for takeoff and passengers should be seated and buckled up. Jack and Debra returned to the sofa and buckled themselves in while George and Priscilla sat in large seats opposite them. The engines roared and the plane began its taxi ride to the runway used for takeoff.

Within in minutes they became airborne as they headed for Paris. The pilot announced "the flight would be relatively smooth, and they would land in Paris in about five hours. The time in Paris is now two-thirty AM and the clear weather with a mild temperature."

"George and Priscilla, l know you are probably tired, but would you mind spending about thirty minutes with us to provide you an update on our progress. Debbie and I have been very busy and thus far have some interesting and positive results for you."

"You have our full attention. But first, do you want a glass of wine?"

Absolutely, we both do, and we prefer reds."

The ordered the wines and Jack waited for the attendant to leave before he began to speak.

"What I am to tell you is all good, but you must keep it to yourselves and take no actions which could easily blow our cover. Quite frankly, we have the start of a case against the employees now, but there is a lot more to learn to really seal the verdict. We will do our best to keep you informed and we hope you can contribute to our planning but right now, all information is only between the four of us. Debra and I will decide when it is time to turn the feds loose. Agreed?"

"Talking for both Priscilla and I, we trust you based upon your experiences in these matters and your honesty to us. We promise you; we will only act on what you ask us to do."

"Thanks to both of you. Cheers!" as he raised his glass and took a drink.

"Wimsley, Silverman and Rivera, I will call them the three amigos, have not been working for the best interest of the company. Their actions in no way benefits Blanton Arms and if fact could very well be quite detrimental to the company. They may not realize it, but Blanton Arms maybe in danger of losing multiple military contracts while the three amigos continue to fatten their wallets.

I can also say, they like many crooks do not act like the smartest people. I easily entered all of their personal computers and retrieved the data I wanted. Some of it is incriminating, but this case is far from being over. Debra and I have a number of priorities which we hope will provide us all the incriminating evidence we need."

One of those priorities I had asked you about is a record of all your trips to Europe the past two years and your activities which can be verified. Do you have it or is it yet to come?"

"We should have it at our hotel when we arrive, and it will be faxed by our assistant to our private fax machine in our suite."

"Thanks George. We have arranged a number of meetings with close acquaintances to help us sort through some issues. I will be meeting one of them tomorrow at our hotel.

Debra will probably visit Belgium in a few days to meet a contact with knowledge of Russian arm purchases through the dealer network.

Next, I will fly to Finland to meet a friend known as the world's greatest hacker.

We need him for a very special job. I am good but he is great and fortunately, we have been good friends for many years.

We also have some friends in Interpol who can possibly help us on a few other issues about the arms dealers fueling the flow of illegal purchases, the banks where they launder their money and the infamous three amigos.

As I previously said, we have confidence on the path we established, but it is long and treacherous, and we don't want to make any missteps. That's all we have folks and Debra and I would be happy to answer your questions."

"Did I hear you correctly, you have incriminating data against, the so called three amigos?"

"You did hear it correctly, but it is not conclusive enough and although I still have a lot to read, I believe I may find a substantial amount of additional information.

"You two have learned more in two days then maybe the FBI has learned in two months. I am damn pleased I recognized Debbie because we maybe would have been hung out to dry."

"We have no doubts about it. Debbie and I after reading the documents smelled something wrong but could not put our finger on it. In fact, before we even went to the White House function, Debbie told me, it appears the Blanton's could be involved in a set up?"

"George, I am happy you suspected something weird had happened. Thank goodness you had sense to call us and to sit and explain your side of the issue for which we had no knowledge. We believe you both and we are confident it will be okay.

Now, I assume you both are tired and we all should get a few hours of sleep. We will be busy tomorrow."

"Thanks to both of you and now Priscilla and I will call it a night. Sleep well."

Chapter 26

Everyone slept well until the pilot announced they would be landing in thirty minutes. They all slept about four hours but the excitement of being in Paris and continuing the investigation woke them up and got their adrenalin running.

The plane landed at Orly International exactly at the time predicted and taxied for a few minutes to the private terminal on the west side of the airport. They gathered their belongings and exited the plane and would clear customs and immigration inside the terminal.

Twenty minutes later their passports had been stamped, their luggage inspected, and they went outside to wait for the limo taking them to the Shangri-La Hotel. The vehicle arrived as they exited the building and the driver carefully placed their luggage in the back of the car. They entered the limo and seated themselves and the driver began the long ride to the hotel.

About forty-five minutes after leaving Orly, the limo pulled up to the main entrance of the hotel and the doorman greeted Mr. and Mrs. Blanton as returning guests and welcomed Jack and Debra as new guests to the hotel.

They made their way into the lobby and waited while George retrieved the room keys from a staff member sitting at an elegant desk. Then staff members ushered them into the elevator to take them to their individual suites.

They knew delivery of their luggage would be very soon and the staff member with Debra and Jack asked if she could assist in unpacking their luggage. Debra said no, it would be fine, and the staff member quietly left the suite.

"Well, arrived safely here in Paris or is it Shangri-La. Do I get another gold star?"

"Not now but I will give you a loving kiss." And she snuggled up to him and gave him a long sensuous kiss and he held her close for a few seconds enjoying the feel of her next to him.

"Unfortunately, Franz will be here shortly and either I or both of us must go to work. If you want, you can take a nap and I will meet with Franz."

"My choice, I'll nap, and you work." And she smiled as she spoke.

Their luggage arrived and it didn't take long for them to unpack and put away their belongings.

The very spacious and well-appointed suite surprised Jack and Debra. It had plenty of sitting room with plush upholstered sofas, a desk with a computer, printer and fax machine, two large TVs, a well-stocked bar and quite a few munchies. The bathroom had duel marble sinks, a large tub and standalone shower, a warming towel bar, and lots of fancy soaps, creams and shampoos.

Together they oohed and aahed as they roamed the suite. When they opened the drapes, to their surprise, the Eiffel tower stood directly across from their suite. No more than a couple of hundred yards away.

"Jack, I am not sure we should get used to this luxury. Remember, we have a day job and hopefully soon, we will again be retired. Then again, we might as well enjoy this while we can."

"It is nice living in first class. I'm going to set up my computer and do some work until Franz calls me. Enjoy your nap on the spacious bed and those luxurious sheets while I slave away."

She smiled again, gave him a quick kiss on the cheek and plopped down into luxury.

Jack once more began reading Silverman's emails. He had completed 2017 and began reading early 2018 emails. In early January the majority of the emails contained mostly good wishes, good fortune and good health for the new year. Silverman also made one comment about doubling our take this year. Jack thought, maybe greed is the new norm for the three amigos, and he knew greed is a dangerous thing when you are a crook.

He began reading February emails and about mid-month, Silverman reported to the other two, they now had close to $500 million in their bank account plus they could expect another large order through Serbia destined again to Ukrainian separatists. Further emails discussed even more additional orders and Silverman stated he expected the business to grow rapidly this year.

The bell to their suite rang and Jack went to the door where a staff member handed him an envelope from the Blantons. He opened the sealed unit and took out a copy of their previous itineraries to Europe and Russia for the past two years. He started to read it and the phone rang. Franz said hello and he would wait for Jack in the lobby.

"I'll be down in about five minutes. Make yourself comfortable."

Jack placed the Blantons itinerary data on a dresser and left the suite. He took the private elevator to the lobby and immediately spotted his old friend Franz comfortably sitting in one of the oversized chairs in the lobby. Jack walked over to where Franz sat, and he startled Franz.

"Franz my friend. It has been three years since we last met and I am happy to see you again."

Franz stood up and gave Jack a big hug. "I am fine my friend and I am so glad to see you once more."

"Do you want some lunch Franz?"

"I didn't drive all the way from Munich just to say hello. Let's eat."

Jack put his arm around his friend and the walked to the desk and asked the staff member which restaurant served lunch.

"The one in the left corner of the lobby is very special sir. I recommend it for you and your friend."

Jack and Franz headed in the direction of the restaurant. A staff member greeted them and quickly seated them at a table with a window view of the city.

"Let's have a drink first Franz, then order and then we can talk."

In a moment, a waiter asked them if they would like a drink. Franz wanted a tall glass of cold beer and Jack selected one of his favorite scotches on the rocks.

"Franz, how about your family? Are the kids all grown?"

"Yes, we now have two in college and only one remains at home. My wife and I cannot complain. We both enjoy good health and we hope it lasts for quite a while. What about you Jack? Have you found a wife yet? Your, not getting any younger you know."

"Funny you should ask because I am dating a lady who I like very much, who like me worked for the government. In fact, she is with me on this trip and is helping me on a special project. I will tell you more after lunch."

Just then their drinks arrived, and the waiter also left menus for their use whenever they deemed ready.

"Prost Franz."

"Yes Jack, Prost."

They briefly chatted a bit before ordering lunch and held off on any serious discussion until after lunch. When they had finished lunch, Jack asked Franz if he wanted to stay in the restaurant or get more comfortable in a corner of the lobby where they could talk more freely.

Franz preferred the lobby and Jack signed the check and they walked back into the lobby to find a quiet area with few people so they could talk business. They seated themselves and then Jack began his speech.

"Franz, I appreciate you have travelled a good distance to see me. I have an opportunity for you which needs completion in the next two weeks. I promise you I will cover all your costs and you will also receive very good compensation if you can achieve the results needed. Are you available for the next two weeks?"

"I am available, but it depends on the deliverables. What do you want, and can I do the job?"

"Good reasonable question. My girlfriend Debra and I teamed up to work with the intel agencies in the USA to investigate Blanton Arms. We know almost five hundred million dollars of Blanton goods has passed through European borders in the last two or three years illegally. We also know dealers and Blanton executives are getting greedy and looking for even bigger orders."

"Jack, how can I help you?"

"Franz, here are my requests. I need the names, locations, email address or even phone numbers of the dealers selling Blanton Arms products to the highest bidder. I would also like to know the name of the banks laundering the money and where they are located. Intelligence tells us the goods probably go to Russia, Ukraine Separatists, South African Rebels and who ever offers big amounts of Euros or Dollars. It's not only insane, it is out of control and legal arms dealers get a bad rap because of a few bad apples. Can you help me and maybe help yourself and get paid well for your effort?"

"It sounds okay and I understand what you need, but it could put me in danger, serious danger."

"I realize what you say is true, but I can assure you I will do my best to hid how I got the information because I also want to protect myself. I believe it can be fixed to make it look like the info originated from Blanton employees and intelligence agencies in the USA. I assure you, I can do this, and nobody will ever know the true source."

"What is the compensation Jack?"

"Fifty thousand dollars in cash plus expenses."

"Jack, it's a large amount and it would be a lovely payday for me. I trust you can hide the source of information and with two kids in college, I can definitely use the money. You have a deal. Two weeks, right?

"Yes, it is very important because it will take me or the US agencies a week or so cross check all the three suspected executive emails to find corresponding names, email addresses and the dollar value of orders. Finding this info in Blanton Arms employees emails will result in immediate arrests and it will put them in Jail."

"Sounds like a big sting to me and it will help future business to get these guys out of circulation. Very frankly, only about two dozen of these guys sell Blanton goods and I know a number of them, and I also know who they sell their arms too. So, I must say again, it's dangerous out there and you must hide the source of the info and let it show it came from Blanton Arms computers."

"Franz, it's my promise to you and I always keep my promises. The Blanton Arms employees have stolen millions from the company, and they deserve to get punished for their actions and the data the FBI finds in their emails will include the info I receive from you. It will not show any source except Blanton employees. The information discovered by the FBI will then be shared with the proper Interpol people and arrests will be made across Europe to get these guys off the street."

"Jack, It, getting late and I have to get back to Germany tonight, but I will begin work immediately and I promise two weeks. I enjoyed seeing you again."

"Drive safely my friend and thanks for your help. Let me know if I can assist you in any way and keep me informed as to your progress."

Chapter 27

Jack went back to his suite satisfied Franz would obtain the information he needed. And now he and Debra had their priority one and two in-process.

Next on the list would be tracking the money. Debra and I can take on this task after we get a report from Franz and then Boris and I can also work on it when we meet in Finland.

Before I tackle number four involving Interpol, I will need to complete one, two, and three. Number five concerns the Blantons and we now have the data. Between Debra and I, we should be able to complete the study in one or two days. Number six regarding Russia, will present problems and will be dependent on how much Boris knows and if he is willing to cooperate.

Debra had woken from her nap and had been talking to her contact in the Netherlands. They promised to meet in two days in Antwerp at the downtown Holiday Inn.

She gave Jack a hug and wondered how his meeting with Franz ended.

"I think things will happen pretty fast. Franz knows just about everybody and he knows who has been involved in each illegal deal. He has to gather a lot of information and it is dangerous he promised to get it done in two weeks. "Can we make an offer to your contact to motivate a quick response?"

"Maybe Jack. I know her as Anna, and she has been my friend for a number of years. I would think depending on the information she can provide; she should get $25,000 to $50,000 thousand. I'll see if she has a high interest level, what she can deliver and then how fast she can respond."

"Debra, I'm going to take a nap now as jet lag is catching up to me. Wake me in two hours and I should be over it. While I nap, can you study the itinerary data George supplied covering the last two years of their European trips? It's in a folder on the dresser over there."

"Actually, I like fun jobs, especially when they expose how the rich and famous travel and where they stay. I could write a travel blog and make us some money! Go to sleep now dear."

Jack probably didn't hear her because he fell into a deep sleep the moment his head touched the soft pillow.

Debra picked up the envelop with the information George had given to Jack. She removed the contents and began reading the first page which had a date of March 2016 and the Blantons had been in Switzerland for about ten days. They had skied in the alps, took a tour of Bern and then visited an orphanage in a small town called Saint Gallen, just west of the Austrian border. After reading about eight more pages of similar travel notes, it became obvious the Blantons supported a number of orphanages in Europe.

Debra continued to study the Blantons travels. They always travelled using their private jet and stayed in expensive hotels and resorts. Each country they visited included a visit to one or two orphanages. At this point, she decided to call Priscilla and ask a couple of questions about the orphanage's visits. She dialed her suite number and Priscilla answered the phone after the second ring.

"Debra, funny you should call as we wondered if you and Jack you would like to join us and go to one of our special restaurants this evening near the Eiffel Tower?"

"Absolutely. What time is suitable for you and George?"

"Well, as you probably know Parisians do not usually go to dinner before eight. Is it too late or okay for you and Jack?"

"Eight o'clock is fine. The reason I called though, as I read some of your travel itineraries, I noted you always visited a number of orphanages. Is there a reason for so many visits?"

"It's very simple to answer. George and I team with a foundation here in Europe which supports over 140 orphanages in twenty or more countries. We like to visit them periodically to see if our funds get properly used, the facilities look in order and the kids look happy and appear being well-treated.

"There should be no doubt about the generosity of you two and Jack and I can vouch for it. Can you have the person who provided the itinerary sort it by city and orphanages visited in chronological order and amount of funds donated to each orphanage. All of this data and other data we gather, will be used to wipe the slate clean regarding the false charges raised against you and George. Jack and I trust both of you and the data strengthens our trust. Thanks, for the dinner invite and we will meet you in the lobby around eight for what I assume will be a fabulous French meal."

'Thanks Debra. I will get the information in the format you suggested and yes, we will have a fabulous French meal. See you at eight."

Almost two hours had passed since Jack took his nap. I should wake him and tell him the good news on about my new discovery and raise his appetite for tonight's dinner.

"Jack, wake up. It's your spoiled sweetheart."

He rolled over and smiled and reached out his hand to her and then gently pulled her down beside him. "Hi, honey I had a good nap. What did you do?"

"Well, while prince charmer slept, I toiled away reviewing the Blantons trips over the last two years and what they did here in Europe was strictly charitable. Lastly, the Blantons invited us to go with them to their favorite Paris restaurant tonight and we will meet them in the lobby at eight."

"Debra, who in the hell did the research on the Blantons and gave it to the intel people. What a bunch of hogwash. We spend a few hours, and we have data and witnesses to verify the honesty and integrity of these people. I will definitely raise my voice when I speak with the Director."

"You can do it honey but the reason I am here now is to use up some of your energy and then you will be very hungry by eight." She giggled and he laughed.

Chapter 28

Jack and Debra greeted the Blantons in the lobby, just about eight o'clock.

"It's not too far from here and if you don't mind, we can walk. Only about six to seven minutes away but great food, said George."

"We are looking forward to it and I am hungry. Debra made me work and I used up all my energy. I need a refill."

They arrived at the restaurant and the Blantons again were greeted as old friends. They introduced Jack and Debra to the staff and then the maître de escorted all of them to a large table ornately decorated with flowers and bright shiny glasses and tableware.

They seated themselves and George asked the waiter for two bottles of their favorite wine, Chateau Latour Pauillac, a well-known expensive Bordeaux. The ordered their meals and the food tasted beyond good. Phenomenal described every dish for presentation and taste and they each tried a little of everything and washed it down with good wine. When they finished their main course, the table reset for dessert. Each dessert tasted wonderful and Debra made the comment, "I better not eat this way every day."

They finally decided to leave the restaurant around 11:30 and slowly walked back to the Shangri-La. In the lobby, they wished each other a good night and headed for their separate suites.

After returning from the restaurant, Jack and Debra sat and talked for some time discussing various aspects of the case and the potential outcomes.

"What time do you leave for Antwerp?"

"My train is a four, so I will probably should leave here about two. And I hopefully will return the following day. When do you plan to go to Finland?"

"I will probably meet Boris in two days, and we might be together for at least two days and maybe more. What I want to do is really difficult but if we are successful, we will hit the lottery."

"Debra, I think we should ask George and Priscilla to stay another two weeks. I want them to participate in the putting together a long report of our findings. I don't want to leave anything hanging nor should there be any doubt about the three amigos being the real criminals."

"We can talk to them tomorrow. My guess is they will agree."

"We have had a long but wonderful day. I'm tired and we both should get a full-night's sleep as from now on, the days will get longer."

The got ready for bed and kissed each other good night and both fell asleep pretty quickly.

Jack and Debra were still sleeping when the phone rang around eight in the morning and Jack reached out to answer. "Hello Jack, it's me Franz."

"Is everything ok?"

"Even better than ok, Jack. I have just about finished getting most of the data you needed, and along the way, I uncovered another deal worth 180 million being negotiated by one of Blanton Arms dealers.

What is weird about this deal concerns not only the value but where it is destined. It's reportedly going to the Islamic Revolutionary Guard in Iran. I heard they negotiated for a delivery in about six months. The original delivery destination is unknown at this time, but there is no doubt as to the final destination. I learned the order is cast in concrete and definitely going to Iran."

"Franz, great reporting. You have earned the money I promised you."

Thanks Jack, it's a short list of bad guys, but I have enough details about them to get them off the street very soon. It will be in your hands in about one week. Hope I didn't wake you."

"With news like that Franz, you can wake me any time. Goodbye my friend and thanks once again for your help."

"Who called Jack?"

"Frantz. Let's get up, get dressed and have some coffee and maybe a small breakfast and then we will talk."

Jack called room service and asked for a bowl of various fruits, some sweet rolls or Baguettes and a big pot of coffee.

"Ten minutes sir."

Their breakfast arrived within the ten minutes room service had promised. The staff member set the order on the small dining table and set out place settings for two. He then poured coffee for each person and announced they could now be seated and then he left the suite.

They drank coffee and had some fruit along with the baguettes and sweet rolls. As they finished their breakfast, Jack suddenly jumped up as if he had been struck with a high voltage line.

"What is Jack? Are you okay? What's wrong did something bite you or what?"

"Sorry Debra, I didn't mean to scare you, but I just got the wildest idea and from whence it came, I don't know. Remember I said whoever did the report didn't know what they were doing. Well, I believe they did."

"Jack, what you just said to me sounds like we have a traitor in the FBI. Do you really mean it?"

"It's exactly what I mean. We need to know the guy investigating Blanton Arms and who wrote the report? I may be wrong, but the three amigos may have a friend on their payroll and the friend plans to destroy the Blantons."

"What do we do now, Jack?"

"I know exactly what I am going to do. I am going to completely read all my illegally gained folders and hopefully I will find one name, maybe one clue and maybe one FBI agent about to be crucified."

"Need help?"

"No, you have to go to Antwerp today and I will comb through these files until I find what I need. It may take me two or three days and I will probably delay my meeting with Boris but right now, this becomes the most important priority."

"You get started and I'll do my thing and the day will come when we can just enjoy ourselves and not be locked into a project."

"It's my hope too Debra and we will get there, but not today."

Jack then took his computer and sat at the large desk and began his review of the information on the thumb drive.

He went back to the Silverman files he had originally partially studied and picked up where he had previously stopped. But even before he started, he had a question for Debra.

"Honey, do you remember any dates in the dossier which referenced when the investigation of Blanton Arms began?"

"If I remember correctly, it started with an arms shipment in early 2017 and one thing lead to another and the investigation began. Give me a few minutes and I can verify it for you."

"Thanks honey, I believe you have it right, and I'll start looking around the beginning of 2017 and see where it leads me."

He scanned through Silverman's emails to the beginning of the year in question. He wasn't interested in orders or money amounts but rather he zeroed in to find a name or a reference unfamiliar to him. He had a decent memory and could remember names pretty well and so he began his search looking for the proverbial needle in the haystack.

He went through January pretty quickly, then February, March and April. At the end of April, Silverman had sent an email to Wimsley and Rivera and referenced a lunch he had with Adam. Silverman stated it went well and maybe good things could come of out of this meeting.

"Jack, the beginning of February 2017 is a good place to start."

"Thanks honey, I am there now. By the way, please remind me to make a copy of this thumb drive and give to you so we will always have a duplicate."

Adam, Adam who? Why is Silverman informing the other amigos about Adam? My instincts tell me this maybe it and he again began reading emails starting in May. He could find no reference to Adam. Neither did any reference to Adam show up in June, July and August.

September became very interesting. The three amigos had agreed to open an account for Adam at their Moldova bank in the amount of two million dollars Nice bribe but chump change to the amigos because they now had almost $500 million hidden away.

Adam had been bought and paid for and Blanton Arms had avoided any serious investigation and he had placed all the fault in the laps of George and Priscilla Blanton.

Chapter 29

After Jack discovered the facts involving Adam, he picked up his phone and dialed the number of the Director. The phone rang twice and then he heard the Directors voice.

"Good morning Jack. You know it is five am here?"

"Sorry sir, I didn't think of it."

"Jack, you sound sad. What's bothering you?"

"Sir, I discovered a bad weed in the FBI. I had a feeling for some time, the author of the dossier did not know the Blantons. I went back to reviewing the Silverman emails and I found more than one referencing Adam. It may be the guy doing the investigation of Blanton Arms and the one who wrote the dossier about the Blantons. Adam has no last name, but he has a nice account in the bank owned by the exec's at Blanton Arms."

"Jack, it's very troubling to me because Adam is the guy doing the investigation of Blanton. Adam Sanderson to be exact. I can handle this, but I don't want it to interfere with your investigation."

"Sir, Debra and I have about two or three weeks to locking down what we set out to do. We believe the Blantons to be one hundred percent innocent and we have a slew of information to justify our thoughts. We have started gathering info on about twenty of the Blanton Arms shady dealers. Any action before the next two weeks will create problems for us."

"Adam isn't going anywhere, so just continue your search and it will be ok. Two weeks or so will not change anything."

"Thanks sir. Later this week, we expect to have data about the corrupt dealers. Once your people complete and verify the data, we want the information to come from the FBI to Interpol. Adam should have no knowledge about this matter as it puts Debra and myself plus a couple of sources in dire danger. I remember what you told me about big bucks attracting big bullets."

"I fully understand Jack. When you get the data, you want to share with Interpol, send it to me and I will see it gets to the right person for transmission to them. In the meantime, stay safe."

"Thanks sir."

Jack told Debra about the call and he had told the Director, we would need about two or more weeks to finalize our investigation. "I don't need to change my plans to meet Boris and I hope we can bring this to a speedy conclusion. I still have a ton of emails and other data to study, but I may just pass it to the Director to add to the evidence you and I have gathered about Blanton Arms. He can get knowledgeable people to sort through it and besides when they go after the three amigos, they will grab all their computers, files and anything not well hidden."

"Jack, I am about to head to the rail station. Please behave yourself while I'm away and stay safe. I don't want any harm to come to either of us, but we are playing in a dangerous ballpark."

"Honey, I am getting concerned about our safety. From now on, we should not travel without our guns and it starts now."

"I agree Jack and I have a place to hide mine in my overnight bag and I will carry it to all my meetings.

He stood up and walked over to her and wrapped his arms around her and held her close for a full minute. He then lightly kissed her and said, "stay safe honey and your hubby will be waiting for your return with open arms."

"Thanks, Jack, I'll miss you too." And she picked up her overnight bag and slowly left the suite.

Chapter 30

A private car from the hotel took Debra to the largest Paris railway station where she would board an express train bound for the three-hour trip to Antwerp. it would allow Debra to use the time to think about her meeting in Antwerp with Anna.

She had not seen her friend since she retired over three years ago, but they had stayed in touch with each other at least a couple of times per year. Debra knew Anna had the sources and the capabilities of getting the information she would require, and it would add to information Jack had gathered. All of it together would help the authorities convict the three amigos.

She sat back in her seat and closed her eyes to rest for a few moments and remembered the sweetness and warmth of being with Jack. I haven't been in love with anyone for years she thought and now I believe I found my perfect match. God, I hope he stays safe and I get to hold him for the rest of my life. Her wonderful smile lit up her face and if anyone had been watching, they would see a beautiful woman in love.

See opened her eyes just in time to see fields of tulips of every color quickly passing by as the train sped towards Antwerp.

She had about another ninety minutes before arrival and again closed her eyes and dozed almost to the time the train arrived in Antwerp.

Before she realized it, the train had pulled into the station and it slowly came to a stop. She picked up her belongings and exited the train and would walk the short distance to the Holiday Inn Hotel.

Anna had been waiting for her arrival in the hotel lobby and when Debra walked through the entry doors, there stood her friend Anna to greet her.

"Clare, it is so good to see you. It has been three or more long years since we stood together. They gave each other a hug and together stepped over to the reception desk to check into the double room previously reserved by Debra.

"Do you have a reservation miss?"

"Yes, Clare Aldridge."

"Yes, I found you. May I see your Passport please?"

"Debra reached into her purse and removed her Passport to present it to the receptionist."

"Thank you, Mrs. Aldridge. Are you only staying one night, and will the charges remain on the credit card on file?"

"Yes."

The receptionist gave them each a key and they took the elevator to the third floor and easily found their room.

Anna asked if Clare if she needed to rest or she suggested they might want to go to the cocktail lounge have a glass of wine and talk there for a while. Debra replied, "sounds good to me and it will give us a chance to catch up to our current status."

They returned to the lobby and headed towards the lounge, found a deserted spot to sit and they each ordered a glass of red wine. They started to bring each other up to date regarding their current activities while they waited for their wine to be delivered.

"I'm still single Clare but I recently met a nice guy who is an airline pilot. Not sure where the relationship is going but it is pretty sweet now."

"Clare told Anna, she enjoyed her life and her husband had a good job in the computer industry. She also added she had a consulting contract with the government to update them about arms trading in Europe, Russia and Asia. Basically, this is the reason I came here to again meet with you. Let's finish our wine and go to our room to discuss the purpose of my visit.

"That's' fine with me Clare. Whenever you're ready we can go."

They left the lounge area and returned to the room and Clare began to speak.

"Anna, I know you have some good sources in Russia regarding the arms business. I am only looking to get a few questions answered and I know you pay for your information and so do I. Hence, if I give you a few questions, I am willing to pay you well for the answers."

"I appreciate your offer Debra, and I will do whatever I can to provide the information you desire. If it gets expensive, I will let you know and you can just say, yes or no. We have worked together before and we were always able to get along well and be honest with each other. Where do you want to start?"

"Okay, here is my first question. In your estimation, what amount of Dollar or Euro shipments of illegal arms have been supplied to Russia the past two years? Then, do you have knowledge of the manufacturing sources of the weapons being imported?"

Anna had taken out a paper pad to make notes. "You ask easy questions to answer. There will be no charge yet."

"I estimate approximated 100 to 200 million Euros a year crosses the border into Russia. The second question is a little harder, but I would say the goods come from a few ex-soviet puppet states and maybe 50 million or more from the USA."

"From the United States?"

"Yes, from the US. Clare. Can we delay answering the question now as tomorrow afternoon, we will be able to answer the question much better? In the morning, we will have breakfast with one of my good sources Sergio, who will provide you a broad picture of the total arms activity in this part of the world."

"I can wait for question one answer until the afternoon. what is our schedule for tomorrow?"

"Well, we have a very busy day. As I told you, we will have breakfast with Sergio, a very knowledgeable source about the entire European, Russian and Chinese arms trading story.

Then, later we will meet with an old friend of yours, who now is also my friend and a good source for Russian intelligence information. Do you remember Anatoly Goodsnofsky?"

"Yes, I remember him well. He lives here?"

"He not only lives here but he works with me. I now know him as Ethan Van de Berg. After he deflected from Russia, Interpol gave him a new history and changed his appearance. You will probably not recognize him, but it's him. He always says, you saved his life."

"I am glad he is still alive, and I am fortunate I could help him when he came close to losing his life. I knew some other people who helped to smuggle him out of Crimea and get him safely into Germany. It's a long story but I am happy to hear he survived."

"He looks forward to seeing you. He says he owes you a gift."

"It's not necessary. I had a job to do and he needed help."

'Clare, I believe most answers you are seeking involve arms sales and both Sergio and Ethan are able to provide detailed answers to any question you might ask. It is getting late and we have an early appointment so let's get a good night's sleep."

"Your right Anna. All my questions are about the arms business in Europe and Russia. There is no sense you and I discussing them when the answers will be available tomorrow from some experts. I am sure everything I want will be done early and I plan on leaving in the late afternoon and return to Paris.

About ten minutes later, each of them, selected one of the two beds and quickly they had gone to sleep.

Chapter 31

Both Clare and Anna woke early, showered and got ready to meet Sergio for breakfast around nine o'clock, not too far from the hotel. They left the hotel about eight-forty and walked about three blocks to the restaurant where they would meet Anna's contact. Sergio stood outside the restaurant.

"Good morning Anna. Glad to see you again.'

"Sergio, this is my friend Clare who has some questions which I am sure you can answer."

"Glad to meet you Clare. I'll do my best to help you."

They entered the restaurant and found a table far from the front door. They each ordered coffee and began to scan the menu to decide on the breakfast meal. They ordered their food and they talked about many things before their meals had been served knowing the real questions would be discussed after they had finished their breakfast.

About twenty minutes later, each got a coffee refill, had their empty plates removed and Clare began opened the discussions.

"Sergio, Anna told me about your expertise concerning arms sales between Europe, China and Russia. I know a little about the subject from prior assignments here but in three years, a lot of things have changed.

Hence, I asked Anna to meet with someone to bring me up to date on the arms business today. I sure hope you can enlighten me."

"I will try my best Clare. Today is very different from your previous assignments in this area. There are more players, some legal many illegal and the market has grown larger as if the world did not enough weapons of mass destruction. I am ready to answer your questions and we should not be in any hurry as the restaurant expects us to stay for as long as we care to stay."

"Thanks Sergio, my first question involves the Russian/China/Iran relationship. Everyone knows Russia has a great relationship with China and Iran, who themselves have large manufacturing capabilities to produce weapons. Do they each still represent, a major sales channel to enlarge Russia's stockpile of weapons?

"Good question. Russia continues to expand its hoarding of arms as if manufacturers planned on going away. It is kind of crazy, but nobody can predict which country or manufacturer will come up with a new Uzi or an AK-47. All of them continue to innovate and search the marketplace for the latest gadget. To answer your question more specifically, Russia wants to maintain good relations with China and with Iran and so regardless of the lack of anything new, they buy in many instances just to keep the relationship. China and Iran return the favor by purchasing an equivalent number of weapons from Russian industries. I think the only people making money producing weapons would be the workers and of course the transportation companies.

Clare laughed and then said, "I have to laugh Sergio because you are absolutely correct. You give me 300 widgets and I will buy 300 widgets from you and we will remain good friends."

"That's right. I hope that answered your question. What else do you want to know?"

"You did answer my question very well. Now I have another one. "Russia is well known to be a major manufacturer of arms. If this is true, why do so many illegal arms end up going into the area? Why do they accept the use of the "dirty dealers" or is this the only way of getting technically advanced weapons from many countries?"

"This is a tough question. You see, Russia is trying to gain favor with many of the smaller countries run by dictators or autocrats. To gain a foot hold, they don't want the world to see them as being the supplier of arms to everyone, so they have a number of surrogates. I call them thieves, out getting weapons from whoever, at ridiculous prices, to give to these smaller countries. Russia of course picks up the tab and looks the other way. The country's receiving the weapons become indebted to Russia and they will act as Russia wants them to act. It is a wild west out there right now and who knows how it will end. Speaking of ending, I have another meeting scheduled within the hour; can I answer another question for you?"

"No Sergio, you have helped me a lot and I appreciate your giving me the time and opportunity to meet you. Thanks."

At that point, they said their goodbyes to Sergio, and they all left the restaurant.

"Clare, we have about an hour before we meet up with Ethan. Want to just stroll around until then?"

"Sure, let's do some window shopping as we say in America."

"We also say it here but it's in Dutch."

They both laughed and began slowly walking towards the area where they would later meet Ethan.

They looked into various shop displays along the way without ever entering any of them. They reached the area to meet Ethan just about the same time he arrived, and Anna correctly told Clare, she would not recognize him as Anatoly Goodsnofsky.

"Hello Clare, do you remember me?"

"Not really. How would I know you?"

"Picture yourself back in a small village in Crimea and a guy by the name of Anatoly Goodsnofsky had a death sentence hanging over his head. You somehow managed to get him safely out of the situation and then into Germany. Many things have changed since that time including me. I moved to Antwerp and I am now known as Ethan, happily married with two children and I have never forgotten you and what you did for me."

Ethan then walked to Clare and gave her a big hug. She almost started to cry.

"Clare, I did not mean to startle you, but a flood of memories overtook me for a moment."

"Me too Ethan and I also suddenly replayed the scene in my head. My god, I am so happy to see you well and happy to know you have a good life."

"Let's walk to a park nearby where we can continue to talk, Ethan suggested.

They entered the park within a few minutes, found an empty bench so they could talk for a while. Clare still had about three hours before her train would leave for Paris.

"Last night, I asked Anna a question she did not want to answer at that time. She said let's wait to tomorrow and you will get a better answer. I did not know at the time who I would meet, but I am happy to meet you again. So, now I will ask you the question which couldn't be answered last night. Actually. It's two questions.

"In your estimation, what is the Dollar or Euro amounts of illegal arms shipped into Russia during the past two years? Then, do you have knowledge of the manufacturing sources of the weapons finding their way into Russia?"

"I estimate approximated 150 to 200 million Euros a year crosses the border into Russia. The second question is a little harder, but I would say the goods come from China, Iran, North Korea and a few ex-soviet puppet states and maybe fifty million or more from the USA."

"You said, fifty million from the US?"

"Yes, Clare, this is true, and it is a long story and regarding the volume and I believe every word of it. How it became this way is interesting and lets you know how Russia and the former KGB operated. I must confess, I only witnessed the beginning of the story. I know what and how this is is happening in the United States and the truth is the FBI has a mole in their organization placed there by the Russians many years ago.

He went to high school with me in Russia and we both spoke excellent English and then we got recruited or pulled into the KGB and each of us trained in espionage for more than three years. I can tell you more, but I am going to give you a gift I have wanted to give you for a long time for saving my life. The papers I am about to give will allow you to piece the entire story together. It starts with a picture of him and I at our high school graduation and then there is another picture of us receiving our certificate from the KGB after we finished our three year espionage classes. All of theses are signed by him and me as memories of our friendship. Next I have two letters he sent to me after settling in America and he signed both letters with his old and new name. I never heard from him again, but a mutual comrade friend told me he was doing very well in America and gave me copies of fourteen emails from about a year ago between him and his Russian handler in Moscow.

From all of this information, you will be able to piece together the real story of Adam Sanderson."

"How long ago did he did the KGB, send him to the US?"

"I lost contact with him after a few months, but I believe approximately twenty plus years ago, which makes him now about forty-two or forty-three years old. I really do not have to much more to share with you Clare, but this is my gift to you for what you did for me a long time ago."

"Ethan, thank you for what you have shared, and I can only wish you all the best and stay healthy and happy with your family."

They hugged again and Ethan went out of the park one way and Clare and Anna, left the way they had entered.

"Anna, I decided you have given me more than I ever expected. Send me info about wire transferring some money to you and I will send you $50,000. It will be sent tomorrow, and I want you to share it as follows: $10,000 for Sergio, $25,000 for Ethan and the balance for you. Please promise me you will do as I wish."

"I will Clare. I promise I will."

"I have about an hour or so before I can catch the next train back to Paris tonight. I have a lot of work to do and the information from Ethan has caught me by surprise. Let's go back to the hotel so I can retrieve my stuff. The room was prepaid and the check for the bar will be added to the bill, so you are free and clear my dear."

"Thanks Clare, I hope you get a promotion for the information Ethan and I gave you."

They walked quickly back to the hotel and Clare got her overnight bag and they went to the lobby to say their goodbyes.

"Thanks for everything Anna. Stay safe and keep in touch.

"Ciao."

The station was only a short walk from the Hotel and Clare had about a half hour wait to get on her train. She went to the ticket booth and obtained a reserve seat and then sat to wait until the station announced a track number.

Next, she called Jack. "Hi sweetie. I want you to meet me at the Paris railway station tonight in about four hours. I will be on the express train from Antwerp."

"Are you okay?"

"I'm fine and I have some very shocking news for you but not over the phone. See you in about four hours. Ciao."

"I'll be there. You will remember me, the tall handsome one.

Chapter 32

As Debra sat in the railroad station awaiting her train back to Paris, a woman sat down beside her. Debra did not pay too much attention to her but then a man with his hand in his jacket pocket sat down on the other side of her. Debra instantly felt for her safety. The woman talked first, "Clare, we have not seen you in a longtime, but we did know you would be visiting your friend Anna and we do know why you are here and also why you came to Paris."

"I'm Marie and beside you is Rick with a rather deadly weapon in his pocket aimed at you. We will not kill you, but we expect you to cooperate with us or you will die. We are now going to leave the station and we expect you to go without raising any suspicions." Then Marie grabbed her arm and slowly lifted her from the bench and the three of them left the station via the main entrance of the station where a large black car awaited them.

Debra had been in these circumstances before but then she had her own weapons but at this moment her weapon was in her overnight bag now in the hands of Rick. She decided to comply with these people and hope for opportunities to free herself later.

Rick opened the rear door and pushed Debra inside and then threw her overnight bag into the car and Marie slid in beside her. Rick then sat in the front seat and nodded to the driver.

The car headed out of the city and nobody talked the entire time of their journey in the car. It had already turned dark and Debra could not recognize any city landmarks or determine what direction they traveled.

About, forty minutes after leaving the station, the car pulled into a long winding unlit lane and stopped about a quarter mile up the road in front of what looked like an old farmhouse.

"Get out of the car Clare and Marie will escort you into the house. The driver and I will be in shortly so make yourself comfortable."

Marie took Debra's arm and guided her to the front door of the house. Marie then pushed on the door and pulled Debra inside. "Sit over there and be quiet."

Debra concentrated on controlling her emotions and she had no clue about who these people and what they wanted from her. She did sense they wanted information from her, and they probably received information about her from Adam.

When she had called Jack earlier from the station, she normally would have put her phone in her purse but for some reason she had placed it in her pants pocket and during the ride, she shut it off and moved it down and into her long stockings while Marie dozed for a moment during the ride. She could only wish they don't search her.

Rick and the driver entered the house and sat down near Debra. Rick, began to ask her questions, "Tell me why you and your husband visited Paris? We know some of the story but would like to hear it from you."

Debra had to make a quick decision and because she didn't have any idea what they knew, she had to tell them something close to the truth. "I came to Paris with my husband strictly for a vacation. I came to Antwerp to meet with Anna and learn about illegal arms sales into Russia. I am retired from the government and do consulting periodically to earn some money and they gave me an assignment. It only involved getting some number estimates from this part of the world about the dollar value of illegal weapons flowing into Russia and report back to the government as to what I learned. It did not involve people nor types of weapons or where they came from or where they were going. It turned out to be a very simple assignment."

"That is all you are here for and nothing else?"

"That is, it and there is nothing else. This may be a surprise to you, but I am not consulting to any of the intelligence agencies. I am consulting to a group in the US congress trying to determine why Russia is building up its stockpile of weapons."

"You want us to believe you travelled all the way from the United States just for that information?"

"Yes, and to have a vacation with my husband in Paris paid for by the government."

"Who is your husband and what does he do?"

"He is retired, and he used to develop computer software for games."

"Marie, did we make a mistake here?"

"I don't think so. I thought she came here to look for people but maybe I am wrong or maybe she just doesn't want us to know."

"Marie, put her in the back bedroom and lock the door. Maybe her memory will improve over night.

Rick nodded to the driver to get the car, "We will leave now but will return later."

What Rick did not tell Debra that he and Marie heard the same story from Anna, and Clare as they knew her, could not be a threat to anyone but they did not want to take chances.

Rick and the driver left, and Marie took Debra by the arm to bring her to the bedroom. In two swift moves, Debra threw a quick elbow into Marie's stomach and then another quick jab to her throat and Marie fell to the floor unconscious. Debra quickly dragged her into the bedroom and tied her to the bed and left the room.

She grabbed her purse and overnight bag and went out the door. She stopped to retrieve her gun from the bag and then ran down the unlit lane towards the main road the car had previously travelled. She reached the main road in a few minutes and turned left to head back towards the lights of Antwerp.

She found a clear area and pulled the phone from her stocking and called Anna.

"Anna, I have been kidnapped from the rail station and taken to an old farmhouse but, I have managed to get away. I am on a main road headed back towards Antwerp, but I am sure it is very far away. The people who took me knew my name and they knew you and may have talked to you today. Do you know where I might be, and can you help me?"

"Oh my God. Clare, I know those people and I have a clue of your location. Did you turn off the highway onto a small road on the right or left?"

"The right side."

"How far are you from the road where it meets the highway?"

"Maybe less than one kilometer."

'Further down the highway, in the direction of Antwerp and about two more Kilometers is a gas station. It will be closed for the night. Go there now and hide out in the rear and I will be there in less than thirty minutes."

"Thanks Anna. I will wait for you. What kind of car do you have?"

"Silver Mercedes and when I arrive, I will flash my lights twice. Avoid all contact with anyone."

Debra then called Jack.

"Jack, just listen I am in trouble and Anna is on her way to get me. Please take the next train you can get to Antwerp and bring your gun as you may need it. I am safe now and have my gun handy, but I have got to hide and wait for Anna. Text me when you arrive in Antwerp and we will find you. I Love you. Ciao."

'I love you too and will be there ASAP."

Debra walked on the edge of the highway and if she saw a car approaching, she dropped to the grass off the side of the road. After about a twenty-five minute walk, she spotted the gas station and went to the rear of the building to hide until Anna arrived.

She had been there about ten minutes when she heard a car approaching and it stopped and slowly drove to the rear of the building. The lights flashed twice, and Debra moved from her hiding place and ran to the car.

As soon as Debra closed the door of the car it began moving and heading back towards Antwerp.

"Anna, you are my hero tonight. I have called my partner to take the next train to here and he will let me know when he arrives. Where do we go now?"

"We definitely cannot return to my house or the hotel. But there is another hotel not far from the station we can check into, at least for tonight."

They drove for another twenty minutes and parked the car in nearby parking garage to avoid parking in front of the hotel. They went to the reception desk and asked for a room for the night. Debra handed the receptionist her passport and a credit card in the name of Clare Brown. The woman handed her a key and the took the elevator to the floor where they would find their room.

"Anna, this is not real is it?"

"Clare, I do not know how those petty thieves learned about you and me, but they can also be dangerous. We will stay here until we can figure out a plan. How did you get away from them?"

The driver and the one called Rick left to go somewhere and while Marie escorted me to a bedroom, I used my self-defense training and she is now tied up in the bedroom. Now let's worry about what they do when they find I am gone."

Chapter 33

Jack originally waited at the station for the eight o'clock express train from Antwerp to arrive in Paris. He wondered what sort of news could Debra be bringing back to him and why did she want me to meet her here at the station?

He had been there about ten minutes when the train arrived exactly on time and he stood outside the area where the arriving passengers disembarked. Within a few minutes, all the passengers had left the train, but he not see Debra. He tried calling her, but she did not answer, and a message appeared stating her phone had been turned off.

He sensed something had to be wrong because the only reason she would not be on the train would be because she had been stopped from boarding. Whoever did this to her better not hurt her or they will wish they never met her.

Now, after her most recent phone call, he once again waited for at the Paris station, but this time it would be his turn to take the express train to Antwerp. He waited nervously to hear the station announce the track to board the train and travel the three hours worrying about her safety and how he would handle the situation.

The train left exactly on time and he knew the time would move ever so slowly before he would arrive in Antwerp and hopefully reunite with the woman he loved. About twenty minutes before arrival, he texted Debra and told her his arrival time into Antwerp.

Debra and Anna discussed the risk of leaving the hotel to meet Jack but decided it might be too dangerous for all of them. Debra then texted Jack the name of the hotel and room number. Within a minute, she received a simple answer; Stay safe and I will be there soon.

About thirty minutes later, someone knocked on the door and Debra looking out the peephole, could clearly see Jack. She quickly opened the door and jumped into his arms.

"Debra, glad to have you back in my arms."

"Thanks for coming here so quickly. I have so much to tell you."

He took her hand and tightly held it as they walked to the room. "Okay, I am here now. Let's sit and relax for a minute or two so I can catch my breath and get my brain working again. Maybe you should introduce me to Anna?"

"Anna, this is Jack, my partner and best boyfriend I ever had in my life. He is very skilled in many facets of spying but like me, retired three years ago. The two of were picked for a special assignment to find evidence of some bad guys in the United States and part of our investigation involved meeting you."

"Before I forget, I promised you I would wire you some funds today but sorry, you will have to wait but you will also receive a bonus if and when we can find the guys who kidnapped me and perhaps remind them, we also know how to play rough."

"Debra, can I call you Debra now?"

Debra laughed and Said, "Sure."

"Don't worry about the money, let's first figure out how we get to the people who tried to hurt you."

Debra, tell me about what happened yesterday when you went to the rail station?"

Debra related the entire story to Jack as it had happened.

"Anna, what do you know about these people and when did they contact you?"

"Jack, I don't really know them, but I do know about them because after Debra left, some small-time hoods burst into my apartment and started asking me about her. They knew about her and wanted to know why she came here. I told them she had been gathering information about arms sales into Russia and nothing more. Then they left.

I know They work with some of the illegal arms sellers in this area. How they knew I would meet Clare or Debra; I really don't know. Tomorrow, I can call a few close associates who may be able to provide the answers and give us some help in finding them. Then, the next steps belong to us."

"I have a car; I know my way around the entire area, and I can get us some additional hungry workers who know the ropes and can shoot straight."

"Anna, we have money and can employ probably three to four hired hands who have their own weapons."

"Let's find the clowns who did this first, then bring in the hired guns."

"It has been a long day for all of us. We should now go to sleep until morning and then put our contacts to work. You two ladies each have a bed and I will sleep on the sofa."

"Good night all."

Jack woke up early and took a quick shower and by the time he had finished the others were dressed and ready to go.

Anna suggested they all go downstairs and have breakfast and she will also get on her phone and start asking some questions. They all left the room and went to the lobby and had a nice breakfast and then sat and drank coffee while Anna made some calls to contacts.

She had made three calls and then suggested they should return to the room and wait for responses to her inquiries. She also suggested to Debra to talk to the reception desk and extend their stay by two or three days. They then returned to their room and sat and waited.

Debra suddenly remembered she had to tell Jack about Adam. "Jack, I just remembered I have to tell you a story about Adam. Anna is here and can collaborate my story."

'You mean Adam Sanderson?"

"Yes, he is a Russian mole. Planted along time ago.

"Oh, my god." Jack almost fell off the couch."

"Your serious?"

"I am very serious, and I have documentation as further proof. I will tell you the story exactly as it had been told to me and Anna, then you must talk to the Director immediately."

Debra related the complete story to Jack as it had been relayed to her by Ethan and gave him the papers and photos Ethan had given her plus the emails between Adam and his Moscow handler. When she had finished, Jack appeared to be in complete shock.

"Jack, are you ok?"

"Not really but I will be in a moment after all of this stuff sinks into my brain. Two shocking stories in one day is frightening especially since it involved you, but now this story you just told me is beyond my capacity to think straight."

"For me it is sad to think of all we have gone through, and especially you Jack, on this assignment to now learn it is all due to a mole in the FBI. I could almost cry."

Jack got out of his seat and walked over to Debra to give her a loving hug. He also had tears in his eyes for it made him sad when he heard of people betraying the country he loved so much.

"Debra, I need your help to settle down before I call the director. Please hold my hand for a few moments so I can return to reality."

After a minute or two, Jack once again became rational and picked up the restricted phone to make the hard call to the Director.

"Good morning sir. Hopefully you are seated because I have some really sad news to give you. Adam Sanderson is a confirmed Russian mole. Trained by the KGB and sent to the United States for whatever purpose fit the Russian agenda at the time. This time, he had orders to infiltrate Blanton Arms and bribe the executives with a few million dollars to give the Russians needed technology and weapons to possibly use on our troops or on our allies. Sir this is true and factual and comes from rock solid sources along with extensive documentation. Debra uncovered this and she knows her sources and what is real and what is fake news. This is real, and we will send you a written history of Vitaly Kuznetsky, who you know as Adam Sanderson along with verifiable documentation."

"Jack, I don't know what to say at this moment. I know you and Debra have impeccable resumes and there is no doubt as to what you have told me. A lot of wheels will now be accelerated up to get a handle on this issue.

How much more time do you need to complete what you and Debra were doing?"

"I believe, I can compress it to about ten days to two weeks. Maybe earlier but not much sooner."

"I can live with that Jack; I don't want to spook anyone at Blanton Arms or in the FBI. We have ways of getting it done quietly at least for a while. You told me you had gotten into the three amigos emails, etc. I want you, starting tomorrow to look at them every day or maybe twice day and keep your and Debra's other things going on simultaneously. It is obvious to me the Blantons are innocent but keep this information quiet and only between you and Debra. Thanks Debbie and thanks Jack. I'll be in touch and I have to go now. There are a number of calls I have to make to ensure we keep this train on the track."

Chapter 34

Not long after Jack had made his call, Anna's phone rang and from her comments, Debra and Jack understood the call originated from one of Anna's contacts, she asked a few questions and then thanked the person and said goodbye.

"Jack, Debra, we will now begin planning our day. The jerks didn't leave the area but are holed up in a house about forty kilometers from here. It will take us about thirty or more minutes to get there. But I suggest, we don't go alone because there may be more than three of them and my contact said be careful because they are well armed."

"Anna, how fast can you get two or three of your workmen for a day job?"

"I will let you know in a few minutes."

"Anna then made a phone call and asked who she called if he had plans or would he like a nice paying job today?"

She must have got a positive answer because her next question asked if his two cousins also needed some work. Whoever she had talked too must have replied yes because the next thing she told him that they were to meet in thirty minutes at the truck stop on the E 217 near the interchange of the E427 and have their work equipment with them."

"Jack, we are all set to confront them, and it could turn ugly. Are you and Debra ready to accept the consequences?"

"Anna, you know Debra and I work for the United States government and we have done this before but here is a suggestion. Why don't we confront them from a distance with our associates and learn what they may have in the house they occupy. Then, we call in Interpol and leave when they arrive?"

"Will they let us leave?"

They will after I talk to them. Wait a minute and let me make a call.

He looked up a number on his phone and hit the call button. "Dennis Wilson please. Tell him it is Jack and it is urgent I speak to him."

"Dennis how are you. Great. Look I have a problem In Antwerp along with my partner. We are going after some Illegal arms dealers here in the area who have threatened to kill us if they catch us. We have some local fire power, but I think it would be better to use your services. Our plan is to surround their house and let them think we are going to have a shootout. But instead I will call in your troops to make a major arrest and we quietly fade away. Do you, think you can arrange this?"

"How much time can you give me?"

"One to two hours would be okay."

"Done. You have always helped us Jack and we want our relationship to continue. Give me some coordinates so we can act fast once you call me. You will then have two minutes to leave the area and we will do the rest."

'Thanks Dennis. I appreciate the kindness and later this month, I will call you with even better news. In the meantime, until we get near the place, I cannot give you the coordinates, but I will have them for you in thirty minutes or less."

"Sounds good to me Jack and you and your partner stay safe."

Anna it is all set, and we can explain to your workers what our plan is when we meet them at the truck stop. Is this okay with you?"

I think I need another car because my car is too recognizable. Fortunately, there is a rental agency in the hotel lobby. So, let's get started."

They all went the lobby for Anna to obtain a rental car and when that had been done, they left to meet the rest of the group at the truck stop. During the drive, Jack asked Anna if she could find out who the kidnapers worked for and if they had any relationship with the Russians.

"I will find out for you and give you an answer today or tomorrow."

The drive to the truck stop only took about twenty minutes and Ann's contacts had arrived and anxious to join them. Anna parked her car in a deserted section away from the restaurant. She then requested her associates to join her along with Jack and Debra to discuss their plan before heading for the farmhouse.

They all gathered around Anna's car and Jack opened the discussion.

"Hi, my name is Jack, and this is Clare and yesterday after meeting with Anna, Clare became a prisoner of the people we now plan to confront. Fortunately, Clare had the smarts and ability to get away before they could harm her. I don't like people who try to hurt my friends and it is the reason we are now here. Anna will explain how we intend to even the score."

"Guys, you know me well enough and that I also care about my friends. I also care about my safety and yesterday before the thugs kidnapped Clare, they also burst into my house and threatened me. Today, we get even, and I promise they will not like what we are about to do. Our plan is simple. We will surround the house and let them know we are there and also let them know, we are armed if they are interested in a bloody battle. When they then threaten us, we will play games with them like firing a few shots from every side of the house. They may fire back but all of us will remain in protected cover.

Once we feel they may be getting ready to do more serious shooting; I will give everyone a signal and we quickly leave and return to Antwerp City Center. In actuality, we are turning the bad guys over to Interpol who will arrive in less than one minute after we leave, and Interpol will put them out of action for quite a while. Interpol only knows Jack and does not know about anybody else involved in this set-up. You will be well paid for your help today and it is to remain a silent story."

A few minutes later they left in separate cars and within minutes they were driving in a rural area and soon they were approaching a very deserted farming area and then a house appeared on a small hill overlooking the recently cultivated land. The passed the house and turned on a dirt road about one kilometer beyond the house.

They stopped well hidden from the house and discussed how they would approach their target from different directions. While they stopped,

Jack texted Dennis their coordinates and told him he would send an alert when they would be ready to vacate the area.

They agreed how to proceed, and one car continued up the road for a short distance and the driver would walk to the house using the cover of a large patch of fruit trees. The other car and Anna's car turned around and headed back towards the house, Anna's car turned into the driveway leading to the house and the other car continued down the main road.

Anna's car stopped about 100 meters from the front door and blew the horn. Debra stepped out of the car staying behind the car door. Jack slid out the other door and took a position behind the rear of the car. Both had their guns drawn. The front door of the hose opened slightly, and Debra waved to Rick as he stepped out of the house and he also had a weapon. Before he could raise his arm, Jack fired a shot that knocked Rick back against the front door, and somebody dragged Rick back into the house

Debra fired two shots at hitting the front windows of the house and other shots were fired from the side of the house and more shots were being fired at the rear of the house. Jack and Debra quickly got back into the car and Anna turned the car and headed out of bullet range. Jack sent an alert to Interpol and Anna signaled to her hired guns to leave now. As Anna's car reached the main road, a number of unmarked cars began turning up the road towards the house on the hill.

They all arrived back at the hotel safely and Jack and Debra decided it would be better if they returned to Paris. Anna agreed and they went to their room to retrieve their belongings and then, went back to the lobby to check out.

"Anna, we had a good day and now what do we owe you for the car, people and something for you?"

"Look, you two helped me get some thugs off the street and my straight shooters don't need much."

"Anna, I promised you fifty thousand originally. Will a hundred thousand cover everything?"

"That is more than enough Debra. Save some for your Paris vacation."

"It is okay, you and your contacts earned it. Jack and I will catch the next train and we will stay in touch with you. We will try to return to a normal life."

Chapter 35

Debra and Jack left the hotel for the short walk to the rail station and hoped for a few days of rest. They safely returned to Paris and back to the elegant Shangri-La hotel.

They awoke in the morning still somewhat in a haze but awake and both knew neither one of them had slept well and under the circumstances it would be understandable. Jack called for room service and ordered an array for food for them. Eating may help them get some energy back and settle their stomachs.

Debra took a long hot shower and emerged a bit more peppy than last night. They sat in the living room of the suite awaiting their breakfast. The doorbell rang and the room serve staff entered, set the table for them and placed all the food and drinks on the table before exiting the suite.

"Good morning darling, a good cup of coffee and a decent breakfast will be good for us to start our day. Can I pour your coffee Debra?"

"Thanks Jack and as a matter of fact, I am hungry. Thanks for ordering so much food."

After completing their breakfast, they each poured themselves another cup of coffee and went to the living room to sit and discuss what had occurred over the last week. Jack summarized the past few days as the week of horrors and hoped this next week would be more controllable.

"What do you have planned for today, Debra?"

"Well, I hoped to relax but I have to send the Director a full report about Adam and I will call the Blantons and try to convince them to remain in Paris for another two weeks. I will use the excuse of there being a number of things happening in the States regarding Blanton Arms and the three amigos which cannot be revealed at this time, but not too much of anything else."

"It sounds good to me Debra."

"Is there any way I can help you? I know you still have a lot to do. Didn't you want to meet with Interpol or are you awaiting Franz's report?"

"No, I don't think it would help us or reduce what we have to do. In addition, when Franz sends me his report, I will immediately forward it to the Director for retransmission to Interpol. I promised Franz the information to Interpol would originate in the USA via confiscated files of the three amigos. I will probably spend most of the day continuing my study of the three amigos folders to learn if there is additional information unknown to us. The Director also asked me to keep tabs on the all the three amigos to learn if they have any knowledge of current events."

Debra then dialed the Blantons suite and Priscilla answered the phone. "Hello Priscilla. We are still gathering important information relevant to the case. We have confidence we will finish all our investigations within the next ten days, but it could drag out for another few days. A number of actions are underway in the USA involving Blanton and the three amigos. For these reasons, we would like you to remain in Paris or in other parts of Europe if you desire for two more weeks. Is this possible?"

"As matter of fact, yes because George and I want to visit a few orphanages while here and if that is fine with you and Jack, we will leave later today but we will remain in touch. I assume we will return in five or six days at the most. You people stay safe."

"Thanks Priscilla. You and George also stay safe. And we'll see you when you return."

"Well dear, I got that done, can I be of any help to you?"

"It is still nighttime in the States and I am going to look in on our boys. You can help by starting to read Wimsley's email folder and see if anything stands out and raises your suspicions."

"I don't understand it. I came to Paris to spend time with my hubby but all I do is work, work and more work."

"No complaining my honey. Working honeymoons are in fashion. I thought you knew that?"

"Well okay but one of these days, you owe me a real honeymoon where we can find lots of sunshine, a jacuzzi, waiters with appetizers and fresh drinks and shimmering palm trees."

"What is the matter, you don't like Paris?"

"What's not to like about it. I'm in Shangri-La."

They both began to laugh and then gave each other a big hug.

"Off to spy we go. I'll do Wimsley and you do a good job tracing those three amigos."

"Yes dear."

Her laptop sat on the dresser in the bedroom and Debra went in to retrieve it and then, she returned to the living room and sat in the comfortable large leather chair. She plugged in the thumb drive into the computer, turned it on and located the folder of interest and began scanning the contents until she located the Wimsley folder.

She started reviewing emails from the early days of 2018 and unless they contained order information or financial transactions, she quickly moved on to the next one in the folder. She had a legal pad and pen to make notes if the email contained anything suspicious.

In late January, she read about an order destined for Albania to later ship to Syria. Nothing unusual she thought and continued her reading of emails in February and March and still nothing jumped out for her of any serious concern. Just the usual nickel and dime stuff done on a daily basis.

As she began reading April there seemed to be more discussion of growing orders and a mention of Adam trying to control the international business related to Russia. Silverman had sent Wimsley and Rivera a message complaining of Adam being too pushy and maybe too friendly to Russia.

Silverman told the two he felt pushing too much stuff to Russia could be a big risk to Blanton Arms because it may draw the feds into the equation. This could be dangerous he said, and they should meet soon to discuss the issue and then have a conversation with Adam.

Debra made a note of Silverman's concern and then continued reading May and June emails. There were no further emails mentioning a meeting about Adam or anything about a meeting with him. July was no different and as she continued into August, an email again from Silverman talked about a meeting with Adam and from the tone of the meeting, it appeared Adam knew they had accumulated more than $600 million and yet he had only a token payment of two million.

Debra knew a good part of the orders came either from Russia or one of their surrogates. Adam felt he deserved more because he had set the stage for them to do all this business and yet they treated him as a financial stepchild. He told Silverman he had helped them make a lot of money and they should give him a better slice of the pie.

Silverman became unsure as to how to proceed with Adam's demand because Adam knew just about everything they had been doing and because of his government connections, he could easily black mail them.

Debra thought for a minute. It sounds like Silverman is caught between a rock and a hard place and from what I know, Russia and Adam know of every move the three amigos take to sell their goods illegally and hide their money. This could now get very interesting and maybe dangerous for either the amigos or Adam.

She returned to her reading of the emails where she had left-off hoping to find if the mini-feud had accelerated. Late August and early September showed not a hint of Adam and Debra began to wonder if the amigos tried to figure out how to eliminate Adam from their operation or give him a bigger slice of the pie. Maybe the Russians told Adam to back off as they still wanted shipments.

Her answer showed up in the last week of September when another email from Silverman confirmed an additional ten million dollars had been transferred into Adams account. This will probably end the feud, or would Adam become greedier?

"Jack, I have been reviewing the Wimsley folder and the only strange occurrence concerned a mini-feud between the amigos and Adam. He pushed for more money because his rational said he had made them a lot money and they were oblivious to him. The feud when on for a couple of months and finally they added ten million to his account.

It appears this quieted him down or maybe his Russian handlers slapped his hand. Tell me. Isn't it possible for the Russians to gain access to the money at any time?"

"Great question Debbie, I know my capabilities and I know how good Boris can be and I would say, in a day, we or the Russians could take them and the bank to the cleaners."

"All six hundred million?"

"Maybe more, because Adam has about twelve million and I would guess their partner has maybe a hundred million. It could all be snatched away, and it would be very hard to trace where it ended up."

"My brilliant husband. Before or simultaneously with the take down of the three amigos and Adam, why not donate a nice amount to the Blanton's trust and fix it as if the partner stole it or the Russians wanted some of their money returned."

"Damn, I have wife with a safecracker's mentality. It's wonderful. What a pair we are going to be. We can do a new job every time we want to take one of those expensive trips."

"Your funny and I love you."

"I love you too sweets but, in all honesty, you have a great idea and Boris and I can do it. We just have to time it in line with the takedowns of the entire cast including the partner in Moldova. It could also be a nice payday for Boris, as he can have Adam's share."

"It would be a nice windfall for the Blanton's trust. It's almost the same as a court directed damage award for pain and suffering."

"Well said honey and now it's time to return to our mundane jobs."

"Okay."

Debra returned to reviewing the Wimsley emails while Jack got back to peeking inside the three amigos computers.

Chapter 36

Unknown to Debra, as a follow-up to Silverman's April email he had sent an email to Wimsley and Rivera suggesting they should meet to discuss the possible threat of Adam being pushy and too friendly with Russia. They all agreed to meet in the evening at Silverman's house in three days.

Wimsley and Rivera arrived together, and Silverman greeted them at the door and escorted them into his den.

"Make yourselves comfortable and can I get you a drink? Bob, what would you like? Larry, what about you?

"Bob requested Baileys on the rocks."

"I'll just have a cold beer," replied Larry.

"Give me a minute and I'll be right back with the drinks and then we can start to talk."

When they each had a drink, Paul began the discussion.

"Guys I sense a future problem with Adam. I feel he may be pushing too much stuff to Russia and this is a big risk to Blanton Arms. Why, because it may get the feds involved and this could be dangerous for all of us. I need some guidance here guys and help in how we approach this problem and get Adam to understand the trouble we face if we continue sending arms to Russia.

"Paul, Larry, I know we all have a big stake in this arrangement and maybe we have to tell him what you just said. Let him know if the feds come knocking at our door, then all of us are in trouble. We will continue to do well with less Russian orders because they can reroute these orders to their surrogates and the Russian concern becomes less of a problem."

"Good suggestion Bob. Any comment Larry?"

"I think this has to be handled soon as I see a number of Russian orders working their way through production now outnumber a lot of other customers."

"I agreed with you both, but I don't see it as an immediate problem. What I suggest is you hold off a couple of months and let's see what happens. If it is still a problem, Paul can arrange a meeting with Adam and more than likely, it will cost us a few million, but the ROI is still good."

"Thanks guys. Your input is appreciated, and I will do my best to keep Adam at arm's length and will keep you both updated as things occur."

Larry and Bob left the house and Silverman made a note to himself to stay in touch Adam and try to keep him happy.

Although Silverman had brief conversations with Adam about the subject, two months later, nothing had changed, and Silverman had arranged a meeting with Adam to discuss the Russian order dilemma. They would meet at Adams apartment in the early evening.

Adam greeted Silverman at his apartment, and they began their meeting in Adam's living room.

"Adam, we are getting concerned with the growing volume of Russian orders currently in our factory. We worry the feds may receive information from their European contacts and begin investigating the company. We would like to suggest you arrange the majority of future orders to be sent through surrogates thereby hiding the source of the order."

"Paul, I have done my best to get you many orders of significant dollar value and you and your companions have made a lot of money off my efforts. I can change the direction of where the orders are issued and transported but this is just another example of me doing something for you guys while you do nothing for me. I want to start getting a little more respect from you guys."

"What do you mean by respect Adam. We respect you and appreciate what you have done for us. So, tell me how you interpret respect?"

"What I mean is I am tired of being a stepchild who continuously feeds money into your piggy bank while financially you guys leave me high and dry. It seems it's okay for you three big wheels to make six hundred million and pay me a puny two million. What the hell do you call that after I gave you lessons how to get really rich. I opened doors for you and showed you how to avoid the pitfalls. Remember when I gave you my pitch, you and your buddies had forty million in the bank. I give you contacts; you get orders, make a ton of money and shove it to the guy responsible for making you successful. Again, you're asking me to do something you guys can't do and yet you snob me as if I don't matter."

"We gave you two million dollars."

"Yes, and I have given you six hundred million and what you gave me is chicken feed. Do you think that is fair? In any other organization, I would be rewarded like a star. If you feel the status quo is okay, you better reconsider how much you need my support. Even my friends in Russia feel you should put more into my pot. In fact, keep that in your head that I have friends in Russia and a place to run to if it gets to hot here. Where can you run to when the house catches fire?"

"I hear you Adam. Give me a clue as to how much will ease your concerns?"

"Look, unknown to you are my expenses. The people helping me get orders also like money and I am their banker. I think a good starting point is ten million to support my efforts. Later, if we decide to disband, another ten million as severance pay."

"I have to talk to Bob and Larry before making any commitment."

"Okay, but I will not wait too long and make sure you tell them how pissed I am."

"Understood. I will give you an answer this week."

"I will await your answer. Send me a message stating 'ten days until my vacation' when you approve my request."

Silverman left the apartment knowing he and his partners were caught in the middle because of the knowledge Adam had of our operation and his potential threats. He would suggest to his partners to accept the offer.

Later that evening, he sent an email to Wimsley and Rivera rehashing his meeting with Adam. He told them ten million was a small amount to pay against our $600 million in the bank. Maybe we should make it fifteen or twenty million because we need a happy Adam. He later received an agreement from both to make the ten million payment.

"The next day, he sent an email to Adam telling him he would be going on vacation in ten days.

Chapter 37

Adam had left the meeting with Silverman very unhappy with the response even though he knew they would accept his ten million demand. 'Well let them be stupid because either they don't realize my worth or they are just too greedy' he thought.

A few days earlier, he had received an interesting email from his old Russian friend Nikita, who now went by the name of Louis and was living in France. He asked Adam if he wanted to partner in a new arms business based in Southern France?

After his meeting with Silverman, Adam was smart enough to know his days with the Blanton bunch were numbered and he decided it would be a good time to work with his friend. He would be happy to be back in Europe as he never really accepted America as his home. He and Louis knew a lot of arms dealers in all parts of Europe and his relationship with Blanton would steer many to work with him.

He emailed back his interest and told him he could very quickly enlist a few American manufacturers to sell their product in Europe. He would use the same sales pitch he had successfully used with Blanton and he knew most of these companies didn't mind being devious or skirting government laws if significant orders and profits came their way.

He then called his friend to negotiate a deal. "Louis my friend. I like your proposal and I want to join you in this new venture. Here is what I can do. I can line up at least four or five American companies to supply us a broad line of arms. Guns and ammo, rocket launchers and even ground to air missiles. I would assume we will be partners and because of my current relationship with Blanton, I would like this to happen fast."

"It's a wonderful idea and I would like nothing more to join forces with you Vitaly, my old friend. I have enough money to keep us happy for the next year but with our common contacts and a few good suppliers, we can get a lot of business. Tell me what you need to get us started in business within one to two months."

"Thanks Louis. I will need a French passport with a new name and some catalogs showing our products. I suggest we use the name American Rifle Importers as it will impress the American companies I will approach. Once I have the information, I can begin signing up manufacturers quickly. Lastly, within a few weeks, I will relocate to France with my new identity and at that time, I will be able to put a lot of cash into the company to pay for inventory."

"Excellent, I promise to have everything you need in about two weeks and I will overnight ship you full details of the company formation, your new identity information, product specialties and French business cards. Let's plan on opening our business in one month and you join me here in France shortly after we officially open."

"That timeline works good for me Louis and it will be good to have a business where we are working for ourselves. I look forward to receiving all the information and I'll keep you informed as I cut some deals. Bye for now."

Adam was pleased knowing he would soon be in business with his close friend and no longer have to deal with the greedy Blanton bunch. They probably will get caught eventually and I want no part of that scene. I will try to get their money once I move to France.

He then began his research of possible suppliers to his new company to create a broad product line to attract known dealers to sell the American Rifle importers products.

A week after his discussion with his friend, he received everything Louis had promised. He began to organize a schedule of meeting with his target companies over the next two weeks and begin his recruiting campaign.

At the end of the two weeks, he had convinced three companies to allow American Rifle to sell their products. Two other companies also expressed interest but had not yet made any decisions. He had notified Louis of his success and he felt they were off to a good start. Adam also believed what he had already accomplished would bring in a lot of business rapidly and the profits would flow into the company.

He began to make plans to leave the country faster than he had previously planned. He now had three things to make him happy over the next few days. The ten million from Blanton, his successful start of his partnership in the new company and finally leaving the United States after twenty years as a Russian spy.

Chapter 38

Jack had been carefully monitoring the three amigos accounts to assess if they had any suspicions of the FBI surveilling them. The three amigos still talked about orders and about their growing bank account and Jack concluded nothing bad had occurred.

As he began to look at Silverman's emails for today, he immediately saw the pending order for one hundred and eighty million dollars destined for the Islamic Revolutionary Guards in Iran. Jack had not yet reported this potential order to the Director, but he should in case it is being readied to be shipped and then it could be stopped during the export process. He knew, neither he nor the Director would want these arms going to Iran.

After this thought, he sent an email to the director informing him the details of this pending order in addition to the potential final destination. He then continued his search into Wimsley's and Rivera's accounts, but they had nothing new in them and no indication anything had gone bad.

Within an hour after reviewing the amigos email accounts, Jack received a large envelop from Franz. He carefully opened the envelop to find detailed information on twenty-two know illegal arms traders in fourteen different European countries. The data given to Jack included names, resident addresses, know phone numbers and in many cases email addresses. Included along with each name were detailed descriptions of arms specialties, sales channels and purchasing channels. He noted four dealers had listed Blanton Arms as a source of weapons and Franz had included the names of banks in six different countries who were possibly laundering money for the illegal arms dealers.

He read the documents provided twice to ensure he had not missed any vital information and began to write down key information which he could then compare to information he had pulled off the three amigos computers. When he started to compare data from the listings, he found Silverman's emails contained the same email addresses of fourteen dealers on the list. Yet only four dealers had successfully purchased products from Blanton Arms. This finding proved Blanton had dealt with a large number of illegal dealers, but they had not always been successful in obtaining a weapons order.

Further review of Silverman's data allowed Jack to identify specific orders for the four dealers Blanton had provided weapons too and the dollar amount of each sale. All further analysis can be better handled back at the agencies and he felt, the list looked complete and with suitable information for both US intel and European Interpol.

Jack then, immediately faxed the information to the director and followed it up with a detailed email regarding what he had learned from the small sample of data he evaluated and how the information should be handled to ensure Interpol knows it came from US intelligence agencies and did not come from European sources. In fact, Jack stated it is possible to tie the data to the three amigos emails, and this would be the best solution of protecting the international sources.

He followed this action up with a call to the Director. "Sir, I have sent you all of the illegal European dealer network information via fax and an email. I want to ensure it has been received."

"Thanks Jack. It is being reviewed by a secure team as we speak, and I will advise you of our actions within a few hours. You and Debbie stay safe. We'll talk again soon."

Jack would hold off talking to Interpol until he had been advised they received the information from US agencies. He had to also wait to see if or when Adam and the three amigos would be arrested and charged. Once he received the plan of action by the American authorities, he would meet with Boris to decide what to do with the large amount of dirty money sitting in the Moldova bank.

While Jack had been reviewing the data Franz sent, Debra had continued searching the Wimsley data. Most of the information had been found in Silverman's and Rivera's emails didn't justify any further searching. In early 2018, she found an email sent to the banking partner, but not copied to the other two amigos.

The email had a strange tone and it appeared to Debra, Wimsley may be trying to undercut his partners. He wanted the bank manager, also a partner, to create another account for himself and the bank manager. He asked him to put fifty million into the account, twenty-five million for Wimsley and twenty-five million for the banker.

The banker is to inform all of the amigos; he had been forced by Moldova government inspectors to either pay a large bribe or have all the funds confiscated and then shut the bank down. In addition, every new large deposit received by the bank, ten percent would be paid to the same officials. Debra knew that in reality, this money would go into the new Wimsley/banker account.

Debra immediately went to Jack to discuss her recent finding. "Jack, there is no honesty among thieves."

"What did you find now Debra?"

"Wimsley and the amigos bank manager have struck a deal to keep more money than the other partners. They all have been bitten by the greed bug and you and I know, it will be the downfall of them all."

"Debra, I think it is time to put the Three amigos and Adam behind bars. It is also time for us to act quickly to move all the money before the arrests and avoid potential actions by the Russians or others to take place. I have uncovered sufficient evidence to charge the three amigos and Adam of fraud, money laundering and illegal arms sales. I will call the Director now and recommend they immediately arrest the entire group."

Chapter 39

Within twenty minutes after the Director received Jacks request and the data supplied by Franz, he called in two close associates to discuss the findings.

"John, I have received information from Jack regarding all the illegal arms dealers in Europe and especially those associated with Blanton. This information is to remain confidential and in no way is Adam Sanderson or anyone else be made aware of its existence. I want you to immediately have a couple of agents review the information and compare it to what we already have from Blanton. If it agrees with our data, let Pat know and then he will forward it to our Interpol contacts for further action by them. Please specify to Interpol that this information came from our investigations in the United States. No mention is to be made of any European sources and I want Interpol to be notified today."

"Understand sir, I already have two agents with familiarity of Blanton emails."

"Pat, the same rules apply to you. No information is to be supplied to Adam. While you wait for John's group to attest to the data, I want you to immediately prepare five teams of four men each plus additional agents to remove equipment and documentation which may contain evidence.

Three of the teams will simultaneously raid the homes of Wimsley, Silverman and Rivera. One of them is to arrest Adam Sanderson and the final team is to raid the headquarters of Blanton Arms and arrest the three executives whose homes are targeted. In all cases, computers, cell phones and complete file cabinets are to be confiscated from their homes and Blanton headquarters."

"Both of you are to stress to all involved agents that this action is to remain confidential until our objectives are met. I don't want to spook Adam as other agents will be at risk."

About three hours later, John informed his associate. "Pat it is a go. The report from Jack contained information found in numerous Blanton files. Good luck on your assignments."

Within a few minutes all five teams were dispatched and they were told that all raids must happen simultaneously to ensure no warning to those being charged takes place.

FBI agents raided the homes of the three amigos and confiscated all relevant equipment and personal files but not without some conflict.

At Silverman's home, an agent rang the bell and knocked on the door.

"Who is there?"

"FBI, open the door."

"I'm not opening the door; I'm calling the police."

"This is the FBI and we have a warrant to search your home and if you don't want to open the door, we will break it open."

"I've called the police, so you better get out if here."

"Lady. Your choice."

An agent with a large sledgehammer took one swing at the lock portion of the door and the door flew open and they faced a screaming woman.

"Lady, we said we were the FBI and we have a warrant to search your house; so, find a seat and let us do our job."

About a minute after the agents entered the house, the local police arrived to find three FBI vehicles and a clearly marked FBI agent standing in front of the house with a warrant in his hand. The police immediately recognized this was a serious raid.

Within a few additional minute's agents began removing objects from the house while the wife sat sobbing on a bench in the entry way. Within ten minutes, they had removed what they needed and left the premises.

At the Wimsley and Rivera homes the raids went much easier.

Simultaneously, a total of six agents entered the lobby of the Blanton Arms headquarters to join the director of security along with two of his staff. The FBI had previously telephoned them to meet in the lobby.

"Nice to meet you Mr. Lyons. Per our conversation, I hope you have not notified anyone of our being here today. In my hand I have a warrant identifying all of the legal actions we are justified in taking today."

"No, I have not notified anyone sir and up till now, my two assistants were totally unaware of the visit."

"Good. You will stay with me and another one of my agents. Your assistants will each be joined by two agents. We have two parts to this operation. First, we are here to arrest Mr. Silverman, Mr. Wimsley and Mr. Rivera and nobody is to use their cell phone or notify anyone we meet as we go to their offices. Is that understood by all of you?"

"Yes sir."

"Secondly after we arrest our suspects, you will assist other members of our team to gathering certain items of interest for removal from the building. This is consistent with the warrant I have shown you upon our arrival. Is this understood?"

"Yes sir."

"Fine, now let's begin by each group going to the respective offices of our suspects."

Silverman, Wimsley and Rivera were arrested without incidence on charges of gun smuggling, money laundering and income tax evasion. All their company computers, phones and files were also confiscated and the three were transported to local FBI holding area where they would be formally charged and undergo interrogation.

Adam Sanderson's residence was also raided but somehow, he must have been spooked by something because he could not be found. An APB was issued immediately with his vehicle ID along with pictures of him to local law enforcement. FBI agents and local police immediately began a stakeout at all entrances to the Russian Embassy.

Jack and Debra had to be notified of Adam's freedom as it could be dangerous for both of them.

Chapter 40

Jack and Debra awaited a response from the Director regarding Jack's request, and it wasn't long before the phone rang. Jack picked up the phone and knew it had to be the Director.

"Jack, I have some good news and bad news for you. The Three amigos have been arrested and are undergoing interrogation as we speak. They will then be held without bail in a federal jail. The bad news is Adam is loose and could be in contact with his Russian handlers. We will continue trying to trace his phone and we have an APB out for his car. We also have FBI and local law enforcement agents watching all entrances to the Russian Embassy. We do not know for sure what will happen or when."

"Sir, I planned on going to Finland tomorrow to remove all of the groups assets and put it in a safe place. Based on what you have just told me, Debra will join me on the Finland trip for her safety. We have had some proof of other dealers knowing our whereabouts and perhaps thinking we came here to spy on their operations."

"Don't change your plans and yes, take Debra but you two be careful as there may be some hired guns in the area. We don't exactly know what Adam knew about our plan, but something spooked him. All, I can tell you is stay safe and keep your eyes open."

"Call me at any time and keep me updated."

"Yes sir, I will."

Jack told Debra what the Director had explained to him and there could be an outside possibility of Adam having an awareness of our plan.

"Maybe the Blantons had been watched by the Russians and know where they went and who went with them. I think we have to assume this could be true. If so, we have to be alert and stick close together. I want you to go with me tomorrow to Helsinki because I have a hunch the bad guys know our address."

"I understand and I guess it is time to again unpack the guns."

"I'll call downstairs to make reservations now. Do you have alternate ID's with you so we can drop the Mr. & Mrs. Aldridge in Finland?"

"I have the Clare Brown ID's and we should switch after we clear immigration and customs in Helsinki."

Within a few minutes, Jack received a call from the staff confirming an early morning flight on Air France and a private car to take them to the airport.

"We are booked to fly early tomorrow. Let's get our stuff ready and give me the guns as my suitcase has two areas where the guns will not appear on an x-ray search by security. I also have other ID's with me, and yes, we will switch after clearing customs in Finland."

"Let me send Boris an urgent message to see when we can meet in Finland. Debra, what you have read in Wimsley's email, tells me, it is time to drain the bank now before Adam or his Russian friends get a chance to do what Boris and I want to do."

A few minutes after he sent the message, he received a return message from Boris simply stating tomorrow evening in Helsinki Tower Hotel. But then, he received a phone call from Anna.

"Jack. I just received information from one of my contacts. In a roundabout way, Adam setup the kidnapping of Debra to learn about your plans and location. It is not known where he is at this time and we don't know who he has contacted."

"Thanks Anna, we are about to move, fast."

"You and Debra be careful, and I'll stay in touch if I get further information about him. Bye."

"Debra let's get packed and check out now. Adam knows where we are and it's time to leave. Anna confirmed your kidnapping was arranged by Adam. It's probably too late to get a flight to Helsinki but we can get a hotel at the airport for tomorrows flight."

"Jack, I suggest we take only what we need for a couple of days and let the Blantons arrange to get the rest of our stuff later. We can be out of here in twenty minutes or less."

"Good idea, we won't even check out but just get a car to the airport. I will text Boris about the urgency of meeting."

Jack then sent Boris a text simply stating meeting is a go and has become urgent. He ordered a car to get them to the airport went to the bedroom to quickly pack a few things including their guns. Within ten minutes they were downstairs awaiting the private car.

"Debra from now on, we have to include Adam in our plans and move quickly."

Chapter 41

Jack and Debra left the hotel in a private car to the airport. The driver left them at the Air France terminal, and they headed for the arrival area where they could arrange an airport hotel stay. They spent the night comfortably and safe. Early the next morning they took the hotel shuttle back to the Air France terminal.

When they arrived at the airport, they paid close attention to everyone near them, but it did not appear they had been followed. They had no difficulty checking in or clearing security and again they stayed on alert as to who might be on the plane with them.

They comfortably sat in first class and their flight left on time and since the flight would only be a couple of hours, Jack had time to think of what he and Boris could safely accomplish. He knew they had a good chance of being able to move the money but to where and how without raising suspicions, could be questionable.

At the same time, they were on their way to Helsinki, Adam was driving to New York to fly to France the next morning. He had changed his appearance and had a French passport in the name of La Roi Boucher. He also had thoughts of stealing the money resting in the Moldova bank and he was sure another two days would not matter but he was not aware of the arrests of the three amigos.

Jack also continued to think about the money. I know the three amigos account has at least $500 million, the Adam account $12 million, the Wimsley/bank manager account $50 million plus and the Bank Manager's account perhaps $100 million or more. This may reach $700 million and if we are successful, how do we divide it up for useful purposes and to who will benefit?

Jack had already decided that Boris would get the Adam account for his reward of helping Jack and for providing the necessary equipment and know-how to allow them to successfully obtain the funds. Beyond Boris's payment, there still remained a lot of money to be safely and meaningfully distributed. The big question would be how many people or organizations and who makes the decision about how it is to be divided?

The Blantons deserve some but realistically, they and their trusts are well endowed so it would not serve much of a useful purpose to just make them richer. He thought of the poor country of Moldova, the home of the corrupt bank and they could certainly use some funds.

He also thought of the Interpol and the large expense needed towards capturing not only the twenty plus corrupt dealers in fourteen countries but also the bank manager. The help they would provide would benefit many European countries and the United States.

Then, what about his own government who will end up spending millions in investigating and trying the case against the three amigos and Adam. There is also the past and future loses to Blanton Arms for the actions of their crooked executives with the potential of cancelled military arms orders.

He and Debra could discuss it while relaxing at the hotel after landing in Helsinki but before meeting Boris. These are important decisions and Debra is a good strategist and levelheaded. I know she will help us make the most logical and meaningful decisions.

By the time, he had thought of all the various financial options, the flight began its descent into Helsinki. Ten minutes later they were taxiing towards the terminal and Jack flipped open his seat belt ready to depart the flight along with Debra and together they would go to the hotel to meet Boris.

They exited the plane, went through the immigration checkpoint and then retrieved their suitcases to pass through the customs checkpoint. Once cleared, they entered the general terminal, found seats in a partially deserted lounge and selected new ID 's for both of themselves and they would register at the hotel using their new aliases.

They exited the terminal and caught a taxi and told the driver to take them to the Helsinki Tower Hotel. They arrived at the hotel about twenty-five minutes after leaving the airport property.

After registering at the hotel and texting Boris their room number, Jack then told her of all the possibilities and options he had envisioned during the flight and could not decide what would be the right thing to do with so much money.

"Jack, I heard about all your possibilities, but I didn't hear about the villa on Lake Como in Italy or the beachfront property in Hawaii and my Lamborghini."

Jack laughed loudly and then she continued. "Never mind honey, we will suffer with what we have now. So now, let's get real. The Boris amount is fine. Moldova is good but the how to accomplish this is still an unknown and is questionable without some legal entanglements. Then there is Blanton Arms and the American government. Am I correct or did I miss something?"

"Yes, you forgot the money for Interpol. They will serve as a very reliable partner to the United States in this effort. You did get the rest of it all right, but resolving who gets what is part of the issue and then the question is, how to do it?"

"Jack, it's too much to digest at one time. Give me a few hours to really think about it and we can attack it later when we know the real amount. I suggest, you and Boris go do your thing and park the money somewhere safe and hopeful later today we can reach a workable solution."

"You are right Debra. We shouldn't count our chickens before they hatch. There is another facet to Boris and I meeting, besides the Moldova bank. With the help of Boris, I want to look at two additional things. First, I have the names of four dealers who have assisted Blanton in their illegal sales. Maybe we can drain their accounts in addition to the major ones.

The second item regards six banks Franz sent to me who, I am pretty certain launder money for the illegal arms dealers. I am not sure what we will find or maybe you and I will have to visit two or three of them to verify what we have learned."

While they were continuing the conversation, Boris had arrived at the airport in the early afternoon and he caught a taxi to take him to the hotel. While riding in the taxi, Boris texted Jack a short note. I'll be in lobby in ten minutes.

The taxi got Boris to the hotel in about eighteen minutes and after Boris retrieved his bag from the taxi, he entered the lobby of the hotel just as Jack exited the elevator.

"Boris, over here, it's great to see you my buddy. It been too long and three years since we have been together in person. Check-in and then let's go upstairs to talk where it is a lot quieter and by the way, I will introduce you to my partner Debra."

Boris went to the reception desk and quickly checked-in, picked up his room key and returned too where Jack stood in the lobby.

"Jack, I will go to my room first and drop this stuff off. Then I will go to your room to meet Debra and we can talk for a while and then maybe we can have a good dinner together."

Sounds good, I will wait for you in our room.

Five minutes later, Boris entered Jack and Debra's room.

"Pretty snazzy Jack. I guess we'll have to work hard to pay for this luxury?"

"I think if we do it right, we can buy the hotel. Please have a seat and let me introduce you. Boris, this is Debra and my partner in investigating a few crooked guys. She will hang out at the hotel while we work."

"No hurry Jack. I have no set plans for the next three days and then I must return to Russia."

"Actually Boris, there is a need to hurry. One of the bad guys, a KGB implant into the FBI has disappeared. He has money in this bank, and I am afraid he may try to get at all of it very soon. If possible, I hope you have everything setup and we could possibly start tonight."

"Well, I had hoped we can do our work in a day or less and then move on a little wealthier. I have all my equipment and everything else ready whenever you want to start but let's just chat for a few minutes, then go have a quick dinner and for dessert, we eat a rich bank."

"Great, so, how is your family? Is your son as tall as you now? And the daughter, what about her?"

"Jack, thanks for asking. Everybody is fine. The son is in love again for the sixth or seventh time and the daughter is sticking to her studies and will graduate college this year with her master's in computer science. I worry now, I am going to have some real competition."

"My goodness, I remember her when she turned ten. They grew up so fast."

"How's your life Jack?"

"Well, I have this beautiful lady who is also an ex-agency person and the intel people teamed us together for this assignment as consultants to the government. I expect if we are still friends when this project is over, then we can both retire again and plan the rest of our life."

"That is great Jack and I am happy for you. Wait until I tell Natasha. She will be overjoyed for you. Of course, she will want to know, when is the wedding?"

"Did I say wedding? But if it is to be, your invited along with your lovely wife. Those are the happy things but now we have to talk business and I want to tell you more about why we are here."

"I figured we would eventually get around to it, Jack."

"Debra and I have been given an assignment to investigate an American company, Blanton Arms and their illegal shipments of banned weapons into Europe and Russia. This has been ongoing for almost two or more years and we and our government know they have made a lot of money illegally exporting forbidden arms into Europe but destined to be shipped to a number of America's enemies. They could not have done this without the help of the Russian mole in the FBI.

I want to drain the bank of the illegal assets and plant them someplace where we can eventually divide them to a few large payouts as compensation to those involved for their efforts and losses. It will not include Debra and me.

"If we are successful, I want you to have the mole's account of $12 million or so as your reward for helping me now and for your previous successes in the past."

"Jack, that is too generous of you but on the other hand, Natasha and I would like to retire, and I have been told, it is always good to retire rich."

"Your right Boris and you deserve it. There is one other thing which I will need your help. After working the Moldova bank, I want to look at additional accounts in the Moldova bank and see if we can find the names of four known dealers with Blanton. If they have funds hidden there, then we also take their loot. Then there three or four banks in four countries which I believe are laundering money for the illegal arms dealers. And if we could look at them, it would be helpful information for Interpol and the American agencies. So, those are the goals for tonight, but we should we leave for dinner now and begin our bank holdup adventure after dinner?"

"Not a holdup Jack, it is a plumbing job. We will drain the pipeline."

They all laughed and got up to leave the room and to go dinner.

Chapter 42

They decided the best place to have a quick dinner would be in the hotel and they chose a Japanese restaurant specializing in Tappan Yaki style cooking. They seated themselves at a table with a large cooking surface in front of them and the three of them ordered a standard meal of steak and fried rice with a few vegetables. The meal lasted about an hour and they left the restaurant. Debra said goodbye to Boris and Jack, and she took the elevator to go to their room.

"Boris, I assume you have another place where we can do our magic act?"

"We do, and it's only a few minutes' walk from here."

Boris and Jack left the hotel and walked a short distance to the location where Boris had placed his equipment for his description of draining the pipeline.

"Jack, we will visit an apartment of a local hacker who owes me a few favors. The equipment here is new, advanced and untraceable. I purchased and installed it and when we finish, it will again be cleansed, leaving no traces of our actions whatsoever and all of it will return with me to Russia."

"Boris, you are the best. Now it is time for us to go to work."

"Before we start Jack, we have two very advanced computers with lots of power and memory. However, first we have to load some software I developed onto each computer and then we will be ready to roll.

This will take about twenty minutes for each of the computers. Then, it will be you and I working as team to hack our way into the bank computers. We will have to proceed slowly at first until we learn what firewalls and security systems the bank has installed and then we have to figure out how to overcome each of the roadblocks we encounter."

They each began to install the software developed by Boris and the computers reacted according to plan and after the software had been loaded, each computer had to be tested using other software Boris had developed before they could be safely used as the entrance devices to gain access to the bank.

Boris told Jack what to look for in the programs they would use. He figured it would take some time and practice before they both could understand what had to be done and what keys needed activated and to carefully follow what would be shown on the screens in front of them.

Twenty minutes later, after testing and practicing, both felt confident they were ready to proceed.

"Ok, Jack what site is our target?"

"The Moldova National Bank located in the capital city of Chisinau. I assume it is the only bank with that name."

"Let's give it a try and I hope their firewall protections do not present a problem and can be overcome easily."

"Boris, it is a very poor country and I doubt if they have any sense of the outside world and as a small local bank with lots of small deposits except of course, for the three amigos and their pals. Hence, I doubt if they worry about hackers in Moldova.

"Sometimes, I get surprised what some banks have for protection. Some are very lousy and others very up to date. Let's hope this one is lousy, and if true, we should be able to operate very fast."

"Boris, just let me know what I am to do to help you."

"Okay, I am on their site and now I will knock on their door and see if anyone answers. So far, I see nothing in the way to stop me. It is almost too easy."

"They appear to be doing packet filtering, but those programs can usually be easy to get around. Hold-on now and watch this on your screen as I'm about to try what is called a go-around. It makes the packet filtering used in their system believe I am acceptable.

We will know in a minute or two if it works. Fantastic, it worked and now I can creep along and study accounts. I want you to carefully watch and see if you recognize any account and let me know right away so I won't bypass it."

"Go slow Boris as some of the accounts maybe coded and I will have to figure out if it is the ones we need. Actually, just looking at the amount in the account should tell me right away as I would guess, there cannot be many millionaires in the neighborhood."

"No hurry Jack and the bank, at this hour, more than likely is probably closed for the day and this will even make it easier to work as the broadband traffic will be very low."

Boris continued scrolling through dozens of accounts while Jack looked for account value as a possible hint towards finding the three amigos accounts. It could be a long process thought Jack.

"Boris, stop. You have accessed an account with over ten million. Move back a couple of accounts and can we get a name on the account?"

"I'll try. Look and see if this is familiar to you?"

"It's coded. I need to study it for a minute. It reads AABNP with $12.75 million. First deposit two million. It's Adams account, the KGB guy and then later another ten million had been deposited. Definitely Adam. The code is American Adam Blanton Partner is my best guess. Boris, take it all and put it into your account and make sure you remove all traceability."

Boris worked another few minutes to complete his task and finally, he assured Jack the money went to his bank and the path on how it went there had been totally eliminated.

"Well Jack, I earned my money. It's now into my bank and my personal account. Can I go home now?"

"Not yet Boris, we have bigger fish to fry. And I am happy to see that nobody else has grabbed the cash. I am sure they will try by tomorrow when the bank manager learns the three amigos and maybe Adam have been arrested in the United States."

"Got it. Let's finish tonight and surprise them tomorrow with no money left for them to steal. Here we go again but too many small accounts. Maybe the big accounts could be all stashed in one place. It is not uncommon for banks to do that as it makes for easy accessibility for them."

Boris continued to work slowly through the hundreds of accounts contained in the bank's system. After about ten minutes of scanning, he thought he found what he had been looking to capture.

"Look at what I found now Jack, three more accounts, all coded similar to the first one and all with big bucks deposited into them. Jack look at the codes, all with the same ending as the KGB guys account. Take a look at them, WSRBNP, WPBNP and GPBNP. Does this make any sense to you?"

"To easy Boris. These guys are not very bright. The first is Wimsley, Silverman and Rivera Blanton Partners, the second Wimsley, Petrolin Blanton Partners and the last is Gustov Petrolin Blanton Partners.

WSR is the three amigos, WP is an account setup by Wimsley and Petrolin to skim some money from the other two amigos, in other words, the two of them got greedy. The last code we know as the bank manager and partner of the amigos."

"What is the total cash amount of all three and is it still in all the accounts?"

"Yes, it is still safe for the moment but not for long. Are you ready for the big number? $870 million."

"Definitely a lot more than I thought Boris."

"So, now where can we safely park it for a couple of weeks?"

"Jack, I have a bank in Estonia, who knows me very well. I have parked amounts like this a few times without any issues of deposit or withdrawal. They charge one percent plus they get to use the float. It's okay for me but it's your money."

"I wish it was mine, but it sounds okay and I trust you know the bank. Eight million earned by taking a risk. Not too bad but obviously for us, it is worth the cost."

"It will take me another twenty minutes to move the funds and then quite a few minutes to cover my tracks.

"Move the funds but don't leave the bank yet. I have four names of arms dealers used by Blanton and I wonder if they also use this bank to hide their money. I have some other names of illegal dealers and they may also be bank customers. Maybe if we are lucky, we can capture a few more million?"

"Before you start Boris, I suggest we don't look for any account less than five million dollars. Here is the first name, Janos Baksa."

"Jack, it is easier if I only look for large dollar amounts and then when I find one, I will give you a name."

"That works for me."

Boris began scrolling again but this time he returned to the section where he had found the amigos large dollar accounts. He began only stopping for accounts five million and above and then called out a name.

"Jack here is one, Omar Ikovonish."

"No, not him."

"Petro Tkachenko"

"Yes, how much in his account?"

"Fourteen million."

"Take and send it to Estonia."

"Got it and done. Next Yuri Slodebronich."

"No."

'Here is two more. Janos Baksa and Stefan Kovacs. One has eight million and the other over nine million."

"Take them both as they show up on the Blanton list."

"Okay, that is complete, and you have one left. Is that right?"

"Yes, Mustafa Yavoz."

"Easy, he is in the same area. Just a few accounts away and has the most money, twenty-one million."

"Now that I finished that, it will take me about ten minutes or so to exit the bank safely and to cover all my tracks."

Take your time Boris, we just added forty-nine million to our haul.

"Once, you have completed your task, can we then look at the other banks on my list?"

"Sure, just let me finish this process before we can start looking at the other banks. It may take as long as thirty to forty minutes to completely remove all traceability.

Boris carefully transferred each account's total dollar value to an account at the bank in Estonia. He finished everything including erasing all the tracks and traceability codes in just under thirty minutes.

"I am now ready Jack. Give me a bank name, city and country."

"BPB-Belabank in Belarus."

"Jack it has seven branches. In what city is the branch located which you would want to enter?"

"Try Pinsk on the Ukraine border."

"I'm there and they have very tight security but let me play for a minute or two. Nothing doing and I believe I could work my way in, but it would take hours to do.

"Skip it and try Bostova-Banka in Sabinov, Slovakia."

"Let's hope we have better luck with this one. I'm knocking on the door, but it doesn't want to open. Again, it would take a lot of time and effort. I can stay another day to try these out but even after getting into the bank, what I am looking to find?"

"I only have one name at each of these banks and it maybe, too difficult to find. Try one more please. UKR- Bankovite in Vinnytsia, Ukraine."

Boris worked for a few minutes before he said, "Jack, I hit another stonewall. These banks are much smarter than the Moldova bank. I could work on all of them but going very deep into the system takes time and it also gives the bank's security software notification of someone trying to enter and then other firewalls become activated to stop the potential intrusion. Taking too much time also increases the risk of being identified."

"Boris, we succeeded in our major priority and took a lot of cash out. The data concerning these banks is being given to Interpol and they will have the means to get what they need.

Let's leave and go drink Scotch and Vodka toasts to our success."

At that moment, his phone rang, and it identified Debra on the phone screen.

"Hi honey, anything of real importance? We should be done in about one hour and then, Boris and I are about done for the day."

"No, I just want to talk to you about the money. Do you have it yet?"

Of course, we have it and it's partially parked at our villa on Lake Como and the balance is at the beach front property in Hawaii. I also ordered the Lamborghini in red. Wasn't that the instructions you gave me?"

"My hero, call me back later and let me know where we are going to celebrate our windfall."

He could hear her laughing and he could see the beautiful smile on her face.

"Debra, I assume Jack?"

"Yes, we will meet her when we finish and go out to celebrate our mutual good fortune."

Boris continued to work for another thirty minutes and then he erased each hard drive with another program he had developed and as the software completed the job, the computers automatically shut down, clean and untraceable.

"I will retrieve my hardware tomorrow and then, me and my equipment are on our way back to Russia."

"Boris, before we leave, I want to ask you a couple of questions regarding Russia's arms business. If you don't want to answer it will not be a problem and I will understand."

"Jack, just ask and if I can answer, I will."

Russia manufactures lot of weapons, but it seems, they also buy a lot from other friendly sources and they also buy big numbers from illegal sources and I just wonder why?"

"Jack, many of our Russian citizens ask the same question. Are we preparing for a war and if so, with who or do it just to show how mighty we are as a nation? We cannot get a reasonable answer to these questions and the funding for this overbuying habit costs everyday Russians a lot."

"The illegal part is very troubling as they pay big ruble or dollar amounts, and nobody knows why. An example of the high payments is what we just moved out of the Moldova bank. It is all profits from illegal arms and where these arms go is known by only a few. I hope that answers your question and now after all my hard work, I am thirsty."

"Thanks, Boris, for your honest answers and I agree, it is time for a drink."

Jack and Boris left the building and slowly walked back to their hotel, met up with Debra and they all headed for the nearest bar.

After they were comfortably seated, they each ordered a drink and after the drinks arrived, they began to toast each other.

"Nostrovia Jack," "Nostrovia Boris." After such a good day, they had to toast each other in Russian, then in English, French and finally in Finnish. As much as they tried, the bar bill did not reach the level of their haul today.

Chapter 43

When they had drank enough, they left the bar and said their goodbyes and walked back to the hotel and then went to their individual rooms. Boris would leave the next morning and Jack and Debra decided to stay another day.

They slept well that night and woke around nine am. They both showered and Jack ordered room service breakfast which about twenty minutes later showed up at their door.

They ate and drank coffee and did not talk very much about yesterday's success. When they had finished eating and poured themselves another coffee, they then began to discuss the money issue.

"Debra, can we talk about the money distribution now?' I believe we should try to resolve the split and then ask the Director to guide us towards a legal solution."

"For a woman, money is always a good way to start a conversation. In all seriousness though, did you and Boris accomplish one hundred percent of what you set out to do and did you finish?"

"Yes, we did finish and the total now sitting in a safe bank totals around 919 million dollars for us to possibly divide up. I have my ideas and

I would like to hear yours and then we can decide upon the best choices. Any time you are ready."

"Jack, it's a big pie to divide up and here's my thoughts. The Blantons should get some, the American government some and maybe Interpol for use to clean up the current illegal arms mess throughout Europe."

"OK, I understand the Blantons have been wronged but to give them money doesn't make anything any better.

My choices would be as follows: 200 million to the Moldova government to improve their banking laws and perhaps their infrastructure. It's a very poor country.

I think $300 million to the US government to cover costs of investigations, court costs etc.

Next $200 million to Blanton Arms to cover costs of reorganization, potential loss of future orders and to cover what they lost during the tenure of the three amigos.

After all of that, we still have over $210 million left and I like your idea about giving some, maybe 100 million to Interpol to assist them in cleaning up the illegal arms mess. This would leave $110 million left to distribute and maybe we just increase the amounts a little bit to everyone I've named, and we would be down to zero."

"Jack, I agree on everything, but I still think the Blantons have been wronged and should get a piece of the pie."

"Ok, I agree then how about the $110 Million?"

"That would be fine, and I will cancel our purchase in Italy but not Hawaii or the red Lamborghini."

"Actually, the American government has to decide. I'll have to talk to the Director and others as to how we do this legally. In other words, the US Government confiscated this money and they will decide how it will be distributed."

"Let's wait and speak to the Director about the money later today. I also want to get an update concerning the status of Adam."

"Speaking of Adam Jack, we should notify the Blantons about this news and perhaps, all of us should consider a move to another country for the balance of this trip to stay safe. We should also get the Director's input on this subject."

"Your right honey and but we should wait about four hours before calling the Director."

"Jack, I still have shopping to do. Whether it's one day or just four hours does not give me enough time. So, let's go out and see what Helsinki wants us to buy today."

They left the hotel and walked in the direction of the main shopping district. They window shopped for a while and then bought some interesting Finnish art from a gallery and Jack bought Debra a beautiful earring set and she in turn bought Jack a model ship he had admired.

They always appeared very happy together, smiling and walking hand in hand. They finally made their way back to the hotel to make the important calls to the Director and the Blantons.

Jack dialed the Director's number and he answered almost immediately.

"Jack and Debra, I want to sound the alarm to both of you. Adam is still loose and for all we know he could have left the country. We have no way of knowing if he exposed either of you or anyone else. The remaining question is to who he would expose you too?

I strongly suggest you and Debra assume somebody knows about you two and will try to eliminate the both of you. In fact, if Adam is aware of you, he may be looking for you or putting feelers out to find you and Debra. Stay alert and on your toes at all times."

"Thanks Paul, concerning this subject, Jack and I would suggest, we can contact the Blantons and all of us leave Paris and move to another country. I will call the Blantons after we complete this call and we will advise you later, where we intend to go."

"Good idea Debbie. You and Jack stay safe.

"Thanks for the info about Adam, we will keep our eyes open."

"Ok, Jack, let's talk about money. Tell me what you have and what you want to do."

"Regarding the money situation, maybe there is a diplomatic way to get the bank manager into the United States. We have some banking costs, but we will net around $910 million and it sits in a bank in Estonia. Debra and I have discussed a number of possible ways it may be distributed

Jack then told the Director what he and Debra thought would be practical distributions but there has to be some negotiations within our government and Interpol and certainly with Moldova.

"What I am suggesting sir, is if we can offer the Moldova government a 200 million dollar grant to improve their banking system and infrastructure, maybe they would hand over the bank manager. Also, maybe a 100 million dollar grant to Interpol will also assist in getting the bank manager and all the corrupt arms dealers we have identified off the street."

"Jack, great job in getting the money. Some day you can tell me about how you did it. Meanwhile, let me get with some diplomatic and legal minds ASAP and try to rapidly bring this to conclusion in which all parties are happy. I will try hard to get this accomplished in one or two days. "How fast can you get the money into an American bank?"

"Certainly, in an hour or less during banking hours, after a definite decision is reached by all parties."

"Thanks Jack and Debra. You have done a fabulous job for both our country and the Europeans. Now, stay safe and we'll stay in touch with you. Bye for now."

Chapter 44

Adam easily cleared customs and immigration check points in New York and boarded his flight to France as Boris and Jack were hacking the Moldova bank. As the flight headed across the Atlantic towards France, Adam thought of the money stashed away for him and how he might get his hands on most of the profits deposited by the three amigos. He had his Russian hacker sources and had confidence of getting the money in the next two days.

Landing in Paris, he cleared customs and awaited a connecting flight to Marseilles. He texted his partner his arrival time and then received a shocking text back. All of the Blanton executives had been arrested and arrests of known illegal European dealers was actively being pursued by Interpol.

Adam swallowed hard and almost lost his breath. He had ten minutes to board his flight and quickly texted his Russian handler to immediately move the money from his bank. He had not received a reply when he boarded his flight and knew he would not get any further information for at least two hours.

As his flight was landing, he switched on his phone and when he had service, he saw he had a text message from Russia. It simply said, bank is closed by Interpol and funds are either removed or frozen.

He sat staring at the seat in front of him and only moved when his seat companion rose to leave the plane. Adam was in shock knowing he not only lost his twelve million but all the other money as well.

He slowly made his way to the arrival area to collect his luggage and meet his partner.

"Monsieur, why do you look so sad?" asked his partner.

"Louis, I just learned all my money hidden in a Moldova bank has disappeared. At least twelve million dollars and a few hundred million more I could have stolen a few days ago."

"Why did you wait?"

"I did not know of the pending arrests of the executives and now I have to start over."

"La Roi we will make back a good amount of what you lost in a few months. Do not fear because the Americans do not know where you went and your new name and our business. We will succeed because you have lined up some good and greedy suppliers and there will always be dealers who just want to make money."

"Thanks Louis but is still a hard blow to my head. I know the two American agents here in Europe probably had something to do with this and I will find them and have them killed. I had the girl but the idiots I hired were stupid and she got away. It will not happen again."

Chapter 45

After finishing the call to the Director, Debra dialed the number she had for George Blanton and he immediately answered the call.

"Where are you guys?"

"We are in Helsinki and were successful with our project but it's story to relate to you later. Now we all have a problem." She went on to relate the Adam story and the possibility of all of us being in possible danger.

"We suggest we all move to another country where we might have a safe refuge but can continue our work."

"Debra, Jack. I can do this. Priscilla and I can be airborne in about two to three hours. We can tell France air control; our plan is to return to the USA. We leave Paris and about one hour later we head for Helsinki and meet you two at the airport. We then all the head for Norway where Priscilla and I have some good contacts and a safe house for us to stay for however long we have too. We can then send the plane back to the USA and everyone will think we went home."

Sounds good George. We still have our stuff left in our suite, and it needs to be packed and taken with you and then call us when you have your ETA."

"We will take care of everything and we'll see you in Helsinki."

"Are you ok honey?"

"Yes, I am fine Jack. It's just getting used again to looking in the mirror over my shoulder to see who is tailing me and now it involves both of us."

"Debra, I have not shot at anybody since Antwerp and I still know how to do it and I promise you I will do my best to keep us safe."

"Thanks honey. We will get through this together. It will definitely be a memory in our relationship.

In Helsinki, while Debra and Jack began preparation to leave, a different situation had already started involving the Moldova National Bank and the bank manager, Gustov Petrolin.

He had arrived early to the bank after having received information of the arrest of the three amigos. Upon learning about arrests, he went into each account and discovered every one of them, including his personal account had a zero balance.

At first, he became very angry asking the staff in the bank, how this could happen. He then became afraid about the news leaking out would cause many citizens to pull their money from the bank. Additionally, the thought of the Moldova government officials confronting him with charges of money laundering and illegal banking practices could also get him arrested and charged.

He had to develop a plan rapidly and save his dreams of retiring wealthy and try to escape the troubles already falling into his lap.

The bank had a safety net of cash in the amount of ten million dollars in equivalent Moldovan Leu, as a safety valve against citizen account holders drawing out all their deposited funds. Gustov decided, it is me or them and I prefer me.

He quickly accessed the safety account and transferred five million dollars into an account in a Romanian bank where it would only stay for a day or two before, he would again transfer it into a safer haven.

He then packed his briefcase with import documents, his passport and other valuable papers. He went back into his computer and deleted all references and emails relating to Blanton Arms, the three amigos and Adam Sanderson. He picked up his brief case and walked out of his office and told his staff, I will return in about one hour.

As he walked to his car and opened the door, he suddenly realized two men had approached his car and stopped him from closing the door.

"Interpol Mr. Petrolin. You are under arrest for falsifying banking records, money laundering and association with known criminals. Please step out of your car and you will come with us."

Gustov face turned ashen and his shoulders slumped as the Interpol agents handcuffed him, picked up his briefcase and lead him away to a waiting government vehicle. They immediately transported him to a local police station for interrogation and confinement.

Simultaneously, Moldavian agents had entered the bank, presented their credentials and notified the banking staff the bank would be closing effective immediately and staff would be questioned and could not leave the premises before submitting to questioning.

At the police station, the bank manager sat in room with the two Interpol agents who had arrested him. "Mr. Petrolin, I am Peter and my partner here is Steven and we are the lead investigators involved with you case. We have a number of questions to ask you." Peter then began the questioning.

"Mr. Petrolin, is it true, you are a partner in the Moldova National Bank and your other partners are named; Robert P. Wimsley, Paul F, Silverman and Lawrence R. Rivera, all executives in the American company, Blanton Arms?"

"Yes."

"Mr. Petrolin, is it also true, you have a banking relationship with Mr. Adam Sanderson of the American FBI?"

"Yes."

"Mr. Petrolin, are you now aware of the arrests of these individuals in the United States for falsifying records, laundering money and other illegal activities.?

"yes, but I didn't know all the charges."

"Mr. Petrolin, are you aware the United States government confiscated all of the illegal gains from you and your partners accounts and when did you learn about this action?"

"Yes, I learned today of the missing funds, but I did not know where they had disappeared too."

"And what did you do upon learning about this action?"

"I gathered my belongings and left the bank and it's when you arrested me."

"You didn't delete all references to your relationship with your partners on your computer knowing it could be incriminating evidence?"

"I did."

"Didn't you also remove the equivalent of five million dollars in Moldovan Leu's and transfer it into a Romanian account knowing you could be charged with grand theft?"

"I did."

Gustov sat in shock as the Interpol agents repeatedly asked him questions of which they knew each of the answers. He knew he either had to cooperate or suffer the consequences which could mean a long sentence in a Moldova prison.

"I believe Mr. Petrolin you fully understand, we know a lot more about you and your operation. We have been studying both you and your bank for some time in conjunction with the Americans. Hence, it is our position, you had better be truthful to us or face the sentencing of the court."

"We also have searched your briefcase and found significant incriminating evidence about other characters for who you had laundered money. In fact, we know of more than one hundred instances you have taken in dirty money for your American partners and other European illegal arms dealers."

"So, Mr. Petrolin, we also have a listing of known illegal arms dealers and we want you to confirm or deny if you had a banking relationship with any of them?"

The agents then slowly read off the list the names they had received from US agents tied to Blanton Arms and other arms manufacturers. Gustov with his head bowed repeatedly confirmed each name as the agent read it.

The agent then began to read the amount of funds which had flowed through the bank from these individuals and asked Mr. Petrolin to confirm or deny the amounts stated.

He knew many of the amounts but could not remember all of them. The agents assured him their data had been investigated and confirmed by the banks records they had studied. The questioning continued but with a new twist.

"Mr. Petrolin, do you know of any additional American contacts within Blanton Arms or contacts within other American or European corporations?"

"There is possibly three or more whose names I have heard but I honestly don't have any records of their involvement. At least two were part of Blanton Arms and the others from smaller companies and I don't remember their names."

"How did you learn of the arrests of the Blanton people and the FBI person?"

"This morning, I received and email from an arms dealer in the Ukraine telling me of the arrests and I should be very careful."

"Did his name appear on our list?"

"Yes."

"Is that when you made the decision to flee or did that occur after you discovered your assets missing?"

"After the discovery."

"I think this maybe enough for today. You will now be held in custody and will more than likely be moved to a more secure facility. We will continue our questioning at a later time. Any questions for us?"

"No."

Another agent entered the room and escorted Mr. Petrolin to a jail cell.

Chapter 46

About three hours after Debra and Jack had spoken to the Blantons, they received a text message notifying them to be at the airport at three o'clock and the plane should be ready to leave by three-thirty.

"We have about one-hour Debra, lets finish packing and check out of the hotel. I will arrange for a private car to take us to the airport. I am very happy the Blantons stayed per our suggestion. They have given luxury vacation a new meaning for me and their ability to get things done rapidly has been very helpful to our assignment."

They then finished packing in less than ten minutes and they took their suitcases to the lobby to checkout. They paid their bill and the private car taking them to the airport had arrived and soon they were on their way back to the Helsinki airport.

It did not take more than twenty minutes to reach the airport and Jack asked the driver to take them to the private terminal. Once inside the terminal, they had all their documents checked and luggage inspected and could board once the Blantons plane landed and taxied to the terminal.

Jacks phone suddenly rang and he could see it was Franz. "Hello Franz.'

"Jack listen closely. You and Debra are on a hit list. Somebody in France has put a bounty on both of you and has reached out to a number of sources to try and find you and Debra. Stay alert my friend and call me if you need help."

"Give me some time to think Franz and maybe I can use your help. I'll call you in a couple of days and thanks for the warning."

"Debra, this is not going to be a vacation. We'll talk when we are alone. In the meantime, I'm happy we are going into hiding because as of now, we are not safe."

"That doesn't sound good Jack."

"It's not."

It wasn't long before the jet appeared outside the terminal. George and Priscilla left the plane to greet them and then they all boarded the luxury jet to take them to Norway and safety.

Once on the plane, Jack and Debra had the opportunity to discuss some of what had transpired over the last few days. They told them of Debra's uncovering a Russian mole in the FBI and then later being kidnaped in Antwerp and safely got away and how it got eventually got resolved. They briefly talked about the arrests of the three amigos.

Learning of the arrests made George and Priscilla happy but expressed their concern of possible repercussions and potential damages for the Blanton corporation. Specifically, what would happen to Blanton Arms, the employees and the company's reputation.

Jack and Debra had separate concerns involving their lives and they knew that had a few fretful days ahead of them.

George told them the flight to Oslo would take about thirty minutes and they had a car ready to take them about one hundred miles away to a friend's home.

They all sat back and had a glass of wine and the Blantons told them although they had enjoyed parts of the trip and the company of Jack and Debra, they definitely wanted to return to their home in Virginia.

"We are also looking to go home but we have a couple of hurdles in the way before we get there," said Jack.

The flight between Helsinki and Oslo is a relatively short distance and before they had finished their glasses of wine, the pilot announced they would be landing in six minutes.

They landed safely and the large jet slowly taxied to the private terminal where everyone would disembark. George and Priscilla lead the way into the terminal where they quickly cleared immigration and customs before exiting the terminal to the waiting car.

George told them, "the trip is about a hundred miles and to the home where we will reside temporarily overlooks beautiful Lake Strondafjorden. We have a good friend originally from the area and he is loaning us his house for up to four weeks."

"It sounds great George and your timing to get us here is perfect because if we remained in Paris, all of us would be in serious danger. Debra and I were hoping this would be the end of our journey but at the moment, I doubt it. We have enjoyed our travels with you, the accommodations and the support you have provided to us, but right now, retirement back in the USA is very attractive, but as long as Adam is loose, we are in danger. said Jack."

They all noticed the beauty of the landscape as they speed along the E16 motorway and in a few minutes, they had entered the city center of Fagernes and now they could see all the shops and restaurants. The continued further out of town and took the exit which ran along side of the lake. Soon they turned into a private residence with an electric gate and a large garden surrounded by stone walls about three foot tall.

In front of them rose a large mansion which looked a little out of place for the area. It sat on a small hill overlooking the nearby lake with a mountain in the background. The car stopped at the front entrance and the massive front doors of the house opened with two people standing there to greet them. They all exited the car and stood in awe of the palatial sight before them.

This would be a vacation to remember if only they were on vacation. A man approached them and welcomed the Blantons and Debra and Jack. He then informed them, he would attend to their luggage and they walked towards the house to enter through large doors.

The lady of the house informed them she would guide them to their respective rooms and after they had gotten settled, dinner would be served at seven-thirty in the main dining room.

As soon as they were in their room, Jack told Debra of the information he had received from Franz.

"Debra, I've given this some thought and here is what I propose. I will only stay here two days and I want you and the Blantons to return home the day after I leave. I am going to gather up my own posse including Franz, Ethan and Boris to try and find Adam. I can also rely on the resources of Interpol and with any luck, we can find Adam before he finds me. I don't want to put you in further danger as they got to you once already."

"Jack, we were so close to completing this assignment and I hate to leave you, but I understand it must be brought to a conclusion. I love you honey."

"I love you too and I hope I'm making the right decision. Let's unpack and then I have a few calls to make."

Jack and Debra unpacked their luggage and toured their large suite; they were in awe of the amenities and appreciated the fine linens, the luxury of the bathrooms and the fantastic view they had of the lake and surrounding lands. After all the suspense which had occurred in their lives over the past few weeks, this setting would be the ideal place to unwind and to enjoy their togetherness if they didn't have a bounty on their heads.

Jack then began to contact his posse. "Franz, it's me Jack. I am still in Europe and guess who put the bounty on my head? The KGB guy eluded arrest and my government feels he is here in Europe and they told me he was possibly looking for me. I would like to come to Munich and meet with you and a couple of other friends and work together towards locating him."

"Sorry to hear that Jack but I'd be happy to help you as I also have some shady friends with Russian contacts. When can you come here?"

"I can be there in two days. Book us four rooms into a hotel. Make one of the rooms a suite where we can meet and work."

"Got it and I will text you booking info."

"Thanks Franz and I'll see you in two days."

He next called Anna and asked if Ethan would be available for a special project in Munich in two days. If so, text me his number.

Lastly, he texted Boris and said he needed help, and could he arrange to be in Munich with a good computer in two days.

Boris immediately texted back and asked Jack to send hotel details and shortly thereafter, he received a text from Anna with Ethan's number.

Then using the number supplied by Anna, he called Ethan. "Hello is this Ethan?"

"Yes Jack. It is me. How can I help you? Ethan you may or may not want to help me and if your answer is no, I will fully understand. Your old friend Adam avoided arrest in America, and it is now believed he is in Europe and is not only looking for me, he has placed a reward for anyone killing me."

"Jack, what is your relationship with Clare?"

"Well, soon if I can avoid any flying bullets, she has agreed to be my wife."

"Thanks Jack, Clare once saved my life and although I gave her a recent gift, this one will be much more meaningful and personal. I will help you Jack. I believe it would be reasonable to meet and do some planning."

"I agree Ethan. I am scheduled to meet another couple of good friends of mine, in Munich tomorrow afternoon who have also agreed to help me. Is there a possibility you could meet with us and we could work as a team?"

"Jack, I have nothing planned for the next week or so and this would work out good for me. Give me the meeting point and I can be there around three pm tomorrow."

"Great, I appreciate your help. I will pay all your expenses and a fee for your service. I will text you the hotel meeting place in the next hour."

"Thanks Jack. I look forward to meeting you."

"Debra, I'm going to call my Interpol friend now and see if he can also help me."

"Dennis Wilson please. Tell him my name is Jack. Dennis how are you and thanks for your previous help."

"Jack, the information we got from you guys was fabulous. We caught a lot of bad apples and almost closed six banks. What can I do for you now?"

"I am not sure you heard the KGB guy was an FBI mole and escaped arrest and could possibly be here in Europe. He is looking for me and trying to end my career."

"We did hear about it Jack and we have an APB out for him. Nothing has surfaced yet but if it does, can I reach you on this number?"

"Sure, and I have some other sources I will work with and if I get any good vibes, I will pass the information to you."

"Thanks Jack and stay alert and safe."

"I'll try Dennis. Thanks for your help."

"Well Debra, I rounded up my posse and we will meet and look for Adam. Now it is almost time for dinner, and I am hungry. I suggest we do not mention anything about my plans."

As seven-thirty approached, they made their way down the broad staircase and quickly found the dining room. George and Priscilla had already been seated and were enjoying a glass of wine. Jack and Debra took seats near them and a maid asked them if they would like a glass of wine. They both said yes and soon two full glasses sat in front of them.

"Cheers, George and Priscilla. You have far exceeded our expectations. We would have never found a place as lovely, as scenic, coupled with the luxury of this home where we find ourselves today. We will always remember your kindness and hospitality. But beyond all that, you have transformed our plight into a wonderful adventure, and we thank you."

"I think you two are very dedicated and experienced people who obviously have given much of your lives to our country. You will never receive the honors you deserve not only for your public service but also for your kindness and thoughtfulness of others in need. We will also remember the day we met at your home and how you trusted and treated us, and you will remain in our thoughts forever. George and I Thank you. Let's raise a toast to ourselves."

They all clinked their glasses together and took a long drink of wine.

After the moment, the maid placed a plate of salad in front of them and they all began to eat. The main course consisted of a pork roast with potatoes and assorted fresh vegetables. When they had finished eating the roast and accompanying vegetables, the table was cleared and set for dessert.

Three separate desserts had been placed before them and each looked wonderful. A bottle of Sherry along with the appropriate glasses had also been set on the table. George poured them all a glass of Sherry and they sat back to enjoy the desserts and Sherry and the conversation.

After about an hour of talking they decided to retire for the night. Jack was happy about that as he wanted to discuss his plans in more detail with Debra.

When they got to their room, Jack and Debra made themselves comfortable and Jack outlined the roles of each of his team and felt they had a chance of getting good information about Adam because of their large network of sources.

"Just stay safe honey and know your love is waiting for you at home."

Chapter 47

Jack woke early and retired to the bathroom to shower and shave. He then dressed casually, and he opened the curtains a slight bit to take in the view. The sun flashed of the lake and the mountains framed the entire area. He felt, he had never been in a more picturesque place during all his previous travels.

"Debra honey. Wake up and come share this beautiful view with me. It is an artist's picture for the eyes to enjoy and I want to share it with you."

Debra arose from her sleep and got out of bed, stretched a bit and then nestled into Jacks awaiting arms. They stood silent for minute or two, feeling the warmth of each other and taking in the beauty spread out throughout the valley and across the lake. She lightly kissed Jack and continued to hold him close.

"Jack please take a picture to always remind us of the lovely scenery set before us and I will remember it not only for its beauty, but also for the love I now feel in my heart for you."

"Debbie, our work is not quite over but I hope are getting close. When this is finally over and we are back home again, will you marry me?"

"I'll give up the house in Hawaii to marry you. Yes, yes and yes again."

They wrapped their arms around each other, and their lips met for a long passionate kiss.

"Debbie, I love you and have for some time but work and dedication sometimes got in the way. I still have some work to do and catching Adam may not be easy but someday I hope we find ourselves free of all our responsibilities except to each other. I am going to be very proud to be your husband."

"Jack, let me get dressed and let's go down for some coffee and breakfast and I have to tell Priscilla the good news."

Jack smiled and laughed, and everyone could see he was a very happy man.

In a few minutes Debra had dressed in jeans and a pretty top and they left the room to go down the stairs. The Blantons had been sitting at the table and when Jack and Debra walked into the dining room, they could see the happiness between the couple.

"May, you guys look pretty spiffy today and you must be so happy for reason?"

'Yes. Jack proposed to me his morning and I agreed to marry him."

"Wonderful, you two are both great people and we wish you all the best life can offer."

"So, when is the wedding and will George and I get invited?"

"Yes, you will get invited and we will make no wedding plans until we return to the USA. When our assignment finally ends and when we return to retirement and normalcy, we will then decide about the wedding."

"It's very wise of you both. Priscilla and I will be happy to assist in any way we can, but we'll leave it up to you to decide. In the meantime, it's so beautiful outside today, how about a walk along the lake and then a leisurely lunch in town?"

"Great idea George. We are going to have a light breakfast and some coffee and then we will be ready to go for a morning walk."

Chapter 48

Jack and Debra finished their breakfast and met George and Priscilla in the formal sitting room. They then set out for their morning walk along the shore of the large lake.

When they reached the lake, they found a wide walking path along the shore and they started their walk heading towards mini forest further up the shore. They slowly walked and talked about various subjects avoiding talk about the assignment or any matter relating to this trip, they just wanted to enjoy mother nature's creations and all its splendor.

They had walked about two miles when Priscilla suggested they return and perhaps visit the Valdres Folk Museum in the town center. They all agreed and began walking back towards the town.

Once they reached the town, the museum sat about a hundred yards away and they reached the front door in a couple of minutes. Once inside they saw the variety and art all related to Norway. The dress section of the museum drew Debra and Priscillas attention and they found an amazing array of unique Norwegian clothing.

They were all relaxed and enjoying themselves until Jack's phone rang. "Sorry folks, it is my boss and I have to talk to him. I'll be back in a few minutes and he went outside the museum to find a quiet place where he could talk to the Director.

"Good morning sir. Sorry for the delay but we are visiting a cultural museum."

"No problem Jack and in fact, I believe some of our problems have ended.

"It certainly is welcome news sir?"

"Well, if you have a few minutes and I will tell you the whole story."

"I do sir."

"Jack after you spoke to me about confiscating the money and the possible distribution, I called together our key intel people plus some State Department gurus, A Treasury person and of course some DOJ attorneys. We spent a good eight or more hours trying to sort out all the money distributions plus the relationship issues involving Moldova and Interpol and at the same time trying to bring this project to a successful conclusion.

Well, we did, and I think you and Debbie and the Blantons will like it and give your blessing to what we decided and have already started to implement.

First, we convinced the Moldovan Ambassador to agree to a 200 million-dollar grant to beef up their banking system and to cooperate with us and Interpol. In fact, the bank manager had been arrested and in the custody of Interpol. He has cooperated and has provided ample evidence about his connections, which help link the illegal arms dealers together with what you received from your sources.

Interpol had no problem working with us especially after we agreed to give them 100 million dollars plus they appreciated all of the input we provided to them about the bad guys. They have arrested twenty of the twenty-two on the list and have assured us the other two will soon to be caught.

Now, let's talk about the Blantons, they are one hundred percent innocent and in no way connected to any wrongdoing within Blanton Arms and their names will be expunged from every false report written. For their assistance and for falsely being accused, the government will pay one hundred million to their charitable trust account.

There will be no compensation to Blanton Arms. But there will be a continuing investigation concerning co-conspirators and the board of directors who had total responsibility for oversight of the company and failed to perform their sworn duty.

The government will retain the balance of 427 million dollars, and it will be apportioned among the number of intel agencies who contributed time, money and personnel to this effort.

Please arrange to transfer all the confiscated money from the Moldova bank to the US Treasury. I will send you the coding in a separate message today and you can arrange the transfer."

"That is the good news sir and I will arrange the transfer today."

"I wish it was all good news Jack. I was hoping to tell you and Debra can end your government sponsored vacation and you both are free to return to a normal life. Debra should return but

you are still on assignment.

We have received intel regarding Adam, and he is now in Europe and he possibly is looking for you.

Interpol has alerted us of this possibility, and I suggest you use your contacts in Interpol and elsewhere to try and locate Adam. Many of us want him back in the USA for trial or taken by Interpol.

"Sir, I was made aware of Adam being in Europe and one of his interests is to kill me. I have gathered some key contacts to see if we can find him. I believe I can find him before he finds me. The search for him begins in Munich tomorrow and with my sources from three countries plus Interpol, we will locate him."

"It's the right decision. Good luck and keep me advised of your movements and stay safe."

Jack returned to the museum after his long call with the Director and located the Blantons and Debbie.

"Sorry for the long delay people but the director had a lot to tell me. In fact, rather than have lunch here in town, I suggest we return to the house and find a cozy corner where we can talk in private. I also have to make an important phone call immediately after we return to the house, but it will take only one or two minutes."

Jack seemed unhappy and the Blantons and Debbie sensed they would hear bad news. They left the museum and walked the few minutes back to the house. George felt the den would be an ideal spot to talk and would ask the maid to bring us some drinks and finger food. Jack said he and

Debbie would meet them in a few minutes inside the house because they had to make an important call.

Jack and Debbie stayed on the porch and sat in the ornate rocking chairs. "Honey, the Director agrees, you are no longer on assignment. He excepted my plan and I'm to remain in Europe until Adam is apprehended. The FBI believes I have the sources to help catch him."

She had tears in her eyes as she reached for Jack. "Jack, I was looking forward to the two of us planning our wedding and being together. Now we will be apart."

"Only for a couple of weeks Debbie, I promise you."

"I understand Jack and I will be ok. I'll spend time with my dad and rearrange our house and begin the wedding plans, but I will miss you and worry."

"I'll miss you too."

"I have to call Boris now and will be inside in a few minutes."

Debra gave Jack a kiss and slowly walked into the house.

He dialed Boris's private number and soon he and Boris were connected.

"Jack, how are you?"

"So, so Boris, I will tell you the news in a moment. First transfer all the remaining funds to the US Treasury Department. I will text you the information shortly after we disconnect. Regarding other news, I told you the KGB graduate is somewhere in Europe looking for me and I appreciate your help. I'll see you in Munich tomorrow."

"Regarding the transfer of funds, it will be transferred within a few minutes after receipt of the coding. Stay safe my friend and I will see you tomorrow regarding the other matter."

"Thanks Boris my friend."

Jack looked on his phone and found the codes supplied by the Director and forwarded them to Boris. He knew he could trust him, and the funds will be in the USA very soon.

Jack went into the house and found the den where he saw food and drink were awaiting him.

"I almost done for today and besides Debbie saying yes to my proposal, I have some other good news to share with all of you. Grab a snack and your drink because this will take some time to explain. Honey, you sit next to me so I can hold your hand because you also contributed a significant amount to this assignment and what we accomplished. Me and my Secret Service adventure may have started this adventure but you, George and Priscilla all contributed to the success of the project which I can now share with you."

Debbie slid in close to him on the coach where he sat, and they all waited for whatever news Jack had to report.

"First, George and Priscilla, you have been cleared of any charges made against you and all evidence of supposed wrongdoing has been expunged from all records. You two are totally innocent and in regard to your cooperation with us in solving some misconceptions; plus, the pain and anxiety to you both caused by the government, 100 million dollars will be placed into your charitable trust account."

"Debra, Jack, we couldn't have been this successful without you two. You listened and you trusted us plus you gathered evidence of our innocence. We could not believe you could do any more and yet you got us an award of 100 million dollars for our charities. You two are too special."

"Debbie and I did our job and sometimes it's not only identifying the bad guys but also includes identifying the innocent. We are thrilled with the outcome for you both and your charities. The inspiration for the gift came from Debra and the government accepted her request without question."

"Regarding Blanton Arms, it's not good news for them. The government will continue investigation of the three amigos and Adam Sanderson. It is known of additional yet to be named conspirators within the company. The government is also investigating the board of directors for failure to perform their stated duties regarding oversight of the company. There is also an ongoing investigation of other unnamed American arms manufactures who also may have been selling arms illegally."

"Adam is now possibly in Europe and intelligence reports suggest he is looking for me. I have been asked to work with Interpol and other contacts in trying to isolate him and get him behind bars. I suspect this will take a couple of weeks for me to accomplish. Debbie is no longer involved in the ongoing investigations, and her assignment has ended. All of you can return to the USA any time soon."

Debbie gave Jack a big hug and George and Priscilla stood up to also hug Jack and Debbie.

"Jack, I am sorry to hear you will not be returning with us? How about we wait a couple of days to do some more sightseeing and just enjoy our freedom. A lot of our stress has now been washed away.

Let's have two days of enjoyment of the area and then the plane will be here, and the three of us can return to our hopefully normal lives."

"Thanks for the offer but I must leave in the morning and I will meet with some others to try and capture Adam. I wish you and Priscilla well and thanks for looking out for us. Debbie will accompany you back to the states whenever you plan on leaving. Now if you will excuse me, I have some urgent calls to make and to pack for my trip tomorrow."

Chapter 49

After Jack announced he would be living in the morning, George suggested they meet about seven-thirty this evening to go out and have dinner.

"See you both in about five hours." As Debbie and Jack made their way up the stairs to their room.

As they entered the room, Debbie took Jack's hand and said, "you are my hero and I love very much. You keep my spirits up and together we got the job done to everyone's satisfaction. I know what you have to do now is necessary and you are capable of success."

"Thanks honey but you may downplay it, but you also played a significant role in bringing about the success. I love you too and I look forward to our future life together including some hot and steamy nights at our home in Hawaii."

Debbie laughed and her smile could light up the room. She obviously loved Jack and she took his hand and they softly fell into the bed. They made passionate love and then both fell into a pleasant sleep.

Jack had set his alarm and they awoke about four hours later and once again they expressed their love for each other and again repeated the love and passion of the previous time. They held each other close for a long time and finally arose from the bed to shower and dress. All of the expelled energy made them hungry and eventually they wondered down to the sitting room to await George and Priscilla to go to dinner in town.

George greeted them, "my you people look happy and I bet you are hungry?"

"George, now, you leave the young ones alone, they are in love and if I remember correctly, we were young once ourselves."

"Okay, hungry ones, what would you like for dinner?"

"George, you know this place better than we do and based upon previous meals we have shared, we trust your choice and therefore, you pick the restaurant."

"Okay, lets walk into town look at menus at two or three of the places and then choose one. They are all very close together and within twenty minutes we will be sitting somewhere and drinking a fine glass of wine."

They eventually selected a cozy restaurant which specialized in both steaks and fish and as George had predicted, twenty minutes after leaving the house, they began drinking their first glass of wine.

They drank and talked and then ordered their meals. Everyone enjoyed their meal, the desserts and more wine. Jack picked up the tab saying the government owed all of them a good meal. They had spent about three hours in the restaurant before heading back to the house and calling it an evening.

They each bid each other a good night and looked forward to seeing them in the morning.

The happy couple woke up early and took care of their personal habits; dressed and made their way downstairs to greet the Blantons already sitting in the dining room.

"Good morning to the young lovers," said George

Debra just smiled broadly, and Jack laughed and they both sat across from the Blantons to talk while they ate their breakfast and had that important first cup of coffee.

I have ordered a car to pick me up at nine as I have to be in Germany later today. You people can decide how to spend your day.

"Debbie, Priscilla and I were thinking to hire a decent sized boat and we can all sail around the lake and have lunch onboard if it is okay with you?"

"The more relaxation we can get, the better is for us. The lake surroundings look beautiful and it is another sunny day. Everything I like George and I thank you for your hospitality.

"Lake Strondafjorden is about twelve to fifth-teen miles long and stretches from Fagernes to Ron and then Slidre and ends at Ryfoss. We may be able to get off the boat and explore each of these towns."

"When are we scheduled to leave?"

"Probably around ten and it will take us about twenty minutes and walk to the dock where the boat is tied up."

"Sorry I can't join you folks but now I must go upstairs to get my bag and await the driver."

"Need any help honey?"

"No, I am fine, and I'll be back in a minute or two."

Jack returned just as the car pulled into the driveway. "Well folks I wish I could stay but this assignment will not be over until all the bad guys sit in jail. Hopefully I will be back in the states in a couple of weeks to join my future bride. Again, my thanks for all you did for us and travel safely."

"Bye honey and I promise to call you daily. I love you."

They then kissed briefly, and Jack was out the door and into the car.

After Jack left, Priscilla and George continued discuss the area and it became apparent to Debra, the Blantons had been here many times before. Within a few minutes they all rose to depart for the docks and spend a beautiful sunny day drifting on the Strondafjorden Lake.

The captain of the boat welcomed them aboard, untied the ropes holding the boat to the dock and they were soon slowly moving around the perimeter of the lake. The captain named the sights as they moved around the lake and certainly, the Norwegian names would not be remembered for long, but the beauty of the place would not be forgotten.

The lake surrounded by mountains and the town sitting on the shore would be a delight to most people because, it looked like a picture postcard. Debra took a lot of pictures which would always remind her of this time and place.

About thirty minutes after they left, they headed up the northside of the lake towards the small town of Ron. The captain said whatever you want to see in Ron, can be seen from the boat.

As they, slowly drifted by, Debra again took many photos of the picturesque scene in front of them. The mountains in the background stood tall over the town and George commented that it was even more beautiful when it had snowed on the mountain.

As they approached Sidle a few miles further up the river, the boat captain suggested it would be a good spot to stop and take a walk through the small town. He said they would have lunch after they returned from the visit to Sidle.

After thirty minutes, they casually wondered back to the boat and onboard, the captain served a nice Norwegian lunch along with cold beer and other drinks. When they finished the lunch, the boat continued the journey up the lake towards Ryfoss where it would turn around and begin the slow trip home.

The entire trip lasted just over four hours and they thanked the captain for the wonderful cruise. They then spent another hour or so walking through Fagernes, just window shopping and passing time.

They finally arrived back at the large house and decided to just sit on the porch, relax and talk for a while, and the maid would serve them some fresh homemade cookies and cool drinks.

"I hate to be the bearer of bad news, but the plane will return to Norway tonight and we should leave sometime tomorrow after ten o'clock. It will be about a five-hour flight back to D.C. and because of time differences, we should arrive about eleven in the morning and there will be a car there to take us to our respective homes. We will have a few hours tomorrow to talk but I for one will be happy to finally get home and feel totally stress free after this adventure."

"George, I agree one hundred percent but remember, this adventure had enough thrills for a lifetime. Let's not do it again. Eventually, Jack and I will officially retire for the second time."

"Debra, if you feel this episode had been stressful, wait to you start planning your wedding."

"Thanks George. I'm heading up to bed and I'll see you in the morning. Good night."

They all were up early the next morning and met again at the breakfast table. George advised them a car would be here to take them to Oslo airport around nine-thirty and their flight would probably leave for home around eleven o'clock. The household help had brought all the luggage to the porch and the driver loaded it into the car. They all thanked the maid and the chef who had joined them on the porch to say goodbye and then entered the car for the journey to the airport.

The E16 heading south had very little traffic and they reached the Oslo airport slightly ahead of schedule and the car then continued on to the private terminal. The Blantons and Debra again had their passports inspected and their luggage x-rayed and in a very few minutes, walked to the waiting plane. It became a happy moment for the Blantons, and their happiest moments would be when they stepped off the plane onto American soil. Debra was sad and quiet for she knew the man she loved would now be in harms way.

George and Priscilla would return to their home in Virginia for a few weeks before heading to their other home in Florida. Debra would return to Jack's house in Arlington and would meet with various intel officials for a formal but required debriefing and then she would begin planning the wedding.

The flight lasted exactly five hours and within minutes after landing, they entered the private terminal to have their documents processed and their luggage checked. They quickly completed the necessary procedures and the private car driver took their luggage and loaded all of it into the rear compartment of the car and soon they really were on their way home.

They arrived at Jack's house first and they all got out of the car to say their goodbyes. They each hugged each other and promised they would get together again soon.

Debra slowly made her way into the house and watched as the car with George and Priscilla left for their home.

Chapter 50

Jack arrived in Munich about three hours and he took a taxi to the hotel Franz had arranged and when he walked in the lobby, Franz was waiting for him.

It was now close to three thirty and he looked around the lobby to see if someone might be looking for him. A well-dressed man about Jack's age approached him and said, "Hello Jack, I am Ethan."

"How did you recognize me?"

"Anna said look for the most handsome man in the lobby."

Jack, Franz and Ethan all laughed.

"Well, I will accept that as a compliment. Thanks Ethan and glad you are here. Let me introduce Franz. He is a longtime friend and has assisted me successfully over the years. Let me check in to my room and then we can decide what's next.

A moment later Jack saw Boris approaching, and he gave him a hug and introduced him to Franz and Ethan. He then went to the registration desk and completed the check in and suggested to the others it would be better to meet in his room. After entering the room and getting settled, everyone specified what they would like to drink, and Jack placed a room service order.

While they waited, Ethan, Boris and Franz chatted about their respective occupations and interestingly, they had some common clients.

The drinks arrived and after the usual toasts, Jack opened the meeting.

"I am happy the three of you are here because I believe our government and myself need some help in bringing this guy to justice. I do not know where he is or his thoughts. I have been told he most likely is in Europe and he is looking to eliminate me. Hence, I believe or hope the four of us with our broad contact base can locate him. I am open for all suggestions."

"Jack, if I may I would like to start first."

"Go ahead Ethan."

"I have known this guy very well for at least ten years through middle and high school and then KGB training for three years. He is exceptionally smart; speaks perfect English and of course Russian and perhaps other languages. I am not sure why he would be in Europe versus Russia unless the GRU felt he had made some gross errors.

It could be he is afraid to return to Russia, but I can only guess. What I can do is make contact with people I know who know him. Possibly one of them has heard from him or about him recently and can give me a lead."

"Thanks Ethan. Your turn Franz."

"I do not know the guy, but I do know a number of Russian contacts in the arms business. There is a chance one of them either did business with him or had contact with him during the time he was investigating Blanton Arms. I will make send some emails and make some calls and try to verify what I have just said and if Ethan is successful it would collaborate my findings."

"Boris we will need your skills to tap into a couple of computers plus your Russian knowledge."

"Between the three of you, I am impressed and certainly something has to show up between all your combined contacts. I have to tell you; I know Interpol has an APB out for him and they may also provide some clues as to his whereabouts.

Let's quit for today and go have a nice dinner. Franz, this is your town, you select."

Before they left Jack phoned Debra and to let her know he was safe. He also told her Ethan had asked about her and he was glad she would be safely in America.

"Jack, I miss you and we are leaving tomorrow morning. Hurry home sweetheart as your future bride misses you. I love you and have good night honey."

"Thanks, dear. I am trying to stay safe and I will keep you updated as to my travels. Love you too."

After he had talked to Debra, they all left for dinner.

Chapter 51

They met early the next morning for breakfast and both Ethan and Franz had made some phone calls and sent some emails to their contacts. Neither had received any replies yet.

When they finished their breakfast, they then retreated back to Jack' room to wait for any possible responses. About an hour later, Ethan's phone rang, and he knew the number belonged to a former Russian GRU comrade. He spoke in Russian for a few minutes and Jack and Boris understood at least one side of the conversation. The call only lasted a couple of minutes before it ended.

"Jack and Boris, I assume you understood my side of the conversation but let me fill you in with what I heard from my old friend. Adam had contacted him two days ago but would only say he had returned to Europe. My friend felt Adam not only faces problems in America but also in Russia.

Apparently, the GRU assumed they would get some of the millions hidden in the Moldova bank and when they learned the money had disappeared, Adam became the bad guy for not acting sooner to notify the Gru about possible pending arrests of the Blanton executives."

"Thanks for the explanation Ethan. What a dilemma for Adam. If he goes back to America, he receives a long jail sentence and if he goes back to Russia, he probably gets shot. So, now we know he may not be looking for me but rather for safety."

"Jack, it could still be both because if he eliminates you the Russians could say he is a national hero and he gets to go home. What do you guys think?"

Boris answered, "I think Franz, you are closer to being correct than Jack."

"Damn, and I thought I would get off easy. The phone call did not solve our problem and hopefully one of you will get some better information later today."

While they were waiting for calls or mail responses, Interpol had obtained a phone intercept between Adam and a know illegal arms dealer in the Ukraine. The call was traced and Interpole believed Adam at that time was hiding in the south of France posing as an American tourist.

Dennis Wilson, Jack's friend from Interpole headquarters had called to tell him what they had found about Adam because they had a tap on an illegal arms dealer's phone. Unfortunately, they could not learn Adam's phone number but could only say he had called from Marseille.

Jack relayed the information he had received from Ethan and promised Dennis he would stay in touch. He also passed the information he just learned to his posse.

"Ethan, you look very serious. Is something troubling You?"

"Somewhere in my memory is a guy who like me sought asylum in Europe and I believe he ended up in Southern France with a new name and a new face. I am trying to remember his Russian name and I'm interested in him because he stayed friends with Adam for a long time. There is a strong possibility he is sheltering him not for money but for their long friendship. I will get his name soon."

"Any news from your contacts Franz?"

"Not really. Mostly are telling me they haven't heard a thing. I am still awaiting answers from a few more."

"Look, today is only our first day try to find the proverbial needle. We learned some things and we know he is on the radar screen and day by day we could get close. Let's head out to the bar and have a few drinks and hope for a better tomorrow."

They left the hotel and found a local brew Haus and spent most of the evening telling war stories and eventually returned to the hotel for sleep. The following morning, they again met for breakfast and both Franz and Ethan had received some interesting news.

"Jack after breakfast we will return to your room and tell you about our news. Now, I want to enjoy my coffee and sweet rolls."

"Ok"

Soon they returned to Jack's room and Franz began first.

"What I heard this morning from one of my most trusted sources is that Adam has established a new gun import business using the name American Rifle Importers headquartered in France. He is representing two or three US Arms manufacturers. He obviously is not using the name of Adam Sanderson but rather he has adopted a French name La Roi Boucher."

"Guys, he had to have this planned long before the arrests began otherwise, how could he start so quickly?"

"I know how," said Ethan. His friend formally Nikita Ashowitz now known as Louis De Fortete financed the operation and while Adam lived in America, he lined up the manufacturers using his French name. When the fur began to fly, he flew the coop."

"How did you learn this Ethan?"

"About three am this morning his Russian name woke me up. I went back to sleep and when I awoke early this morning, I called one of my contacts and asked whatever happened to Nikita? He told me last year he started an arms import business with an American partner. The business is based in Marseille."

"Did you guys make up this story to please me? Of course, I am kidding but it is weird how easy we found him."

"Now it is my turn to go to work. I have my computer here and it is very powerful. Let me peek into American Rifle Importers and see what I can find. Give me one hour before you do anything else." Boris left to go to his room and to get his computer and returned within five minutes.

"Jack, sit over here with me and together we will try to learn about La Roi Boucher."

Boris immediately went to work and within a few keystrokes had found the business. He then typed in an email address and sent them a brief note of his interest in some long-range sniper rifles. Within minutes he received a response and Jack and Boris laughed.

"What's funny guys?" asked Ethan.

"They just got bite by the flu bug and in a few minutes, we will know a lot more about their business."

Boris continued to work and within minutes he was looking at their order book describing weapons, the buyers and dollar amounts. A couple of more clicks and all the data was saved to his computer.

"Now Jack let's make an appointment to buy those long-range sniper rifles. How's the day after tomorrow?"

"Herr Otto Muller, the meeting is confirmed for ten o'clock tomorrow with Mr. Boucher. The next day they were busy."

"Sounds good Boris. Guys since they confirmed the meeting it is over for you three. I'm calling my friend in Interpol and let them work with me to finish the job. I have a beautiful future wife at home awaiting patiently for me and you guys are invited to the wedding."

'Stick around guys while I relay the info to my friend."

"Dennis please. Just say Jack is on the line. Well Dennis, I am about to give you another promotion.

Adam aka La Roi Boucher is operating a business in Marseille using the name American Rifle Importers. His friend and partner is Louis De Fortete formally a GRU graduate.

"Jack, how do you keep finding these hidden gems? I think you should start buying lottery tickets.

You and your friends can be assured we will jump on this immediately and I would guess make arrests in the next twenty-four hours. I'll keep you advised."

"Dennis don't jump on it yet. I am going to Marseille tomorrow and talk to him about buying some arms and I want to learn about his American sources. I speak French and Russian and I have a number of names of the illegal dealers you arrested. I believe I can accomplish this tomorrow and my meeting with him has been arranged for ten in the morning."

"Jack, it okay with me but could be very dangerous for you. Do you want some back-up?"

"It might help if you have a scruffy looking guy like a bodyguard. Besides, you could wire one of us to listen what he has to say and be close by to make the arrest."

"It all sounds good Jack. Let me propose this. We will put surveillance on his outfit and him and his partner. You show up tomorrow and try to cut a deal for big bucks and learn what you can. You leave and we go in and bust them."

"That will work for me Dennis and I will leave for Marseille later today. Text me a good number for you so we can stay in touch."

"Well my friends Ethan, Boris and Franz, you made me look good again and you heard what I told Interpol. I know we only worked a few days, but I will send each one of you 25000 dollars plus expenses for your efforts. I'm leaving soon and hopefully our bad guys will be in custody later tomorrow and you guys can get back to your day jobs. The next time I see you will be at our wedding. Travel safely and thank you both once more for your help. All of what has now taken place is the result of your mutual efforts."

"Jack we will always be available to help if the need arises. Ethan, Boris and I now share a common friend and we will stay in contact and perhaps work together occasionally. Travel safe my friend and planning your wedding may be more stressful."

"Franz has echoed our thoughts Jack. I was glad we could be of help to you. Now finish up the job and go home to your beautiful lady and enjoy your life."

"Are you going to retire Jack?"

"Franz, it's always good to end your career when you are winning

They all hugged Jack as they said their goodbyes and once they had left, Jack had some work to do.

He called the front desk and asked if they could get reservations to Marseille in the next couple of hours. A few minutes later, they called and told him he had been booked on a flight in three hours.

He next called the Director, "Sir, I have located Adam in Southern France and he is running an Arms business. I will try to confront him in cooperation with Interpol to try and learn which American manufacturers he is representing."

"It sounds good Jack but also dangerous. Be careful and keep your hand on the trigger."

"I'm confronting him with an Interpol bodyguard at my side."

"Stay safe and call me at any time to give me the results of your meeting."

"Thank you, sir."

Jack disconnected the line and dialed Debra's number. She answered after the second ring.

"Hi honey. I miss you and when are you coming home?"

"Soon. I know where Adam is and will try to meet him tomorrow for a fake gun deal. I am being supported by Interpol and if things go right, I could be home tomorrow night.

"Well you missed a lot of the fun of planning a wedding. By the way, it's September 26th and your invited."

She could hear Jack laughing and she also broke out laughing.

"Honey, once you have your travel details, send them to me and I will meet you at the airport."

"When I make reservations, I will text you the details. I love you and can't wait to get my arms around you."

"Love you too and I'll see you soon."

Jack began packing his things for his trip and he would finalize his plans on the plane.

He took a private car to the airport, checked in and boarded his flight for the hour and half trip.

Chapter 52

When he arrived in Marseille, he took a taxi to a downtown Hilton. Once he settled in, he called Dennis."

"Hi, I am staying at the downtown Hilton and I am wondering about my approach to meet Adam. I have names of dealers in Europe he knows, and they are all in Jail. I could use one of their names as a reference as long as I am assured, he cannot contact them in any way for the next forty-eight hours."

"Good suggestion. I'll text you a name in a few minutes. Meanwhile, both of the guys are working in the office and have no clue we are listening to them and watching them. We know they will be in the office tomorrow morning awaiting a call from another dealer about a decent order. I am sending your bodyguard over to meet you for dinner. Your treat."

Thanks Dennis. What is the current hotspot looking for weapons?"

"Sudan. Say it's for the Sudan Military Council through another party."

"Talk to you tomorrow."

About an hour later, Jack received a call from the lobby that his bodyguard arrived and will meet him outside the steakhouse. Jack left the room for his dinner date.

"Jack, Robin Engel. I will be your support person."

'Nice to meet you Robin. Let's head in for dinner."

They were immediately seated and ordered drinks before they started to talk.

"I understand you and Dennis have been friends for a few years. I have also known him for a long time, and we have done a few assignments together. I know the Blanton story and some about Adam. Maybe you can fill me in with further information."

"He was trained by the KGB and lived in the States for more than twenty years. He is very bright and well trained, and we have to be careful what we boast about regarding selling arms since he does know his way around."

"I don't expect to do much talking as I will pose as your bodyguard and say very little, but I will watch their moves carefully. I will be wired and agents on the street will hear us. Maybe we can end this rapidly."

"Thanks Robin. I have similar hopes. I just want to learn a few things."

"Let's eat and we'll meet again tomorrow about ten and head for their office. I should have asked you, how far is their office?"

"Three blocks from here."

"Enjoy your dinner and I'll be ready for tomorrow."

Jack slept well after getting dressed, he ordered room service. He turned on the TV to get into the French speaking habit and to pass the time before leaving to meet Adam. He had received a text from Dennis with the name of a jailed dealer.

His room phone rang at nine forty-five and Robin announced, he would wait for him in the lobby.

Jack had dressed as a businessman and had a gun in his pocket and one holstered to his leg. Robin also wore a suit and together they walked the three blocks and found the office of American Rifle and rang the bell to enter the office.

A French woman asked who was calling. "I have a meeting with Monsieur Bouche. My name is Otto Muller from Germany."

"One moment sir."

"Monsieur Bouche is available to see you. The door is now open."

"Mr. Muller, do I know you?"

"Not Really but I have heard of you, Janos Baksa and I did a few deals for Blanton product but now that is all dead. He had given me your name and besides the sniper rifles, I now need a sizable amount of goods to go to Sudan. I have close ties to the Sudan Military Council. I know you have good contacts in America, so I am wondering what you can offer?"

"Mr. Muller, I have good relationship with three or four American companies making a full range of products. It depends what you want."

"I know most of the American companies and what they have to offer. I'm looking for advance automatic weapons, sniper rifles with night vision, ground to air missile launchers with projectiles and other weapons. They are rearming many groups and have the money backed by Russia. I know that is true because I speak Russian and have talked to their money man."

"In Russian, Adam asked him how he was today."

"Jack immediately responded fine probably due to the rich French food."

"Adam smiled and thanked him in German and Jack told him he was welcome in German."

"Now we can talk business Mr. Muller. By the way, who is your associate?'

"He is my bodyguard."

"Okay. I do business with Reagan Arms, Nova Munitions, Stratford Arms and Ammunition and a couple other small guys."

"I know all three, but Reagan and Stratford have the best product line for me. The question is can they export without issues to here or elsewhere for transshipment?"

"We have no problem Mr. Muller. We have large warehouse here and repackaging is not a problem.

We do require a twenty-five percent prepayment and balance upon confirmed shipment from the USA."

They spent the next thirty minutes speaking about various arms and manufacturers and possible delivery dates.

The bodyguard pointed at his watch and the Jack glanced at his watch and then said; "Monsieur Bouche, I am sorry, but I must leave in about five minutes as I have an important contact meeting with another possible customer and he is on his way back to Russia. I liked what I heard, and I thank you for your time. I will send you my complete list of needs tomorrow and you can give me a quote FOB Marseille. Here is my card and I look forward to your response."

They shook hands and Jack waved his hand to his bodyguard and they turned and left the office.

When they reached the outside walk, Robin raised his hand while they continued their walk back to the Hilton where Robin and Jack said goodbye.

Thirty minutes later, Dennis called; "Jack the two partners have been arrested and thanks again to you we beat the bad guys again. I'm sure the US government will want to extradite Adam back to the United States."

Thanks Dennis. I appreciate your effort and support. Stay safe my friend."

After talking to Dennis, he had to call the Director and then made travel reservations and definitely he must call Debra.

"Sir, I hope I didn't disturb you, but this is a good news call. Adam has been arrested by Interpol and they expect our government to begin extradition action. I hope, I can leave today and return to a normal life."

"Great news Jack and you can give me the full details later. The important part is he sits in jail and the story how he got there can wait. Travel safely and we will talk tomorrow."

Jack immediately called the front desk and asked if there was someone to help with airline reservations. He gave them his request and they promised to get back to him rapidly.

Within minutes the desk returned his call and he had been booked on a direct flight leaving in four hours. A private car would take him to the airport.

He then texted Debra the details and began packing for his long ride home.

Chapter 53

The flight was almost six hours long, but Jack sat comfortably in first class and enjoyed a couple glasses of scotch and then slept for two hours. The plane arrived at the gate and Jack hurried off the plane and headed for the luggage area before immigration and customs. He cleared both in a matter of minutes and there stood Debra with open arms.

He rushed into her arms and they held each other tight for a minute and then passionately kissed.

"Glad to have you back honey and happy to hear of your success. It is good time to retire and pamper your future wife."

"That I promise to do. Let's go home and I will share my adventure story with you but only after we make love and I get some needed rest."

"Jack, I did not plan on you resting."

They laughed and left the terminal hands held tightly.

The next morning Debra made them a large breakfast and after Jack had his coffee, he began to tell the story to Debra. He told her his success was only because of Franz and Ethan knowing the right people and Boris knowing how to get his computer to steal secrets that they were able to quickly put many pieces together.

"I have to call the director today and most likely have a debriefing. Did you have one yet."

"Yes, it only took about an hour, but the director said I had to return with you for your briefing. Maybe we should try to get that also out of the way fast."

"Ok, I promised him I would call him today and remind me later."

He then changed the subject.

"So, honey how about sharing some of the wedding details?"

"I told you the date and we can expect about 150 guests who will eat either filet mignon or lobster and will drink fine wines. The invitations have been selected but not sent awaiting your guest list. The band, flowers and color schemes are complete, and we have to name the best man and the bride's maid. Then we have to choose a person to perform the ceremony."

"You have done all of that since coming home?"

"Sure, it was easy. I called Mario to get a wedding planner recommendation, get your tux ordered and my gown altered. Then I gave the wedding planner a wad of money and she is doing most of the work."

"I won't ask how big a wad of money you gave her but where is all this taking place?"

"The Shangri La of course."

"It must have been a paper bag full of money, not a wad."

"Jack, I assumed we could afford it and it is time to do something nice for ourselves. The whole package is slightly over forty thousand dollars."

"You did a great job and I love you with all my heart."

"Thanks honey. I gave the planner a deposit and you get to make the finale payment and pay for the honeymoon."

"Those are easy to do in fact I have already given it some thought."

"And where are you taking us?"

"It's call surprise and you only get to learn about it a day after the wedding."

"Surprise Arizona for our honeymoon. Are you sure it is not too expensive?"

"Not really, your monthly retirement check should be adequate."

"That's worth a big hug Jack and if it is Surprise, I'll still love you."

"Let's talk about another wedding issue. I need help in selecting a best man. I really don't have any real close friends because of all my years working internationally. What about George Blanton? I like him and he is honest and trustworthy and sort of a dad figure to me."

"An excellent choice Jack. Call him and see if he wants to do it."

Jack picked up his phone and autodialed Georges number.

"Jack, you made it home. how are you?"

"I'm fine. I returned last night. The reason for my call is I would like you to be the best man at our wedding. After serving so much time elsewhere in the world, I really am not close to anyone, but you and I have shared some interesting moments. You and Priscilla have also helped us in many ways and I really would like you to accept my offer."

"Jack, I see as an honor and I will be proud to stand beside you and Debra at your wedding in September. I thank you for the offer and look forward to the exciting wedding. Give my regards to Debra and we will probably see you guys again before the wedding."

"Debra, George said yes. Isn't that great?"

Debra could see Jack was pleased with his decision and now it would become her turn to select someone.

"Jack, help me for a minute. I don't have to many relatives that I am close too. There is one however who maybe I should ask to be my bride's maid. It is my aunt Francis who is my mother's sister. Yes, she is old, but she also stood by me and guided me after my mother died. I bet she would love to see me in my mother's wedding gown."

"I cannot think of a better reason then what you just said, to ask her to stand with you at the altar."

"Aunt Francis, it is me Debbie. How are you?"

"I am good with a few aches and pains from old age, but I am still here. Honey, I heard about your getting married and I expect an invitation to your wedding. I promise you I will be there with bells on or so they say."

"Aunty, the reason for my call is I wondered if you would be my bride's maid at the wedding?"

"Oh Debbie, god bless you. Of course, I will. Your dad told me all about your future husband and he sounds like a nice person and I look forward to meeting him. Just let me know what I have to do, and do I need a special dress or gown?"

"Thanks aunty and if you want a new dress or gown, I will buy it for you. In fact, we can shop together, and it would mean a lot to me."

'Honey call me when you want to go shopping with me, and we will get together then. Love you."

"Love you too aunty,"

Debra had selected a bride's maid and Jack a best man. Her father would walk her down the aisle, but they had yet to pick who would perform the ceremony. Also, they had to plan for a rehearsal at the hotel and a rehearsal dinner for those participating in the formal wedding.

Chapter 54

Jack remembered he had to call the Director to schedule their debriefing. He picked up his phone and hit the button to call the director. "Sir, I am calling to let you know, I made it home safely and we would like to schedule our debriefings whenever it's convenient for you and perhaps other interested parties."

"Welcome home to you Jack. A lot has happened since your Secret Service assignment and there are a few intel chiefs who would like to meet with you and Debra as a team to get some firsthand information mostly about the arms business.

We also have to talk about the amount of money you donated to the government as there is high interest about how you accomplished this large windfall of cash.

Lastly, we have some people who want to thank you and Debra for your service and in particular for your success in breaking up the illegal arms distribution in Europe. Both of you deserve a big round of applause.

I will call you tomorrow with a schedule and I am sure the debriefing will not last more than one or two days.

Thanks for the call Jack."

"Is everything ok honey?"

"Yes, the Director will call us tomorrow with a schedule and he said it would take one or two days to complete the debriefing as a team."

"Debra, why don't you call your Dad and ask him to join us for dinner somewhere as I would like to meet him."

"We are not married yet Jack and already you can read my mind. "I am anxious to tell Dad about our getting married."

She called her Dad and he was happy to hear Jack had come home safely. Dad would you like to have dinner with us?"

"Yes, and I can meet you tonight or tomorrow and there is a nice cozy restaurant not far from my house and the food is very good. How do you feel about tonight?"

"That sounds good. What is the restaurant name and we will meet you there around six?"

"Six is fine and the name of the place is The Pleasant Inn. See you then."

"Jack, we'll meet my Dad tonight at a restaurant near his house."

"Thanks honey."

"Jack, you did invite me to move in with you, didn't you?"

"I'm not sure if you can afford the rent. Afterall, I know you don't have a steady job."

"I hoped you would have compassion for me and be my sugar daddy."

"What are the job qualifications to be a sugar daddy?"

"Well, I need at least six or seven hugs a day, periodic kisses, passionate bedtime and an allowance plus good food and red wine."

"I qualify for all of the above but, how much of an allowance?"

"Based upon my previous pay scale, I would estimate twelve dollars a week would cover my pedicure cost and twenty dollars more per week for hair salons and periodic spa visits and then there is the clothes shopping escapades and the monthly Lamborghini cost. You might also want to add in retirement savings so I can continue my expensive habits into my old age."

"Here is what I promise. I will shower you with love and respect every day left in my life which should be worth more than the items you mentioned. But I also understand they are necessities necessary to maintain a good and reasonable lifestyle. So, I will become your sugar daddy and meet your demands as long as you allow me to hack a major bank once monthly to pay for everything."

"And the parson said, I now pronounce you man and wife."

They were both laughing and obviously very much in love. The held each other tightly and they both felt the stress of the prior week's became a thing of the past. It felt so good to be home.

They left the house at five on their way to meet Debra's dad and to have dinner. It would be about a forty-five-minute drive to reach the restaurant he had suggested. Jack didn't mind driving but he did think it had been nice to have been chauffeured around.

"I believe you and my dad will get along great. He knows quite a bit of the trials and tribulations of being a CIA agent and especially stationed in an adversary country like Russia. You two will have a lot to talk about, and oh, he likes scotch."

"I can vouch for you and let your dad know how good you performed in our most recent adventure. You know as much about stress as I do, and it didn't stop either of us from performing our jobs to a high standard."

They reached the restaurant and parked the car and went inside to await Debra's dad. However, they didn't have to wait because he opened the door to greet them.

"Hi Jack, I'm Rob and I understand you are my daughter's heartthrob?"

"Nice to meet you Rob and yes, your lovely daughter has stolen my heart."

"Hi dad, it's me your favorite daughter and I am so happy to be home and to see you."

'Debbie, I know a little about what you and Jack recently did as I heard from a couple of my old friends. I am proud of both of you, but I am super happy to see you safe and to be able to see you once again. Let's get a table, a drink and then we can talk."

The waitress guided them to a nearby table, left menus for them, and took their drink order.

"Dad before we get our drinks, I have a surprise for you. Jack and I are going to get married. It will be September 26th and I expect you to walk me down the aisle. We still have some debriefings to get over and then we will begin to finish all our plans. In the meantime, we are living together at Jack's house in Arlington."

"Well congratulations to both of you. I wish you all the best a father can offer, and I will be proud to walk you down the aisle."

"Thanks dad. Jack and I believe we have done our last stint with the government and we will probably spend a lot of time visiting places we never got the opportunity to visit while employed. We don't intend to sit around and be bored."

Their drink orders arrived, and Rob raised his glass to both of them. "Here's to the bride and groom. May your life be blessed with good health, good fortune and an abundance of love. I am so happy for both of you."

"Thanks dad."

"Thanks Rob, your blessings are graciously accepted."

"Jack, are your parents still alive?"

"No, sadly they died a few years ago in an automobile accident. I never even got to go to their funeral as my assignment in Russia would have been compromised if I suddenly left Russia. It took me a long time to get over the guilt of not being able to say goodbye."

"Jack, I am so sorry to hear of your tragedy, you never mentioned it to me."

"It has been buried for a long time Debra, but let's make this a happy occasion."

"Welcome to the family Jack; we have plenty of relatives to share and you will fit into our family very well."

"Speaking of family, dad, how is my dog Wally doing?"

"Well he keeps me company and told me he prefers the food at my house over yours and he thinks he has a better range of sleeping options at my house."

"I'm glad he is happy dad and I would appreciate if you could please keep him for a while longer until Jack and I get through our debriefings and complete our wedding planning."

"I may request I keep him permanently as he really is a pleasure for me and like me, he enjoys the outdoors and we get to take long walks together every day."

"Dad, you are now the official owner of Wally. I suggest you get him new tags and get his chip updated, to include your address and phone number."

"Thanks Debbie. You can visit him any time you want."

The waitress returned to the table and asked them if they had made their choices yet. They shook their heads and picked up the menu for their dinner selections.

They placed their orders and resumed the conversation until the orders were delivered and then eating became the priority.

"Dad, this is a nice place and the food is good. Do you come here often?"

"Usually when I have guests. Jack, in the future, I would like to join me on a memory discussion as I probably know a few of your previous partners and other agents since my tenure at the agency overlapped yours."

"I would like that, and I will bring the scotch."

"Now I will definitely look forward to it."

They talked for a short time and then they said their goodbyes. Debbie said she would visit with Jack in a week or so but would call to let her dad know how things were progressing.

During the ride home Jack and Debra discussed some of the events she remembered as a child while her mom and dad were still employed by the CIA.

"I must have envisioned it to be exciting as I also chose it as my career, and it got me to meet my love. That is the story of a successful career."

They arrived home and walked hand in hand up the stairs to their room of passion.

Chapter 55

The next day, the Director called Jack and asked him if he and Debbie could attend the debriefing in two days and promised it would not last more than one day."

"Debbie can you be available for another debriefing the day after tomorrow?"

"Sure, let's get it over."

"Sir, we look forward to seeing you in two days."

Jack then joined Debbie in the effort to complete some of the wedding necessities.

Together they had prepared a list of all the invited guests with names and addresses plus had finalized the invitation style and wording and all of their inputs were forwarded to the wedding planner.

Two days later, they drove to FBI headquarters to meet with the Director and others for a debriefing of the Blanton affair and the Adam investigation.

They entered the conference room and the director greeted them and introduced them to two other individuals in the room.

"Debbie and Jack, I want to introduce you to Tom Hanes of the FBI and Walter Myokowski of the CIA. Both came here to learn about your recent assignment in Europe regarding Blanton Arms.

"Thanks Debra and Jack, they will now answer any questions you may have for them."

"Jack, can you briefly describe you experience which qualified you for this assignment?"

"Mr. Hanes, I served the majority of my twenty-five year CIA career in Europe and I speak five languages of which four of them are used extensively in Europe. My specialty included deep knowledge of weapons and in particular small arms and I became a leading expert on arms sales within Europe and Russia and for the most part the illegal sales of arms."

"Debra, same question for you."

"I had also spent extensive time in Europe and the Middle East and had befriended a number of reliable contacts in both areas. I also speak four different languages than Jack and I also had extensive knowledge of the arms trades both legal and illegal.

Two days after the White House function, the Blanton's called me at Jack's house having obtained my phone number from my dad. They asked if we were available for a meeting with them and we said yes. We met them a few hours later at Jack's house and they were very honest and truthful to us. They acknowledged George had recognized me and through his contacts, verified that both of us were CIA agents and they wondered if they were being spied upon. We informed them, it had to do with an investigation of Blanton arms.

They explained to us of their divesting all management of the Blanton corporation ten years earlier.

Jack and I already knew this as fact, and we wondered how people worth quite a few billion dollars would be trying to profit from illegal arms sales. It made no sense and we saw it as a possible set-up.

We offered them a deal to try and clear their name and catch the bad guys. They agreed and hired Jack to go to Europe as an employee of Blanton. They even flew us to Europe on their private jet and basically, from then on, we started our search for the truth."

"Well said Debra. Do you want to add anything to the story Jack?"

"Sure, Debra and I have numerous contacts in Europe who could assist us in many ways, and I have some computer skills which I used to learn about some key executives at Blanton Arms from information about the names of these people, provided by George Blanton.

The information of the Blantons innocence, came from the executive's computer systems, which I retrieved even prior to my going to Europe and provided proof of the innocence of the Blantons and the guilt of the executives of Blanton Arms."

"Am I wrong in saying you knew early in the investigation of the guilt of the Blanton Arms people?"

"Yes sir, it became very clear to Debra and me, the arms division had a few corrupt individuals cheating and pocketing large sums of money."

"Let's continue and go to your European investigation and what you found."

"When we got to Europe, I had contacted a close friend to meet me in Paris. The name of this person will not be revealed but I have known him for many years, and he is a very reliable and knowledgeable informant about the European arms business. I contracted with him to give me a report on the current Illegal deals taking place in the area and possible ties to Blanton Arms. Two weeks later he fulfilled his contact and this information got passed to the Director. I think Debra can now fill in some other information."

"I of course had other contacts unknown to Jack which I had previously relied upon for sensitive information. I met with this person in Antwerp and she introduced me to a couple of different contacts knowledgeable about the arms business mostly in Russia.

The information received proved to be very helpful and specifically stated that twenty-five percent of illegal arms sales had been manufactured in the United States. If this wasn't shocking enough, I also learned from a former KGB agent a Russian mole had been planted in the FBI and we later learned he spearheaded the investigation of George and Priscilla Blanton.

He also had received more than ten million dollars from Blanton Arms and helped them extensively through Russian contacts to sell large quantities of illegal weapons into Europe while pocketing millions of dollars in profits."

"Tom and Walter, I am sure you are knowledgeable about the arrests of the three Blanton Arms executives and the former FBI agent and the ongoing investigation. Maybe you do not know how the United Sates treasury happened to increase its revenue by almost one billion dollars due to the two people you have heard from today. Jack, can you provide an explanation for us?"

"Can I cite my fifth amendment's rights?"

Whatever you say will stay in this room and we have no recording devices in use."

"I have a very good Russian friend and we have successfully worked together for more than ten years. He agreed to meet me in Helsinki for the purpose of hacking the bank in Moldova owned by the three executives of Blanton Arms and the bank manager. It held the large dollar accounts of not only the executives and the bank manager but also the corrupt FBI agent and other illegal arms dealers associated with Blanton Arms.

Using his equipment, together him and I gained entry into the bank's computer systems and discovered the accounts in question and then transferred the money to a safe place. We left no trails of entry nor any exit traceability.

All of the corrupt gains, except a fee to my contact and a fee to the bank who safely harbored the money, have been transferred to the US treasury."

"Jack, how did you know about this bank?"

"It had been contained in the executives emails I took from their personal computers. Quite frankly, they acted pretty dumb in a number of actions they took."

"Gentlemen, unless you have further questions, I want to thank Debra and Jack for their coming out of retirement and bringing this issue to a speedy conclusion. No questions?

Jack, I would like you and Debra to stay for a short while as there is one more person to meet before we adjourn. Let me get her as she is sitting in my office and I will return shortly."

"Well I guess we did good honey and it actually wasn't too stressful."

"Well we made it thus far and now we only have one person left to answer too."

The door to the conference room opened and the director entered with a well-dressed lady carrying two large envelopes.

"Jack and Debra, this is Mrs. Myerson of the Treasury Department and she will explain why she is here."

'I am very happy to meet both of you and soon, I will share with you why I am here. The United States Government has a number of laws relating to illegally gained monies. The two laws relating to this case are The False Claims Act and The Whistleblower Act.

Both of these acts provide rewards for money recovered by the government and the rewards usually vary between ten to thirty percent. In this instance, the government has agreed to reward each person five percent of the money received by the Treasury. In these two envelopes, is a check for each of you in the amount of forty-five million dollars.

She then handed Debra an envelope and then one to Jack. I also have an additional envelope for Jack. It is a reward for the capture of Adam Sanderson in the amount of one million dollars "The United States thanks you for your service. It was my pleasure to meet you and I wish you well."

"Thank you, Mrs. Myerson. Let me accompany you back to the main lobby. Jack and Debra, I will return in a minute or two."

"Jack is this for real. We have Ninety million dollars?"

"I haven't looked at the check Debra because I am still numb."

"I think we have enough for the wedding, the house in Maui, the villa in Lake Como and at least ten Lamborghinis. I honestly, don't know what to say Jack."

"Take my hand and tell me you love me. That is worth more to me than the checks I hold in my hand."

"I do love you Jack, but I won't give the money back."

"They remained holding hands and laughing until the Director returned. I am happy for both of you and I expect an invitation to the ritziest wedding I have ever attended. You two can leave now and go back into retirement. We will stay in touch in case you are needed again."

"Thank you, sir. You know we didn't do this for the money. We were happy to solve the case and we proved the Blantons innocence and caught Adam."

"Well Debra, what do you want to do now?"

"Find the nearest bar and I am going to start with an El Grande Margarita and maybe followed by a second one."

Chapter 56

The days flew by as they always had something they had to do regarding the wedding. The wedding planner handled all the heavy load, but Jack and Debra always found something which needed to be done before the wedding. With about ten days to go, they went back to Mario's to get Jack's tux and Debra's wedding gown. Jack did not see her in the gown, but Eva did but did not reveal anything to Jack except to say, "you are one lucky groom."

Mostly everything major had been taken care of including paying the bill at the Shangri-La and Phyliss had informed them, the count of attendees now number 147 guests.

"It is going to be a great party for us Jack and only six more days to the rehearsal."

"It has been a while since I have been antsy, but I must admit, I am getting a little nervous."

"Speaking of the rehearsal dinner, I think it would be nice to invite Boris, Franz, Ethan and Anna with their escorts to attend the dinner. They have travelled a long way to see us and this would be a good opportunity to spend a little time with them."

"That is a good idea Jack and I will send an email to Anna regarding the dinner and you should do the same for Boris, Ethan and Franz."

Four days before the wedding they stopped to see Debra's dad and the dog Wally and then they went on to visit George and Priscilla and to join them for dinner.

They would go to an upscale restaurant not far from the Blanton's home. They first sat at the bar and had cocktails and then went into the main part of the restaurant for dinner. Priscilla excused herself to go to the lady's room and asked Debra to join her. As soon as they were out of sight, George asked Jack, "what would you and Debbie like for a wedding gift?"

"George, that is a hard question to answer because we have so much."

"What are your plans for your honeymoon?"

"I told Debra it would be a surprise, but I will let you know, I have rented a villa at Lake Como in Italy."

"Wonderful place. How are you getting there?"

"We will fly first class on Air Italia and leave the day after the wedding."

"How about we loan you the G650 for ten days?"

"George, that would be wonderful, but you and Priscilla are too generous."

"Jack it is a write off on my taxes so don't worry about it. The crew is paid year-round and there are daily parking fees and so it is really a small cost and we have no plans to use the plane during the month."

"In that case, I can't say no and I thank you for such a wonderful offer."

"Here come the ladies Jack, call me with your departure and return times and I will do the rest."

"Welcome back ladies. George and I were about to order but we decided we had better wait for the both of you."

"You have to realize Jack; it takes us ladies time to primp ourselves up to put the sparkle in your eyes."

They all laughed and began to look at the menu. It turned out to be another super meal and after they finished, they each had a glass of Sherry. Debra reminded them; they would see each other again in a few days at the rehearsal dinner.

The bill came and Jack wouldn't let George pay the bill. They said their goodbyes and then left the restaurant and headed for their separate homes.

"What did you and George talk about while we were gone?"

"Not much really. He asked how many people would be at the wedding and mostly we talked about politics and how the stock market might perform over the next few months."

"Well it turned out to be another great meal and I am glad you paid. How much did it cost?"

"With tip almost three hundred dollars but we did owe them a nice dinner."

"I agree and I enjoyed it."

On their way home, they continued to talk about the wedding and began to wonder what did they possibly forget?

"Jack, we have three days left and it's too late to begin worrying about what we might have forgot. All the major stuff is done and as they say, don't sweat the small stuff."

"Debbie, actually, we only have a couple of days left because Friday we have the rehearsal dinner. We will move all our wedding clothes to the hotel on Friday and we will then stay at the hotel most of Friday probably seeing friends who may arrived early.

We also have to pack for a ten-day honeymoon and where we are going is still a secret surprise, but you can bring dressy and casual clothes you might wear in the fall."

"Jack, what if I don't like the place?"

"You already told me a few times; you love it there. But, if not, we'll go somewhere else."

"Now I am really confused but I trust my superhero and I know you won't disappoint me."

"We are home honey and I am tired, so off to bed goes the superhero. I love you and will see you in the morning."

They both arose around eight and had a light breakfast. They decided it would be good to start packing their things for the wedding because in the afternoon, they would meet the Pastor who would perform the ceremony and lead the rehearsal on Friday night.

They met at the pastor's church not far from the hotel. He appeared much younger than Debbie and Jack but as they the discussed the various stages of the wedding rites, they discovered a friendly knowledgeable person.

He asked them a number of questions relating to their religious preferences and asked them to select psalms for him to read which were applicable to their beliefs. He also told them the rites and ritual would last about twenty minutes and there would be a lady singing some popular meaningful songs for them which would extend the entire ceremony to about forty-five minutes.

When he had finished his discussion with them and answered their questions, they said goodbye and they would meet again late tomorrow afternoon.

Chapter 57

Friday arrived and they had already received calls from friends who were staying at the hotel for the wedding and they planned on seeing some of them Friday afternoon before their rehearsal. Both were slightly tense and a little stressed but, they knew everybody goes through this stage prior to a major life event.

Meeting with friends and laughter would ease the stress and the time would go by faster and it actually did and then they had to dress for the rehearsal scheduled for five o'clock.

A large room had been set aside for the rehearsal and on one side of the room a table had been set for dinner for twelve people which included the international guests.

The pastor arrived ten minutes early and the members of the wedding party all arrived on time. The international gusts would arrive a five thirty for the dinner.

The pastor called everyone together and explained to each their role in the ceremony. Debra's dad would walk her down the aisle while Jack and the best man George would wait for her at the altar along with Debra's aunt Francis who would serve as the bridesmaid.

The wedding march music began, and Debra and her dad slowly walked down the aisle and the dad handed the bride to Jack and together holding hands, they stood before the pastor. The pastor began the reading of the ritual and made comments along the way. The entire rehearsal lasted about thirty minutes and then the group retreated to a small bar which had been setup at the rear of the room.

About that time, the international guests also showed up and Debra and Jack showed how happy they were to see all of them. The pastor could not stay for dinner due to a prior commitment to another affair and told the bride and groom he would see them tomorrow.

Jack took Boris, Ethan and Franz to meet George and he thanked them for their help in solving the recent illegal arms case.

The cocktail hour lasted until six and they were all called to the table to dinner as a group.

George and Debra's dad sat together and discussed old times and their numerous fishing trips together. The international group had already worked with each other, and they shared common stories and in particular information about common friends.

Debbie and Jack sat with Priscilla and Debbie's aunt Francis and they had a real nice conversation. The dinner began with appetizers and the main meal had prime rib and baked potatoes and a small salad. The dessert consisted of berry tarts with vanilla ice cream.

The party did not break up until eight and then most of the group headed for the lobby bar where they partied for another two hours. Jack and Debra left earlier to go back home and do a few last-minute chores.

"Tomorrows our big day honey and we both have dreamed of it and waited for it to arrive and now tomorrow at this time, we will be officially man and wife. I love you today and will tomorrow as we say or vows to each other."

"Jack, do you think we should write our vows out as to not forget them?"

"I have said them many times to myself and will never forget them."

"Me too and they become more meaningful then reading them off a paper. Good night honey."

"Good night sweets."

Chapter 58

They woke early and certainly; they should be excited because their wedding day had finally arrived. The hugged each other for a moment and then went down the stairs to have a light breakfast and their coffee. They sat around drinking coffee and talking about the friends they had seen yesterday. They then watched a morning show on TV and decided to do some more packing for their extended honeymoon.

After completing the packing chore, they still had an hour to go before noontime. They again switched on the TV and watched football for about an hour and then switched to the news. The news casters had nothing to report except to talk about Trumps tweets and finally Jack and Debbie had enough TV and shut it off.

They had little to do before leaving for the hotel around three o'clock in the afternoon. They then decided to go to the hotel early and would meet some old friends or other guests to pass the time.

They would begin dressing around four-thirty and Debbie would be helped by her Aunt Francis and Priscilla. The wedding had been scheduled to start at five-thirty followed by a cocktail reception and then dinner at seven.

Finally, by five-twenty, mostly all the guests had been seated, and the pastor slowly walked down the aisle followed by George escorting Aunt Francis to the altar. Jack came down the aisle next and talked to a few friends as he also went to the altar awaiting the arrival of Debbie.

The wedding march music "Here Comes the Bride" started, and Debbie entered the room on the arm of her father and looked like the most radiant bride on the planet. Her mother's gown had been altered and some modern touches added, and the beauty of the gown complimented the beauty of Debbie.

Her father presented her to Jack, and he took her hand and now they both stood side by side on the altar.

"Dearly beloved, we come here today to bless the joining in holy marriage of Debra and Jack, and it is delightful to see so many loving friends here today to witness their blessings.

The pastor continued reading from scripture and then a lady sang an old hymn and finally it became time for Debra and Jack to state their vows to each other.

"Debra, I promise you I will love you and watch over you for the rest of my life. You are my beacon of light and I will care for you through sickness and health so help me god."

"Jack, since the day we first met, you have treated me with respect and kindness and have even risked your life for me. I also promise to hold you dear in my arms and in my heart for the rest of my life through sickness and health so help me god.

"Please now exchange rings."

George handed Jack a beautiful wedding ring Jack had custom made for Debbie and placed it upon her finger. Aunt Francis handed Debbie a ring she had purchased for Jack and she placed it on his finger.

"Consistent with the Laws of the state of Virginia, I now pronounce you man and wife. You may now kiss the bride."

Debbie almost leaped into Jack's arms and they kissed each other lovingly and the guests rose and applauded. Jack and Debra then slowly led the procession out of the room which had served as the chapel and for the first time, they noticed all of the beautiful floral arrangements in the room.

The rest of the guests headed for the ball room where they would enjoy cocktails until the dinnertime and the bridle couple would be introduced soon and join in the festivities.

After about ten minutes, the bandleader called for attention and announced the entrance of Mr. and Mrs. Hudson and the music began playing "At Last" and again, everybody applauded.

Jack handed Debbie a glass of red wine and he also had a glass of wine. They walked around the room looking at the table decorations and floral displays plus the color coordination of the dinner plates and accessories. Phyliss had done a spectacular job decorating the entire room and they were going to enjoy every moment of it.

They continued to walk and talk to the guests and they could sense everyone was enjoying themselves and were marveled by the beauty of the room. Soon, it became time to sit for dinner and Jack and Debbie walked to the head table where they joined her dad and aunt plus George and Priscilla.

The staff first served a small salad and then the main dishes appeared. Soft music played during dinner everyone seemed to be enjoying the meal and the ambiance. Upon completion of the meal, staff quickly cleared the tables and each person received a champagne flute which another waiter filled for the wedding toasts.

The band leader called everyone to attention and Debra's dad stepped to the microphone and asked everyone to rise. Jack and Debra this toast is for the both of you from a grateful father "Here's to love, laughter and happily ever after. As Debra and Jack start their new life, let's toast the new husband and wife."

"Now do we have anyone else who wishes to make a speech or a toast to our newlyweds?"

"Would you two come up and the mic is yours."

"Hello, my name is Franz and you will have to forgive my English as I am from Germany and my buddy here Boris, is from Russia. Both of us have known Jack for many years and we met Debra recently in Europe and both Boris and I feel love for our friend and now his new bride. Please raise your glass and in German we say Prost and in Russian, we say Nostrovia. We wish you the best.

The band then began playing dance music and the first dance had been reserved for the bride and groom and then others including her dad would dance with the bride. The party continued to almost eleven and nobody left early. Jack and Debra each thanked everyone for coming and for making their wedding day so special.

The couple went to all the tables and said their goodbyes and many people asked where they planned to go but Jack would not reveal his surprise to Debbie.

The left the hotel about midnight after packing all their gifts and items from the wedding they wanted to keep and then headed home to sleep after a very long day.

Chapter 59

They fell into their bed and both admitted they were tired and kissed and said goodnight and both were asleep within minutes. They slept peacefully through the whole night.

They woke a little after eight and hugged and kissed and both were happy to now be married. They went downstairs to have their morning coffee and a snack and then went to the living room to begin opening the gifts and cards they had received.

It took them almost two hours to read the cards and make a list of thank you notes they had to send too their guests for the gifts they had received. They didn't open any of the large gifts and would wait until they returned.

"Today will be a rest day for us Debbie as we have been pretty busy for a few days now accompanied with the wedding stress. We have a lot of time because we aren't being picked up to start our honeymoon trip until eight tonight."

"Why so late Jack?"

"It's the earliest I could get a limo."

"You are taking top secret to a whole new level."

"You will soon figure it out because in the limo, I will give you tiny hints and clues and you have to search your memory bank to find the answers to what I tell you."

"How long is the limo ride?"

"It will depend hope fast the driver decides to go."

"Hmm, no clue there. Will it be night or day where we are going?"

"It depends on what time we arrive."

"You are really stumping me but let me make some wild guesses. Your taking me back to Maui because you left your sunglasses there?"

"No, they mailed them back to me."

"We are going to Russia to see Boris and Natasha?"

"No. Debbie it is noon time; let's go find a place on the Potomac to eat and relax."

"No more questions huh?"

"Correct, it is eating time. More clues tonight after eight o'clock."

"Ok honey, you win for now but there will come a time to get even."

They both laughed and went out the door with their arms around each other and got in the car to find a nice place to have lunch.

They found a small café on the banks of the Potomac where they could sit and people watch, have lunch and pass time. They both ordered a glass of wine and toasted each other as Mr. and Mrs. Hudson and then ordered their lunch. They returned home after three and Jack went upstairs to play on his computer and Debra went back to a spy book she had previously started.

Time slowly drifted by and they spent the last hour before the limo would pick them up watching local TV and a few minutes before the limo would arrive, Jack returned to the upstairs to bring the luggage downstairs. The doorbell rang and the driver would now take their luggage to the limo and they would begin their honeymoon trip.

Jack still would not give Debra and indication of their destination, but Debra sensed the limo was heading in the direction of the airport.

"We are going to fly somewhere, right?"

"Yes."

"Thanks for the revealing information."

"I am trying to be helpful."

The limo continued towards the airport and soon the various terminal signs were visible, and Debra noticed the driver had made a turn towards the private jet terminal.

"You rented a private jet?"

"No."

"We are going with someone else?"

"No."

"So why are we going to the private terminal?"

"I thought we might be able to hitch a ride with someone."

The limo stopped in from of the terminal and the driver opened the door for them and said he would bring the luggage inside for them. Jack and Debra walked to the reception counter and Jack presented documents to the passenger agent.

"Thank you, Mr. Hudson, your plane is ready, and you and your wife may now proceed to security. Your luggage will be screened and then delivered to the plane. Enjoy your flight."

Debra eyed Jack but didn't say anything as they went through the security checkpoint. After they cleared security, Jack took Debra's hand and they went out the door leading to the aircraft and then Debra saw the jet.

"The Blanton's plane. You got the Blanton's plane. Are they going with us?"

"Not that I know of."

"We have the whole plane to ourselves including that luxurious bedroom?"

"Yes."

"Are we going to join the mile high club?"

"Do they give rewards?"

"You bet they do."

They both laughed and hurried up the stairway to enter the plane and Jack turned and gave her a soft kiss. "Happy honeymoon honey. Now where do you want to go?"

"To our villa on Lake Como."

"Your wish is my command."